KILLING MIND

BOOKS BY ANGELA MARSONS

Angela MARSONS

D.I. Kim Stone BOOK TWELVE

KILLING MIND

bookouture

Published by Bookouture in 2020

An imprint of Storyfire Ltd.
Carmelite House
50 Victoria Embankment
London EC4Y 0DZ

www.bookouture.com

ISBN: 978-1-83888-731-5
eBook ISBN: 978-1-83888-730-8

This book is a work of fiction. Names, characters, businesses,
organizations, places and events other than those clearly in the
public domain, are either the product of the author's imagination
or are used fictitiously. Any resemblance to actual persons, living or
dead, events or locales is entirely coincidental.

This book is dedicated to Oliver Rhodes
For taking a chance on Kim Stone.

PROLOGUE

I will not feel the fear. I will not feel the fear.

I repeat the words to myself over and over in my mind. The fabric that cuts a tight line across my mouth prevents me from saying it out loud.

My hands and feet are numb, caused either by the cold or the ties that bind me tightly to the chair, I'm not sure which.

The goose bumps on my skin are raised and my breathing is shallow. I know how to control these physical reactions to the fear that is running around my brain. I have been taught.

I don't know how long I've been here. The dense silence around me offers no clues. It feels as though time is standing still. Somehow they've stopped it.

My senses have been muted; there are no smells, sounds, there is nothing I can reach to touch. The blindfold prevents me seeing beyond the blackness of the cloth.

There is only one sound and already I welcome and dread it at the same time.

The metallic clunk that echoes around me when they open the door assures me they've not left me here to die. Yet.

But then I know that it will all begin again: the questions, the accusations, the lies.

Their voices will assault me. Their words thrust into my ears like tiny insects. Left there to crawl and burrow into my brain. I was told they would do this.

They are trying to reach the very heart of me.

I know what they want but I can't give it to them and therein lies my fear.

What will they do when I refuse to say what they want me to say?

CHAPTER 1

Kim could feel the tension emanating from her colleague in the driving seat as he negotiated the traffic island at Russells Hall Hospital and headed towards Dudley.

The cause of his mood could not be attributed to their target destination. Keats had told them not to rush. It was an obvious suicide, he'd said, and needed only their confirmation.

'You doing something nice later?' she asked.

He'd requested the afternoon as annual leave and judging by the hard line of his jaw it wasn't to do anything fun.

'No,' he answered, without looking at her.

'Jeez, Bryant, turn that frown upside down.'

She waited for his retort at the irony of such a statement coming from her.

No response materialised as he turned off the main road and pulled up short behind Keats's van.

She shook her head at his sullenness as she got out of the car.

Groups were congregating at the line of tape stretching between the squad car and the ambulance, their stomachs touching the tape in an 'I was here first' kind of way, possessively claiming the space as though at a music concert, terrified of missing out.

Kim said nothing as she pushed her way through to the front. Bryant followed in her slipstream and didn't offer one apology on her behalf. Blimey, he must be preoccupied, she thought. She'd best not let on to Woody. She was only allowed out of the station because she was accompanied by a responsible adult who was obligated to hold her manners in his mouth.

'Coming through,' she called to the last couple who were holding on to their places as though queueing for a Boxing Day sale.

She flashed her ID and ducked under the tape. A PC pointed to the stairs that appeared to lead to a first floor flat. Another directed her to the first door on the left.

Keats waited for the usual greeting from Bryant, as they normally spent a minute or two taking the piss out of her right in front of her face.

No response came from her colleague as he attempted to look around the pathologist.

Keats looked to her. She shrugged, having just as much an idea about his sour mood.

Keats stepped aside to reveal a room bathed in red.

Her keen sense of smell had already detected the metallic odour of blood. She could feel the sickly aroma wafting around her, sticking to her clothes, attaching itself to her hair. It would stay with her all day. But the smell had not prepared her for the quantity.

'Oh my…' Kim muttered, taking a step over the threshold.

Blood had sprayed around the walls, onto the ceiling and onto the window that was closest to the bed, upon which lay a young woman with a three-inch gash across her throat.

Her hand lay by the right side of her torso, a knife contained loosely in her grasp. Along with the blood that had sprayed around the room, a line led from the wound down onto her breastbone and around into her long blonde hair. Cold, empty blue eyes stared up at the ceiling from a face that, despite its bloodless complexion, was lineless and pretty.

'The carotid?' Kim asked, removing her gaze for just a minute.

Keats nodded. 'She clearly knew where it was and meant to end her own life.'

Kim could understand his reasoning. This wasn't the first suicide they'd attended together but it was the first she'd seen where the person had cut their own throat. More common methods included overdosing, hanging and cutting the wrists. Some of which were cries for help and others definite attempts to end a life. But she'd never seen one as definite as this. If you knew where the carotid arteries were and you decided to take a knife to one of them, you weren't expecting anyone to come and save you in the nick of time.

'How long?' Kim asked.

'I'd estimate her time of…'

'I meant how long would it have taken her to die?' Kim asked, walking around the bed.

The room was sparsely furnished with only a bedside table and lamp to the left of the double bed, which was decorated with a white cotton quilt bearing daisies beneath the blood. On the window sill was a Jo Malone candle still wrapped with cellophane.

'A couple of minutes,' Keats stated. 'After the initial spurting, it takes a short while for the body to bleed out. She would have lapsed into unconsciousness before her heart eventually stopped.'

Kim nodded, coming back to the foot of the bed.

What were you thinking for those few moments? Kim wondered, looking at the peaceful expression on the girl's unlined face. *Were you frightened? Relieved? Content with your decision?*

Kim knew she'd never get those answers.

'No sign of forced entry or a struggle,' Bryant said from behind. She hadn't been aware he'd left the room to check.

'Who raised the alarm?' Kim asked, taking one last look over the body from the bare feet, cotton trousers and tee shirt to the blood spatter on her right hand.

'Woman downstairs took her dog out into the garden before leaving for work at 8 a.m. Looked up and saw the blood on the glass. Knocked the door and called the police. Landlord was here by the time the police arrived and let them in,' Keats answered.

'Door was locked?' she confirmed.

'Landlord said so, and I'd estimate her death somewhere between nine and eleven last night.'

Kim acknowledged the information with a slight nod.

'You ready to call it suicide, Inspector?' Keats asked, knowing they had to be in agreement before he recorded it. Keats would still need to perform a full post-mortem back at the lab, as dictated by the coroner for a suicide, but he would not be searching for clues on her behalf. Her involvement with the victim would end here.

'What's her name?'

'Samantha Brown,' Bryant answered from the door. 'Twenty-one years of age.'

Kim formed the mental checklist in her mind.

No sign of a struggle. No forced entry. Locked door. Method obvious to observers and achievable.

Well, Samantha, if this is what you really wanted, I hope you're finally free of your pain and you'll suffer no more, Kim thought, looking down at the lifeless face.

'Inspector, are you ready to call it?' Keats repeated.

She took a breath.

'Yes, Keats, I'm ready to call it. Suicide it is.'

CHAPTER 2

The crowds had thinned by the time Kim stepped out of the building into the warm early September sunshine.

She guessed with only a couple of days until school term started spectators had been called back to their normal daily lives of going to work or buying new school uniform.

She groaned as the dispersing masses revealed someone who had no such commitments.

'Hey, Inspector, you got…'

'I saw you, Frost, which is why I was walking the other way.'

As the local reporter for *The Dudley Star,* Tracy Frost and Kim had had their moments of understanding over the years but, for Kim, the woman would always be one thing: a journalist after a juicy story.

'So, is it true that…'

'Frost,' Kim said, startling the woman by coming to a standstill. 'How many times have you harassed me as I've left a location?'

'A few,' she admitted.

'And exactly how many times have I offered you any information that even you could stretch into a news headline?'

'None,' she admitted. 'But I just…'

'And that's not gonna change today,' Kim said, resuming her journey. 'But feel free to ask Bryant,' she tossed back over her shoulder. 'Because he is in just the right kind of mood to talk to you.'

'Detective Sergeant Bryant, can you tell me…'

'I'm assuming you're impervious to sarcasm, Frost,' Bryant said in a low voice, as he reached the driver's door of the Astra Estate.

Tracy Frost tossed her blonde hair before flouncing away on four inch heels.

Kim couldn't help but recall the picture of a similar mane of blonde hair she'd just seen, matted with blood. She shook the image away. There was nothing she could do to help Samantha Brown now.

Bryant's phone buzzed as she felt hers vibrate in her pocket.

'Samantha's next of kin,' Bryant observed as Kim scrolled to the message from Stacey.

'I expect the sarge there will pass it…'

'We'll go,' Kim said, noting the address of the girl's parents was less than two miles away.

Bryant turned his wrist and checked his watch. It was almost eleven and he was due to finish his half shift at one.

The motion irritated her.

'Bryant, I know you're taking some "me" time today, but you're still at work now and we've got a couple of parents whose lives are about to be shattered following the suicide of their twenty-one-year-old daughter. News that I really think *we* should be delivering but only if you're sure you can spare the time.'

He didn't look her way, or apologise for his lack of sensitivity. Instead, he offered her the same tone he'd offered Tracy Frost.

'Yes, guv, of course I can spare the time.'

CHAPTER 3

Kim understood the irony of her strong intolerance for people who were in a mood. Her own disposition hovered somewhere between aggressive and hostile and that was on a permanent basis. It was her natural state and anything warmer took a great deal of planning, effort and caffeine.

Which was why she'd chosen to keep her mouth shut during the short journey to the home of Samantha Brown's parents. She couldn't trust herself to say anything positive, so it was best she didn't speak at all.

It wasn't the first time he'd had a cob on. It happened just a couple of times a year and had normally passed by the next day.

He brought the car to a stop outside a detached house in Sedgley.

A half-barrel planter containing trailing fuchsias adorned the area to the right of the front door.

Kim rang the bell and then turned to her colleague.

'I'll do the talking.'

He nodded as the door opened to reveal a slim, fair-haired man wearing black trousers and an open-neck shirt. A pair of rimless glasses rested on top of his head.

'Mr Brown?' Kim asked, holding up her identification.

He nodded slowly as he brought down the glasses to take a better look.

His face creased in concern. 'Detective Inspector…' he said, clearly wondering what they were doing at his door.

'May we come in?' she asked.

'Of course,' he continued, pointing to the second door on the left.

Kim entered what was clearly the man's home office. She noted an A1-sized drawing board in front of a high-backed stool. Two line drawings sat side by side. An antique pine desk held a top spec Apple computer and an open notebook. A captain's chair had been pushed aside. On the left-hand side was a three seater sofa in front of a wall of bookshelves. She guessed he was an architect who worked from home.

'Please, take a seat,' he said, pointing to the sofa.

She had the feeling that the man before her thought he could prevent potential bad news by displaying good manners.

Kim sat and Bryant followed suit as the man lowered himself onto the captain's chair and turned to face them.

'Mr Brown, is your wife…?'

'Myles, please,' he offered.

Kim wasn't keen on using first names, but given the circumstances of what she was about to tell him, she'd follow his wish.

'Okay, Myles, we need to speak to both you and your—'

The door to the study opened, cutting her off.

'Darling, I can't get hold of…'

Her words trailed away as her gaze lifted from the phone she was carrying and saw them sitting there.

The woman she assumed was Mrs Brown and the person not answering her phone was her daughter, Samantha.

Kim worked hard to keep down the nausea that threatened her.

'They're detectives, Kate,' Myles said, standing and beckoning his wife over to the seat.

She acquiesced, holding the phone limply in her hand.

'Is it Sammy?' the woman asked, tremulously.

Kim realised that these were the last few even remotely normal moments the couple would experience until they constructed a new normal around the loss of their child.

Both faces were filled with a mixture of fear and anticipation and yet, once they knew, once the words were spoken, they would wish for this time back, for the time, any time before she said the words.

'Mr Brown, Mrs Brown, I'm afraid I have some terrible news about your daughter.'

Myles reached over and clutched his wife's hand.

'I'm sorry to have to tell you that Samantha committed suicide last night.'

Neither expression changed as the words she'd spoken hovered in the air above their acceptance.

Kim said nothing. She waited.

Kate Brown slowly began to shake her head. She held out her phone. 'No, I just left her a message. She'll call back. You've got it wrong. Look, I'll try her again,' the woman said desperately as the phone slipped from her trembling hands.

Myles bent to retrieve it and when he rose Kim saw the tears forming in his eyes. He had already accepted the truth.

'I'm sorry, Mrs Brown, but she's not going to call you back. We've just come from her flat.'

Kate Brown pushed herself to a standing position.

'I don't believe you. Take me there right now. I'll show you.' She turned and faced her husband. 'Myles, get the car and…' She stopped speaking when she saw the raw emotion in his eyes. She frowned and again shook her head.

'You don't believe them, Myles?'

He nodded as the tears spilled out of his eyes, and he pulled her close.

'My baby, my baby,' she began to wail. Myles pulled her closer. She pulled back once more, checking his face for a final time.

He nodded. 'She's gone, love.'

'But you said she was ready to be left...'

'Shush, love,' he said, pulling her into his chest.

The tears continued to roll over his cheeks as he rested his jaw against the top of his wife's head.

His haunted gaze met Kim's across the room.

'How... I mean...'

Kim held up her hand. 'Someone will be along to talk more with you later, but for now just take care of yourself and your wife.'

The details would come soon enough. As would the need to identify the body.

Kim stood and Bryant followed.

'We'll let ourselves out, and please accept our deepest condolences for your loss.'

They were standard words but she meant them.

'Just one thing, officer,' Myles said, as they reached the door. 'There's one thing I have to know. Did... did she suffer?'

Kim thought about those few minutes after she'd made the cut; moments where the life blood was literally draining out of her. Long, fear-filled moments before she lapsed into unconsciousness.

Kim composed her features, before answering.

'No, Mr Brown, Samantha didn't suffer at all.'

CHAPTER 4

Kim downed the last of her coffee and drummed her fingers on her desk. Bryant had finally left and the events of the morning were playing over and over in her mind.

Stacey and Penn were finishing up the paperwork for a serious assault they had wound up yesterday for CPS, and she really should be looking at the three new cases that had landed on her desk today. And yet she couldn't get the image of Samantha Brown's face out of her mind.

Everything about the scene had been right. Keats had had no doubt and neither had she.

She pulled one of the three new files forward. That was the trouble when you worked murder cases most of the time. You saw foul play everywhere. Occupational hazard, she thought, opening the file.

And yet, Kate Brown had said something about Samantha being ready for something. That hadn't piqued her interest but Myles Brown cutting off his wife's words had.

She closed the file in front of her, a question already forming in her brain.

She'd looked closely at the scene this morning. But had she looked closely enough?

CHAPTER 5

Bryant couldn't shake the feeling that had plagued him from the moment he'd woken up. He knew he'd been short with the guv but his mind had already been on the proceedings due to take place in about one hour's time.

He'd followed this process many times already over the years, but there was a knot in his stomach that today was going to be different.

It was the murder of Wendy Harrison and the case that had changed his life.

As a twenty-six-year-old police constable he had been the first officer to arrive at the scene of the brutal rape and murder of a fifteen-year-old girl who had been missing for forty-eight hours. The horror of the scene had shaken him like no other case either before or since he'd watched over Wendy Harrison's body.

Forty-five minutes he'd waited for CID to attend and in that time he had promised the young girl that he would find and arrest the bastard responsible if it was the last thing he did.

The attending DI had dismissed him as he'd walked around the body, sending Bryant back to the station to complete his statement.

As Bryant walked away he'd felt he was abandoning her, breaking his promise, even though there'd been nothing further he could do. That knowledge hadn't stopped her face haunting his dreams for weeks afterwards.

It was that feeling of uselessness that had propelled him to join CID. He wanted to be the person making the arrests, tracking down the criminals and not the person watching over the body before being dismissed from the scene.

He had closely followed the case, and CID had caught the murderer, but it should have been before he'd had the chance to strike again. Peter Drake had claimed another victim before they'd finally caught him.

So, after letting Wendy Harrison down once, he'd vowed that it wouldn't happen again.

At regular intervals over the years he'd been called upon to do his bit, as he was doing today, to make sure Peter Drake never again saw the light of day.

CHAPTER 6

'You sure this has passed its MOT?' Kim asked as Penn crunched his rust-bucket into third gear.

'Due next month, boss, but she'll do me proud.'

'I've seen better-looking crime scenes,' she observed as the glove box fell open onto her knee.

'Yeah but the old girl won't let me down. We've been through a lot together,' he said, tapping the steering wheel.

Kim suspected this girl would soon be going to the knacker's yard in the sky, but she wasn't going to be the one to break the news.

'Next left,' she said, as they neared Dudley town centre. 'And sharp right,' she added as something on the near side left of the car squealed in protest.

Penn pulled up behind the one remaining service vehicle. Keats's van was gone, the ambulance was gone, the cordon tape had been removed and the onlookers had returned to their lives, the earlier excitement of the day already forgotten. Such a devastating life-changing event for Samantha's parents, but nothing more than a passing subject of gossip for her neighbours.

The single squad car was parked beside the Ford Escort van of the landlord. She was hoping he'd still be around.

The constable on the door offered her a questioning glance as she approached.

'Marm?'

'Just want another look,' she explained as he stepped aside. He would have been told to let no one in but the cleaning crew.

'It's fine,' she assured him. 'And if you see the landlord, tell him I'd like a word.'

The officer nodded as his hand moved towards the radio mounted on his vest.

She took the stairs two at a time with Penn following closely behind.

'It's okay,' Kim said to the second officer guarding the door to the flat. 'Your buddy downstairs is already calling me in.'

He stood aside for her to enter.

Amongst all the bodies crammed into the space earlier she hadn't noted just how small the flat was.

The windowless hallway had three doors. She already knew that the door on the left led to the bedroom. The one on the right was the kitchen and the door dead ahead was to the lounge.

She turned and closed the front door behind her. The door had two separate locks. A latch lock at her eye level that automatically locked when the door was closed and a turn-key lock at waist level. She inspected both closely and found no damage to either. Just as Bryant had said.

'Boss, is there anything you want me to do?' Penn asked.

'Just observe,' she said, walking into the kitchen.

The area was furnished with cheap plain white cupboards and a stainless steel sink. A newish boiler was fixed to the wall next to the window.

The kitchen appeared functional but sparse without any personal touches, no nick-nacks littering the surfaces or wall plaques to stamp the place as her own. A plain white mug and matching side plate sat near the sink, with two pieces of crust left over from a sandwich.

'Doesn't look like my kitchen,' Penn remarked from the doorway. 'Spare counter space is a bloody premium.' He looked around. 'And it's a bigger space than this.'

Kim wasn't much of a kitchen dweller but her own space was littered with bits that she just hadn't bothered to put away, stuff that accumulated over time: a couple of spare batteries; a cookbook that hated her; scouring pads she'd used to clean up bike parts; just stuff that didn't belong anywhere but that her eyes passed over a few times a day. In this kitchen there was a distinct absence of 'stuff'.

She moved along to the lounge. Again, the space was small, dominated by a two-seater sofa and a single chair. A small television sat on a glass unit in the corner. Kim searched for signs of an identity – any mark that Samantha Brown had put on the place – but she found nothing.

'It's like she didn't see this as her home,' Penn said, walking around the small lounge.

Exactly what Kim had been thinking. Had Samantha been displaced somehow? Had she been lonely? Had that driven her to take her own life?

She headed back to the bedroom and stood in the doorway. Whether it was the memory from this morning or the person-shaped patch of clean linen, revealed by the removal of the body, Kim wasn't sure but she could still see Samantha Brown lying there.

Kim tried to pinpoint exactly what had brought her back, just as footsteps sounded in the hallway.

A short, stocky man wearing overalls held out a hand towards her. She looked away as his hand fell to his side.

'Raymond Crewett, landlord.'

'You let the police into the flat?' she asked, heading back into the hallway.

'I did.'

'And did you have to unlock both locks?' she asked.

He began to nod. 'Yes, yes, I…'

He stopped speaking as his eyebrows drew together. He took out his set of master keys, appearing to replay the actions in his head.

'Hang on, no I don't think I did. I opened the top latch lock and then tried the door and it opened. But most folks don't…'

'Thanks, Raymond. If I need anything else, I'll give you a shout.'

'Any idea when…'

'No,' she said, shortly. She did not know when he was getting his flat back.

His admission hadn't helped the feeling in her stomach. Yes, many people forgot to turn the key in the second lock, but not usually young single women living alone.

Raymond shuffled off muttering something about guttering that needed repair.

'You thinking someone else was in here?' Penn asked.

'I'm thinking it's not beyond the realms of possibility,' she said, back in the bedroom doorway.

Penn edged past her and walked into the room.

'Never seen this before,' he said, pausing at the window sill. 'Someone cutting their own throat. Wrists in the bathtub but never this.'

Penn's reaction to the whole scene was not calming the disquiet in her gut. She'd made the return visit to satisfy herself that she and Keats had been correct. It had had the total opposite effect.

'Nice candle,' Penn said. 'Expensive. Mum loves them. Buys herself one a year.'

'Penn, shut up,' she said.

'Okay, boss,' he said, continuing to look around.

She made a mental list of the disparities in her mind.

No preparation. No ceremony. No note. Curtains wide open. Surely it would have been a private thing. Location, why not the bathtub? For some reason people taking their own lives did not want to make a mess. The plate and mug in the kitchen. Who felt like a snack knowing they were going to cut their own throat?

The fact that only one of the locks on the door needed opening. The one that would have clicked itself if someone had left.

The candle in the cellophane had stayed with her. It was the type of thing you bought as a gift. Amongst such a stark flat that held no other personal items, why just one expensive candle?

'Penn,' she said, urgently.

'Yeah, boss.'

'Get me back to the station, now.'

CHAPTER 7

'Absolutely not,' Woody said, shaking his head.

'But, sir, we need to begin a full investigation immediately.'

Penn had driven like a demon to get her back as quickly as possible. She had told Woody everything and requested Keats be instructed to carry out an immediate post-mortem on Samantha Brown's body. He was due to do one anyway, but Samantha Brown would have been classified as a lower priority. The delay might mean a day or two, at the most, but she didn't have that kind of time to waste.

'Any valuable evidence was lost the minute you and Keats made the call of suicide. No crime scene photos were taken, no forensic protocols were followed, not to mention that Keats will already have cleaned her up ready for identification and destroyed anything of any value.'

'But there might be…'

'Stone, I'm not budging. Anything of evidential worth would have been on the outside of her body. The cause of death is indisputable. Even if you're right, and I'm not convinced you are, you've lost your opportunity to interrogate Samantha Brown's body at the earliest opportunity.'

She swore under her breath. 'Sir, we really need to reclassify the manner of death.'

'And we will once you give me a reason to. We're not putting her parents through it, Stone.' He paused and met her gaze. 'If you really think a mistake has been made, look into it, but go gently.'

Kim nodded her understanding.

After all, gentle was her middle name.

CHAPTER 8

Bryant pulled into the car park ten minutes early. He noted immediately that he was first to arrive.

HMP Hewell was located in Tardebigge in Worcestershire. Holding approximately fourteen hundred mixed-category prisoners, it served the areas of Worcestershire, Warwickshire and West Midlands. The prison had its fair share of overcrowding, and drug problems, which had been highlighted when a chance wildlife documentary being filmed in adjacent fields caught the smuggling process in action.

It had also been home to Peter Drake for the last twenty-six years.

Bryant turned off the engine and sat back. Had he still been a smoker, a lit cigarette would already have been in his hand. Ten minutes to spare, anxiety clutching at his stomach, hell, he'd probably have chain-smoked a couple by now.

His palm began tapping on the steering wheel for want of something better to do as he glanced around the car park, waiting for the vehicle he was expecting.

He'd first met Richard Harrison when he'd attended Wendy's funeral, standing unnoticed at the back. Only he hadn't been unnoticed. Richard had approached him as he'd been getting back into his car and asked why he was attending his daughter's funeral.

Bryant had explained his role to the broken man who had just buried his child. At the trial, he had read out his statement and had watched the man fight back the tears. Once he'd done as much as he could, he'd had to let it go. The murderer was safely behind bars serving a forty-five-year sentence. He'd gone on with his life, hoping Wendy could now rest in peace.

Until ten years ago when Richard Harrison had been waiting for him outside Sedgley police station at the end of his shift.

Bryant had not recognised him immediately. He appeared to be half the man he'd been before in both stature and girth. His hair much greyer than he recalled.

Over coffee Richard had explained that Wendy's killer, Peter Drake, had applied for parole having served fifteen years of his sentence. He had also confided that his marriage had broken down and ended in divorce. Throughout their conversation Bryant had gathered that the main cause of the breakdown had been due to Richard being unable to move on and function after the death of his only child. He had lost contact with friends and eventually lost his job due to poor performance. His house and wife hadn't been too far behind.

Bryant had understood the man. He knew that people had to allow themselves to heal at their own pace, find a new way to move on, but had his own daughter been subjected to the same ordeal as Wendy, he wasn't sure he would ever have been able to recover either; both of them, Richard and Bryant, father to only one child. One daughter.

'She was a daddy's girl,' Richard had explained. Whatever happened she had run to Daddy. Needed a plaster, a bedtime story, Daddy made everything better.

'But Daddy couldn't do it this time,' Richard had whispered into his drink, which had all but broken Bryant's heart.

He knew that other parents had opportunities to make good mistakes they felt they'd made. People with more than one child had the chance to make it up somehow to a sibling; do things differently second time around. Richard would never be able to make it up to Wendy. He felt he had failed her and he would never forgive himself.

To help the man out Bryant had made a couple of calls to the prison and a friend he had on the parole board and established that Peter Drake wasn't going anywhere. Poor behaviour and violent episodes towards prison officers had ruled out such an early release.

That had changed five years ago when the man had supposedly found God. In the years since he'd kept his nose clean and firmly out of trouble.

And now every parole hearing carried more risk than Bryant was comfortable with.

Two years ago, Richard had asked him to attend the parole hearing with him. As Wendy's next of kin, he was allowed to attend and take one support person.

In the past Bryant had always trusted the parole board. As an independent body, it was made up of 246 members and 120 support staff who carried out risk assessments on each individual to determine whether they could be safely released back into the community.

He knew that public safety was the number one priority and that they heard around twenty-five thousand cases a year referred by the Ministry of Justice. The risk assessments were based on detailed evidence contained in a dossier together with evidence provided at an oral hearing. Members were drawn from a wide circle of professions and appointed by the Secretary of State for Justice.

Statistics told him that in the years 2018 to 2019 only 1.1 per cent of offenders released had gone on to commit further serious offences. A small percentage but a percentage nonetheless, which showed Bryant one thing: the parole board made mistakes.

As Richard Harrison's car pulled into the car park, Bryant prayed that Peter Drake wasn't going to be one of them.

CHAPTER 9

Myles helped his wife back into the car and had no clue how they'd made it back to the car park.

The moment she had seen their daughter lying on that bed in the mortuary viewing room, something in her face had closed down. She hadn't cried, she hadn't sobbed. In fact, she had not made a single sound since.

At one point his hand had itched to yank away the white sheet that was pulled right up to his daughter's chin to stop it stifling her. Sammy had always hated anything tight around her neck. He had to remind himself that she could no longer feel anything, and he now knew what they were trying to hide. He had no wish to see the wound his daughter had inflicted on herself.

'Sweetheart, I just need the toilet,' he said, leaning down and speaking into the car.

His wife offered just a slight nod of acknowledgment but continued to stare forward.

He closed the car door gently and headed back towards the main building.

There was something in him that felt he could walk out the deadened feeling in his stomach, though he knew it would be with him for a very long time.

He was not as shocked as his wife at Samantha's decision to take her own life. She'd been through a lot and yes, he had felt she was strong enough to try living on her own. He would carry that mistake for the rest of his days, but at the same time a small voice spoke inside him. If she was so determined to end her life, would location have made any difference? When they'd had her at home she had not been under house arrest or twenty-four-hour guard. She would have been able to find a way.

He was acutely aware that his wife had barely looked at him since that detective had told them the news. Something in him wanted to release all the pent-up emotion, the grief, the anger, the injustice, even the hurt, but he wouldn't, couldn't. He knew his wife was no more entitled to her feelings than he was but he would accept her accusatory silence. He would prepare himself for the rage when it came. He would ready himself for the uncontrollable tears once her brain allowed the truth to seep in, but what he couldn't do was allow himself to fall apart. He couldn't allow the grief to swallow him whole. There was still much to be done. And their actions going forward now were even more important than ever.

He entered the main reception of the hospital, strode past the desk and out of sight of the car, even though he knew she wouldn't be watching.

He looked for a semi-private spot along the corridor as he had a sudden thought.

Samantha had been at the core of pretty much every conversation the two of them had had over the last three years. Now she was gone, leaving a void that could never be filled.

He took a deep breath and took out his phone – his real reason for leaving his wife in the car.

He scrolled to the contact he wanted in his list, turning into the wall. As expected the voicemail kicked in. He waited, took another breath.

'Sammy's dead,' he said, and then ended the call.

CHAPTER 10

'Samantha Brown,' Stacey said, looking at her screen. 'Twenty-one years old, born to Myles and Kate Brown in July of 'ninety-nine. Made the school gymnastics team and then later netball, left school five years ago and attended Dudley College, studying graphic design. Appears to have had a great social life, lots of friends but no serious boyfriend, so pretty much studying and partying at the same time.'

'Normal college life, then?' Penn acknowledged.

Kim half listened as she pressed refresh on her emails. Keats had questioned her request for the photographs of the body taken at the scene and after, and she'd assured him she just wanted them for her report. He had agreed to send them. She had ended the call as quickly as she could to avoid further questioning from the astute pathologist. And if she knew him as well as she thought, he'd be poring over those same photos himself right now, wondering if they'd made a mistake.

'Samantha was active on just about every social platform I can find but seemed to especially favour Instagram right up until…'

'Hang on, Stace,' Kim interrupted, as the email from Keats came through.

She began scrolling through the ten pictures she'd been sent, looking for anything that appeared to be out of place or suspicious. Something she could take to the boss.

Right now, she had nothing more than what looked like a gifted candle, lack of ceremony or planning, the possibility that someone else could have been in the flat and her own suspicious nature, and the boss had already shut her down based on these things. She needed something to convince him to let her investigate Samantha's death properly.

She swiped along the photos:

The position.

The knife.

The blood.

The hand.

Damn it, there was nothing there that wasn't still present in her memory.

She began to scroll again. 'Sorry, Stace, carry on.'

'I was only going to say that everything about Samantha's online presence is exactly what you'd expect to see. All pretty normal, as Penn said, except for one thing.'

'Which is?' Kim asked, as her phone pulled up the last picture of the collection: the hand.

'It's all there, but it all ended three years ago and she hasn't posted another thing since.'

Kim looked up. 'Three years?'

Stacey nodded.

Unusual but it wasn't going to get Woody to change his mind.

'Okay, Stace, good work but I'm gonna need…' She stopped speaking as her gaze returned back to the photo of the hand. Something struck her and it was like she was seeing it for the first time.

She turned the phone and looked at the photo from every angle.

'Stace, keep digging, and, Penn, get me a red pen and a ruler. Now.'

CHAPTER 11

Britney reached into her backpack and took out the last few flyers. Once she'd handed these out she could go home.

She smiled to herself as she remembered when she'd first started doing this job. On her third day she'd left the college early when the storm clouds that had threatened all day had unleashed thunder, lightning and torrential rain. With a backpack half full of flyers she had returned home, her clothes soaked to the skin like melted plastic and rain dripping from her hair. It had been explained to her that people couldn't just abandon their jobs due to a spot of bad weather. She had considered mentioning that the storm had lasted for almost three hours, but really, she could understand the point being made. Her work was too important to just abandon it at the first hurdle. Her family depended on her and she swore she would not let them down again.

The following day her backpack had contained the usual three hundred leaflets as well as the ones from the day before. She had never gone home early since.

As ever she was dismayed to see so many of the leaflets littering the ground; screwed up, walked over, having been thrown away once out of her sight.

She wasn't angry, just sad that the recipients hadn't bothered to read all the important information that could change their lives the way it had changed hers.

Britney remembered the day she'd been given the leaflet, almost five years ago and two days after she'd turned nineteen, just another birthday she hadn't bothered to celebrate.

Birthdays didn't mean a lot when you were in and out of the care system. They weren't remembered by the father who had walked out. They weren't celebrated by the mother who had abandoned you because you interfered with her social life, and the short stay foster homes didn't take too much notice either.

Britney shook away the negative thoughts; they were poisonous to her soul. She didn't need them any more. She didn't need any link to her past. It had given her nothing, unlike her present which gave her everything she could ever want. For the first time in her life she belonged. She mattered and she knew it was always meant to be.

She looked around her and smiled. Never mind about the leaflets on the ground. Every single person who walked past her was a potential survivor, someone whose life she could change. Every person was an opportunity. And so what of the leaflets discarded. Maybe someone who needed it would tread on one and read it at a time in their life when they needed something more.

She looked around her, seeing everything with wide fresh eyes. It was her job, her duty to try and help some of these people understand that there really was another way.

Her eyes rested on a single female sitting on the wall alone. Her legs dangled and she idly kicked her heels. She looked at something on her phone and then put it away. As she raised her head Britney saw two things: the acne-covered skin and a quiet loneliness in her eyes.

Britney knew immediately that this girl needed her help.

CHAPTER 12

'Okay, Penn, lie on the floor,' Kim instructed.

'Excuse me, boss,' he said, holding up his right hand which was now covered with small red marks.

She thought for a second. 'Yeah, scrub that.'

He looked relieved. 'Thank goodness for…'

'Lie across the desks instead.'

He tried to read her face for humour. There was none.

'Lie with your head on Bryant's desk and your bottom half on the spare desk.' She pointed to where she wanted him positioned. 'I need to be on your right.'

He did as she asked while Stacey sat back in her chair for a better view, chewing on the end of a red pen. She had painstakingly copied every blood spatter mark from the photo onto Penn's hand.

'Stace, pass me that ruler.'

The constable slapped the twelve inches of plastic into her palm like a nurse assisting a surgeon.

'Hang on, boss,' she said. 'If we're trying to get this as close as possible, that knife in the photos is only about six inches long.'

'Good point,' Kim said, hanging the ruler over the side of the desk. She brought down her hand forcefully and snapped the ruler in half.

'Bloody hell,' Penn said, jolting away from her.

'Sorry,' she said, not realising how close she'd been to his ear.

'Okay, lift up your right hand, Penn.'

He did so and she, without giving it too much thought, placed the ruler inside his fist. Her hand then closed his palm around the ruler, her own fingers splaying as they curved around the knuckles, revealing the blood spatter on the skin. She removed her hand, beneath which there were no red marks.

Without revealing anything she beckoned Stacey over.

'Do what I just did without thinking about it.'

Stacey took the ruler and placed it into Penn's hand. The same thing happened. Her fingers splayed to contain the fist.

Stacey removed her hand to reveal the unmarked skin.

'So?' Kim asked, folding her arms and asking her team what this experiment had taught them.

Stacey was first to answer.

'Samantha's hand wasn't the only hand holding the knife.'

CHAPTER 13

Bryant was tempted to head back to the station but resisted. He'd booked the afternoon off fair and square and it was almost the end of shift.

The parole hearing had gone just like the others. Richard had spoken from the heart and had fought back the tears as he'd explained that his own life sentence could not be paroled; that his daughter was not going to reappear, a grown woman with children of her own. He explained how he still saw every single injury inflicted on her body when he closed his eyes at night. Richard had been no less passionate than he was at the first parole hearing they'd attended. They had then left the room, shook hands outside and Richard had left, secure that enough had been done and said to keep the man behind bars.

Bryant was not so sure.

As he'd sat beside Richard he'd watched the board members carefully. At other hearings they had listened intently, their full attention on Richard as he spoke, empathy and emotion gathering in their eyes, but today he had seen something else. At one point one of the members of the board had checked her watch. The two others had shared a glance or two. He had detected impatience as the still-broken man had pleaded his case.

He had said nothing of his observations to Richard for fear he was looking so hard at the demeanours of the people in the room, he had seen something that wasn't there.

And here he was, he realised, as he brought the car to a stop at a pull-in on the west side of the Clent Hills. At the exact spot where he had been the first officer to lay eyes on the ravaged body of Wendy Harrison. He turned off the engine and allowed the horrific images to play in his head. The viciousness of the assault; the knife wounds that had stretched from her inner thigh to her ankle; the broken bones; the blood; the violation. No man who could do that was capable of rehabilitation, whether they'd found God or not.

The sound of his phone in the silence startled him even though he was expecting the call.

He answered, listened and then ended the call that confirmed what he had felt from the moment he'd opened his eyes that morning.

Peter Drake had got parole.

CHAPTER 14

As Kim filled the coffee pot two things happened. Neither of which surprised her.

She answered the phone to Keats as she opened her front door to Bryant.

'Hey,' she said, serving as a greeting to both. She turned away from Bryant and focussed her attention on the pathologist, while her colleague gave a waiting Barney an apple.

'You really think this is murder, Stone?' Keats asked.

She ignored the inflection in his voice that her theory was some kind of slight on his judgement.

'We both called it, Keats,' she said, to disabuse him of that thought. She was glad that Woody had been quick to start the process with the coroner for reclassifying Samantha's death, which would have commenced with a courtesy call to Keats.

From her point of view, Woody had asked her to inform the family first thing in the morning. The flat had been sealed off awaiting the arrival of forensics, but Kim wasn't going to wait for their findings.

A dozen people or more had traipsed in and out of that property with little regard for evidential value. The killer could have left their name and address and it would never see the inside of a courtroom. And Kim wasn't sure what more Samantha could tell them herself. Yes, she had been in very close contact with her killer but her body had now been moved and cleaned without consideration of it being a crime scene.

Kim explained the results of her experiment with Penn on the desk.

'Scientific study, then?' he mocked.

'Simple but effective,' she said, about to end the call.

And yet she couldn't press the button until she'd said one more thing. Keats was as conscientious as she was. He would not be taking the news of their mistake well.

'Hey, at least we caught it quickly,' she said, quietly.

'No, Inspector, at least *you* caught it quickly,' he said, ending the call.

Kim was tempted to call him back, although she didn't know what she'd say if she did. He would beat himself up no matter what she tried to tell him.

She put her phone down and turned to her colleague. She looked pointedly at his empty hands.

'You know I remember the days you used to bring *me* food or at the very least coffee.'

'Yeah, yeah,' he said, taking a stool at the breakfast bar.

'And now all you bring me is a face like a slapped arse.'

'Sorry but it's the only face I've got,' he mumbled.

Kim took down the black with white spots mug which had somehow become Bryant's mug.

Everyone was entitled to a bad mood now and again, but for Bryant it was so grievously out of character. Okay, forget the pizza or the coffee, but normally when visiting another person's home, the least you took with you was good humour. She stifled her irritation. Given all that he suffered stuck with her every working day, she could at least try and offer a bit of support.

'Well, either straighten your face or bugger off,' she said, mustering as much sympathy as she could manage.

He stared at her for a full minute before his lips began to turn up in a smile.

'Praise the lord,' she said, pushing his drink towards him, having decided that he could stay.

'And I bring Barney a treat cos he wags his tail when he sees me and nuzzles my hand.'

'Well, Bryant, it's safe to say that I am neither going to wag my…'

'I need advice, guv,' he said, forgetting her first name rule when in her home. He immediately held up his hand in acknowledgment.

'And you came here?'

'Yeah, go figure.'

She folded her arms and leaned back against the work surface.

'So, I'm guessing you didn't do anything fun with your afternoon off?'

He shook his head. 'Parole hearing for Peter Drake.'

Kim waited for more. The name was vaguely familiar to her, but she immediately knew it wasn't a case of hers.

Having finished off his apple Barney had come to sit beside her.

Bryant saw the puzzlement on her face.

'That case I told you about years ago that prompted me to join CID.'

She continued to wait. If she remembered correctly it was twenty-five years ago.

'You still go to the parole hearings?'

He nodded. 'Her father asks me to accompany him as his plus one.'

Kim was still confused. 'So, what advice do you need?'

'What can I do? He's going to be released tomorrow and I know it's going to happen again. He'll re-offend and another young girl…'

'Whoa! Easy, Tiger,' she warned. 'First of all, you know no such thing. You might suspect it, just like I suspect that Dorothy next door will put her wheelie-bin in front of my garage door again tomorrow, but I can't kick it over until she actually does it.'

He raised an eyebrow. 'You actually do that?'

She left the question unanswered and continued. 'Bryant, this is not *Minority Report*. We can't assume people are going to commit crimes before they actually do it.'

'But my gut says…'

'It doesn't matter what your gut says. He could send you a signed letter telling you he's gonna re-offend but you can't get him back behind bars until he does it.'

Anger sparked in his eyes until he realised that none of this was her fault.

'He's served more than twenty-five years. Right?'

Bryant nodded. 'Almost twenty-six.'

'We both know that doesn't compensate for a life but no amount of years will do that. It's the best the justice system has got and, although you're not gonna like my opinion, I'm telling you that it's time to let it go.' She had tried to soften the last few words. They both knew what it was like with that one case that haunted you. It was as though it left a small scar on your left elbow that you touched for the rest of your life. She knew she was steering him right and she also knew it was the last thing he wanted to hear.

'And right now, we have another poor girl who needs your attention more.'

'Yeah, I saw the email,' he said, pushing his stool away from the counter.

'You want me to run through…'

'Nah,' he said, shaking his head. 'I'll catch up at the briefing in the morning.' He tapped the counter twice. 'I'll see you then.'

She watched him leave with a distracted pat on the head for Barney.

A strange feeling washed over her as the door closed behind him. It reminded her of walking away from a crime scene with an instinct there was something she'd missed.

Bryant was her friend, he had come to her for advice and she had given it. There was nothing she could have possibly missed. Case closed.

And yet when she glanced at his untouched coffee she got the sense he hadn't heard a word she'd said.

CHAPTER 15

Bryant had left the house early to be at the Crossley residence by six, to enable him to make the morning briefing at the station by seven.

Despite the boss's words the night before, he'd known he had to do this, and a quick call last night had sought permission to visit at such an ungodly hour. The permission had been given begrudgingly and he'd expected nothing less.

The door to the ground floor flat in Lutley Mill was opened by a man who had not aged well.

Damon Crossley had never been a handsome man. His deep-set eyes and high forehead had given him a hawkish appearance. The sallow jowls were heavier with the additional weight gained over the years. But that scowl on his face hadn't changed a bit.

'Yer wanna come in?'

No, he'd got up at 5 a.m. to stand on the bloody doorstep, he almost said, ignoring the hostile tone. It wasn't Damon he'd come to see.

'How is she?' he asked, stepping into the hall.

'How the fuck you think she is?'

Yes, it was a stupid question. He was guessing Tina Crossley was angry, disappointed, shocked and most likely scared.

'Straight ahead,' Damon said, pointing to the small lounge.

Bryant took a breath before entering the room, steeling himself for what he was about to see.

'Hello, Tina,' he said, to the back of her head. There was a bald spot where some of her hair had never grown back.

She half turned so that her left side was facing him, but her right side remained closest to the window by which she sat.

She pointed to a single chair which would mean he couldn't see her right side, but he knew how it looked already. He could just about see the smaller scar that reached from her cheekbone to her ear, and he knew there were two longer, thicker scars on the other side of her face where the skin had been slashed open in a cross that had cost her one eye.

Bryant felt sick just thinking about it, not because of her appearance: that brought him only sadness. His nausea came from the fact that this attack should never have been allowed to happen. Peter Drake had attacked Tina Crossley two weeks after he'd murdered Wendy Harrison.

Other injuries had dictated that she would never bear children or walk again. She'd been found, barely breathing, by a jogger trying out a new path only half a mile away from where Wendy's body had been discovered.

Damon had been her boyfriend back then and had remained by her side. Despite his unpleasant nature, Bryant reminded himself of that fact.

'So, you fuckers have let him out?' Damon asked before Bryant had a chance to speak to Tina.

'It's not the police who are releasing him,' Bryant said, although the man knew full well how it worked.

'All the bloody same,' he said, sitting opposite Tina and resting his elbows on his knees. 'If you lot had caught him before…'

'Stop, Damon,' Tina said, quietly. Bryant saw him swallow his rage. He guessed that Tina had spent enough time over the years considering what might have been.

'I just wanted to let you know that we did everything to keep him in there. Every parole hearing, every…'

'Who's we?' Damon asked, knowingly.

'People involved in the case, Richard Harrison. We all did our best to keep the bastard locked up.'

'Well, it day do any…'

'I still have nightmares, you know,' Tina said, quietly. 'I still dream about him coming to finish me off. I'd wake up screaming but then remember he was behind bars. I can't tell myself that any more, can I?'

Bryant wished with all his heart he could say something that would take her fear away.

From what he understood Tina rarely left the house and was reliant on Damon for pretty much everything.

'We gonna get protection?' Damon asked.

'It'll be part of his conditions that he's not allowed within…'

'A piece of bloody paper?' he asked, incredulously. 'Oh yeah, I'm sure that'll keep him away from the door. I mean police protection; physical presence.'

Bryant had known what he meant. And he could not give them the answer they wanted.

'Any calls from this number will be treated with the utmost…'

'Oh, fucking bollocks,' Damon said, as Tina's shoulders sagged slightly. 'You do know the only time she felt safe was after her breakdown fifteen years ago? When she was behind lock and key. She hasn't had a full night's sleep since then.'

Bryant knew that Tina had suffered a mental breakdown and had been institutionalised for seven months. He prayed the same would not happen again. 'I'm sorry. I wish we could have done more but…'

'I don't even know why you're here,' Damon said, shaking his head. 'We already knew he was being let out so what exactly do you want?'

Bryant had no answer to give. He only knew that he had felt he needed to come.

Damon appeared to look at Tina for some kind of communication.

A slight nod.

'Tina's tired, it's time for you to go.'

Bryant stood and followed Damon to the door. The man waited for him to cross the threshold before speaking again.

'Yer know, I wish you could have known her before. Training to be a nurse she was when the bastard got her. Didn't have fancy-pants ambitions, didn't want to take over the world. Just wanted to take care of folks. She was full of life, hope. Loved laughing, loved dancing. Loved everything till that fucker took it away from her.' The disgust crept back into his eyes. 'If you'd known the person she was back then you'd feel even fucking worse than you do already. Now piss off and don't come back,' he said, closing the door.

Bryant walked away from the flat, haunted by the face of a woman who had not looked his way once.

CHAPTER 16

'Okay, guys, as you know the death of Samantha Brown has been re-categorised as murder. Keats is performing the post-mortem right now, but I think it's best to assume we're not going to get much forensically either from the body or from her home. So, what do we know so far?'

Stacey leaned forward. 'Samantha was twenty-one years old and appeared perfectly normal until all social media activity stopped three years ago. Wide circle of friends at the time, one sister who is two years younger. She had the odd boyfriend by the looks of it and was attending Dudley College. On the face of it outgoing and social. Not sure about the social media absence but no criminal record and no record of her being admitted to any local mental health facility.'

Stacey ended with a shrug, indicating that was all she had.

'Penn, your observations?' Kim asked.

'The picture Stacey paints bears no resemblance to the current home of Samantha Brown. Although she's been there a few months, there's no evidence of her outgoing personality or any personality at all…'

'One candle,' Kim remarked, more convinced than ever that the candle was how the visitor got themselves into the flat. She'd sent Mitch a message asking him to pay particular attention to that item. His terse response had mentioned something about sucking eggs.

'Which tells us it was someone she knew…'

'Or a pissed off neighbour,' Stacey interrupted.

'No radio, music centre or speakers in the property,' Penn noted. 'So, I don't think it was due to the noise.'

'Could she have been off travelling for a few years?' Bryant asked.

Kim shook her head. 'Doubtful. People normally return with keepsakes, souvenirs from travels abroad. There was nothing. And that wouldn't have stopped her posting on social media.'

Although Bryant had been with her on her first visit, they had only entered the bedroom, and so he would not have seen just how stark the rest of the property was. Had he been there he would have made some kind of joke about the place still being more homely than her house.

'Okay, folks, we're all out of here this morning. Stacey, I want you talking to Samantha's friends. Find out as much as you can. What contact have they had with her over the last few years and why did she disappear from social media? And, Penn, I want you talking to her neighbours. We need to know more about this girl now. What were her habits? Who did she see? We need to paint a picture of the girl and her life.'

Who was Samantha Brown?

She was hoping Samantha's parents could help her out with that.

CHAPTER 17

'You've been to see her, haven't you?' Kim asked, as Bryant drove them towards the home of Myles and Kate Brown.

He hesitated and nodded. 'First thing before shift.' He glanced her way. 'How did you know?'

She shrugged in response. She knew because she knew Bryant. There was a core of decency in him as hard as steel. She would be willing to bet he'd offered himself as the official police scapegoat upon which they could vent their anger. He would never hear the words that it was not his fault, that he was not responsible for the second attack. He had been a constable, not a detective but he had carried the guilt for years.

'Bryant, you're not doing yourself—'

'I think we already had this conversation,' he said, cutting her off.

Okay, she got it. Because she hadn't given him the answer he wanted, he'd switched her off altogether. Fine by her. Maybe they could now focus on the case at hand.

'So, how do you think they're going to react to the news?' he asked, as though reading her thoughts.

'Not sure,' she said, honestly. She understood in a perverse way that wrapped up inside the horror might be a sense of relief.

Any death scarred a family. The death of a child, a death outside the natural order of things, took an even greater toll, but a suicide left behind trails of guilt, felt by everyone close to the person. What clues did I miss? Should I have done more?

Could I have prevented it? How did I not see my child was in pain? Why didn't she come to me for help? And for the parents those questions would never go away. Friends and acquaintances would eventually move on to other worries and concerns, but not the parents. Murder brought a whole new set of questions but it somehow removed a layer of guilt.

'But, we're about to find out,' she said, as Bryant pulled the car to a stop in front of the house.

The door was opened by Myles, dressed in plain black trousers and an open-neck white shirt.

He didn't move back as he stared at them questioningly.

'May we come in, Mr Brown?' she asked.

He jumped back as though remembering his manners.

'Of course. I'm sorry, but…'

'In here?' Kim asked, heading for the office they'd used the previous day.

'Yes, yes. I'm afraid my wife isn't up yet. She hasn't left the bedroom since we returned from the morgue yesterday.'

Kim nodded her understanding. 'And is your other daughter at home, Mr Brown?'

He appeared surprised at the question.

'No, she's not here right now.'

Kim idly wondered where she was in the country that she hadn't come home to be with her parents following the death of her sibling.

'Mr Brown, I'm afraid we're going to need your wife present for this conversation…'

'But I don't…'

'Mr Brown, please go and ask your wife to join us,' she insisted.

He gave her one last look before leaving the room.

Bryant stood by the window and she turned the captain's chair, leaving the two-seater sofa free for the married couple to sit together. They would need each other's support once they heard what she had to say.

Mrs Brown entered the room looking ten years older than the day before. Her face was devoid of make-up, revealing red blotchy skin from crying and dark circles beneath her eyes. Her hair was uncombed and unwashed. She clutched a white handkerchief. Kim judged her for nothing. The woman had lost a child. The reality of that had not sunk in, less than twenty-four hours later, and now she was about to make it worse.

Kim noted Kate Brown's expression before she began speaking. There was fear but also hope. As though they were here to tell them there'd been some kind of mistake, even though she'd seen her daughter's dead body.

Kim took a breath. 'Mrs Brown, Mr Brown, I'm afraid we have new information about the death of Samantha that would reclassify it from suicide to murder.'

Mr Brown's legs appeared to buckle beneath him as Mrs Brown's hand shot to her open mouth. Mr Brown almost fell into the seat beside his wife. Their legs touched and Mrs Brown moved her leg away. It was a subtle but definite movement, but Kim could see the change in dynamics between the two of them as clearly as she could see the strip of daylight between their two bodies.

It wasn't unusual for even the closest of couples to drift apart temporarily as they each came to terms with the loss of a child separately.

'M-Murder?' Mrs Brown finally spluttered.

Kim nodded. 'We believe it was someone she knew who did not have to force entry to her home.'

Both of them began to shake their heads in denial.

Kim continued. 'We need to know if she'd had any recent issues with anyone, any arguments; had she mentioned anything strange?'

'Nothing,' Myles said, as Kate looked to the ground. 'She was a kind, gentle girl. She never upset anyone.'

Kim noted that his wife was now pulling on the white handkerchief.

'Mrs Brown?'

She shook her head but didn't look up.

Kim could see from the corner of her eye that Bryant was watching them closely too. Something here was not quite right but she couldn't put her finger on what it was.

'Mr Brown, Samantha attended Dudley College?'

He nodded.

'Until three years ago when she appeared to drop out of college and away from social media?'

'Samantha ran away,' he offered, as his wife's hands stilled. 'She had a fall-out with her boyfriend and she just left. She was gone two and a half years.'

'And you had contact with her while she was gone?'

'Barely… she'd call and tell us she was safe every few months and then six months ago she came back.'

'So, you wouldn't actually know if she had issues with anyone during the time she was away?'

'Well… no… I suppose not.'

'Would your other daughter have any knowledge?'

He shook his head. 'Sammy and Sophie are not close. Sophie won't be able to help.'

'Any particular reason?' she asked, wondering if it had any bearing on the investigation.

'Just grew apart over the years. Typical siblings, really,' he said, dismissively.

Many of her previous investigations had shown her there was no such thing as a typical sibling relationship, but right now the older girl was her priority.

'And whereabouts was Sammy when she ran away?' Kim asked, thinking they could contact the local force and see if Samantha was known to them.

'She moved around, Inspector. She never told us exactly where she was.'

Kim was hearing the words but they weren't erasing the question from her mind. Every single possibility was being closed down.

'Could she have met someone who followed her back here?' Kim asked, wanting to believe what she was being told.

'I don't think so.'

Kim remembered something from the previous day.

'So, when your wife said yesterday that you thought Samantha was ready.'

'We feared she would run away again but we had to trust her sometime.'

Neither his words nor his demeanour were radiating truth to her. There was a secret here that Mr Brown was working hard to keep and his wife was going along with it.

'Mr Brown, maybe your wife could do with a cup of tea?' Bryant said from behind, reading the signs just as clearly as she was. If he could get the husband out of the room for just a few minutes, she could work on the wife. 'She's had quite the shock.'

'Kate doesn't drink tea,' he replied with a slight edge to his voice. He knew what they were trying to do and he resented it.

Gently, Woody had said.

'Mr Brown, if you know anything at all that could help us find the person who did this to Samantha you…'

'Of course,' he said, standing, and she knew they were being dismissed.

Short of calling them outright liars she had little else to say, except for one thing.

'Would you please give us a call once Sophie returns? We still need to make sure she doesn't have any knowledge of someone who might have wanted to hurt Samantha.'

'Of course but we'll have to break the news first once she gets here. She's travelling back from Thailand, gap year.'

Kim nodded her understanding.

She followed him to the door and offered him the reassurance they would be in touch.

She was prevented from commenting on the door being closed swiftly behind them by the ringing of her phone.

'Hey, Keats,' she said, walking back towards the car. Maybe he had found something in Samantha Brown's post-mortem after all.

'Himley Park, Inspector, and I suggest you get here now.'

CHAPTER 18

It hadn't taken a great deal of detecting skills to track down one of Samantha Brown's closest friends, Stacey thought, as she entered the Next store at Merry Hill Shopping Centre.

But what did surprise her was that young women still lived their lives so openly on social media. This particular girl had no privacy settings and documented her every move on Instagram, which is how Stacey knew that she was already at work, what time her shift ended and what she intended to do with the rest of her day.

Perhaps it was the police officer in her that no longer saw young women just living their lives openly and without fear. She saw opportunity for predators looking to see when her home was unoccupied or when she was travelling alone. She feared for these young women who seemed to be oblivious to the dangers that lurked everywhere, even in cyberspace.

'Where might I find Cassie Young?' she asked a woman returning clothes to a jumper rack.

The woman quite rightly frowned. Good. She liked to see a bit of suspicion now and again. Stacey showed her ID.

The woman's suspicion turned to alarm.

'It's okay. There's nothing wrong. I just need a minute of her time.'

'Homewares,' she said, pointing to the other side of the store.

Stacey thanked her and headed in that direction.

She almost stumbled over the woman who was filling a lower shelf with candles.

'Cassie Young?' she asked, although the hundreds of photos she'd seen online told her that this was the woman she was after.

Cassie stood and nodded.

Stacey showed her ID which was still in her hand.

'Is everything okay?'

'You were friends with Samantha Brown?'

Tears filled her eyes as though they'd not been very far away.

She sniffed them back and nodded. 'Not so much the last few years but we were close once. I can't believe she killed herself.'

The news of the reclassification hadn't reached the news yet, and Stacey was happy to leave it that way.

'Can you spare me a few minutes to talk about her?'

'Of course, but I'm not sure how much I can tell you. I didn't even know she was back around.'

Yes, the boss had updated her on the runaway story.

'What was she like?' Stacey asked. The girl she'd seen on social media did not match the friendless girl who had died in a cold stark flat.

Cassie smiled. 'Oh, my goodness, she was hilarious. She was confident and funny. She liked to laugh and enjoy herself, but never too much if you know what I mean.'

Stacey nodded.

'She was always considerate of other people. I remember once we went for a night out in town. Got the train back. Full of life we were, shouting and laughing on a half-empty train. Sammy spotted a woman with a young boy who was coughing and sneezing all over the place. She quietened us all down until we got off the train. She was thoughtful and considerate and always happy and positive.' A slight frown furrowed her well-plucked eyebrows. 'Well, until…' Her words trailed off as she glanced over Stacey's shoulder.

Stacey followed her gaze to the woman standing at the end of the aisle looking concerned. Clearly the news that a police officer wanted to speak to one of her staff members had reached the manager.

Cassie gave her a signal that everything was okay. The woman disappeared around a dinner service display.

'Until when?' Stacey prompted.

'Until she met someone.'

'Go on.'

'Callum Towney. They met at college. He thought he was all that and a bag of chips. Not the type she normally went for but there was something about him that she could not leave alone.'

Stacey took out her phone and made a note of the name. Surprisingly, it wasn't one she recognised from Samantha's old social media accounts.

'He treated her like shit at times, but she kept going back for more.'

'Treated her badly, how?'

'Picking her up when he had nothing better to do. Dropping her when he felt like it. She was completely besotted and then he finished with her completely for someone else, which pretty much destroyed her.'

Stacey was intrigued. It looked as though her relationship with this boy had changed her life and personality completely.

'How did she change?'

'Stopped going out, stopped laughing, withdrew from her old friends; anything I think that reminded her of Callum. I feel awful for this now but I was pleased when Callum finished with her. I thought once she got over it she'd be back to her old self, but she never did.'

'Did she not mix with any of her old friends, interact on social media?'

Cassie shook her head and bit her lip.

'What is it?' Stacey asked. There was something this girl wanted to say.

'I should have tried harder. I always felt that I wasn't patient enough with her. But she made it pretty hard.'

'In what way?'

Cassie hesitated as though choosing her words carefully. 'She started to say mean things. Stuff that was out of character for her. She criticised us all more than she had before. I got a weekend job to save for the new iPhone and she called me a zombie, a follower, started saying I had no mind of my own. There was like this constant disapproval of anything I did.'

Stacey couldn't help but wonder why a break-up with a boyfriend had caused her to be more judgemental.

She bit her lip again. 'I probably should have contacted her more but…'

'And then she ran away?' Stacey clarified.

Cassie frowned. 'Did she?'

'You didn't know?'

Cassie shook her head. 'Her withdrawal wasn't sudden like that. She made new friends, especially one girl with red hair, I think, but it was all gradual, over time, where contact just got less until there was none at all.' Her frown deepened. 'Her parents never mentioned her running away.'

'You saw them?' Stacey asked, trying to hide her puzzlement. She would have thought Cassie would have been their first port of call when Samantha disappeared. She'd been easy enough to find.

'Yeah, I saw them in here about a year ago. I asked how she was and they told me she was fine.'

'Okay, Cassie, thanks for your help,' Stacey said, moving away.

She left the shop wondering what the hell the Brown family was trying to hide.

CHAPTER 19

Penn decided to try the flat beneath Samantha's first. It appeared to mirror the one above, with the lounge looking out onto the road.

He rang the doorbell and almost jumped back at the volume level at which it had been set.

He waited a moment, hesitant to ring the bell a second time. Anyone close by with small children wouldn't thank him.

His finger was poised as the door was opened by a man in his seventies, dressed in dark trousers, a shirt and a light jacket.

'Good morning, sir, sorry to disturb you…'

'Come in, come in, lad. I can't be chatting on the doorstep. My burgers will thaw.'

Penn closed the door behind him and followed the man to the kitchen, where he was in the process of unloading shopping from a bag for life.

'Don't want them to go off after I've paid good money for them.' He stopped and turned. 'I say, before you state your business pop out to the car and see if I've left anything in there, will you, lad?'

Penn opened his mouth then closed it again. Maybe he'd missed it but he didn't remember seeing any car. He put his head out and checked. No car.

He returned to the kitchen. 'Sir, there's no car out…'

'Well, of course there's no car,' he said, rolling his eyes. 'I packed in driving last year.'

'Err… sir, my name is…'

'I'm too old to remember names. You're under forty years of age, so lad will do and you're a copper.'

'How did you…'

'Cos I was one for thirty-four years.'

Penn was impressed. And here he was thinking this guy had lost his faculties.

'And I saw you walking around yesterday with that lady who showed her ID a lot.'

Okay, so not quite as impressed.

'And I've gotta say', he continued, 'she is one good-looking…'

'Sir, may I take your name?' Penn interrupted. He didn't want to hear any more of that.

'Gregory Hall, at your service, lad,' he said, placing three apples in a fruit bowl.

'And you've lived here for?'

'Five years, since my hip operation.'

'Did you see much of Samantha Brown upstairs?'

'Oh, that was her name,' he said, answering the question, and giving Penn a sinking feeling. He wasn't going to get much information here, but it had to be worth another couple of questions.

The man shook his head absently as he took one apple from the fruit bowl and put it in the fridge.

'You're a bit late coming to see me, lad. In my day, we'd have been questioning the neighbours within the hour.'

Penn was not going to explain the reclassification of the death.

'Did you see many people coming and going?' he asked, losing the will to live.

'You think I've got nothing better to do than stare out of my window watching the neighbours, lad?'

'No, sir, I just…'

'Her parents came a lot,' he said, opening the fridge and taking the apple back out. 'Together and separately when the girl first moved in. In fact, I thought for a while that all of them had moved in. I think mum stayed over most nights at first.'

Penn wondered why a twenty-one-year-old woman had required such close supervision in her new home.

'I mean, if you want my opinion,' the man offered, finally taking a bite of the apple.

Penn didn't really but he nodded anyway.

'I think she wasn't all there,' he said, tapping his temple.

Penn said nothing. He'd seen no evidence to suggest that Samantha had any kind of disability.

'Cos, she didn't work, had no friends and was watched closely by her parents…'

'But surely there could be other explanations,' Penn said, trying to keep his tone even.

'And she clearly couldn't keep on top of her bills.'

Penn couldn't help frowning at the judgemental pensioner.

'Don't look like that. I know my stuff. She never answered the door when a man came, so she must have been hiding something.'

'You're assuming he was a bailiff?' Penn asked.

'Well he was a big burly man all dressed in black that she wouldn't let in the front door. So, what else would he be?'

Penn wasn't sure but he knew they needed to find out.

CHAPTER 20

Himley Lake was set in the grounds of Himley Park and was added to the grounds in 1779 by Capability Brown. At the time he redesigned the 180 acres adding waterfalls from a higher chain of smaller pools. The Ward family left Himley in the 1830s because it was too close to the Black Country. Instead they lived in great grandeur at Witley Court in Worcestershire.

Kim remembered being one of the site's 200,000 visitors a year when Keith, her one true foster dad, had brought her on the woodland walks some Sunday mornings while Erica cooked a roast dinner. The trek had always ended with a hot drink at the log cabin café and a stop to watch the sailing club on the great lake. And that was the area she'd been told to head to.

Bryant pulled up on the car park, nestling amongst four squad cars, Keats's van and two forensic vehicles.

Kim could see that uniformed officers were still shepherding people off the site.

The Hall itself was open to visitors from April to the end of September, but the park was open all year round.

As she headed towards the lake, Kim could see that the privacy tent had been erected. That would have been Keats's first priority given the public nature of the location.

Ten metres away Inspector Plant stepped towards her. As ever his deep tan against a shock of thick white hair amazed her.

'Park's almost clear,' he said, tapping his radio. 'Just a couple being escorted from the waterfall around the other side of the house.'

She nodded. 'You made contact?' she asked, nodding towards the house.

'Yes. The management are being as co-operative as they can be at the moment.'

They both knew full well that their concern for the body found would at some stage turn to concern for the running and maintenance of the site.

Inspector Plant and his team would remain at the location for the duration and would liaise with the management, who would keep the owners, Dudley Council, up to date.

She thanked him and continued towards the tent.

'Sunbed or bottle?' Bryant asked, as the tanned officer moved away.

'Holiday home in Spain is what I heard,' she replied, taking the protective slippers from the techie at the entrance flap of the tent.

Keats stepped out and blocked her path. 'A word, Inspector.'

Kim moved to the side, leaving Bryant to cover his shoes. Despite their phone conversation she'd expected this.

'Inspector, I…'

'Look, Keats. It happens. We made a mistake. We both—'

'Inspector, I performed the post-mortem on Samantha Brown at five thirty this morning,' he said, cutting her off.

'Oh,' she said.

Any lingering doubt of his own performance appeared to have disappeared during his few short hours of sleep. She was back in the presence of the Keats she knew and tolerated.

'There was little to note that we didn't already know. Toxicology samples have been sent off but as you know the results…'

'Will take a couple of days,' she said.

'Just one little thing,' he said, as she began to move away. 'Stomach contents. Appeared to be little more than a combination of rice and beans.'

'Vegan?' she asked.

He shrugged. 'Could be but I just thought I'd mention it.'

Kim made a mental note to check with her parents. It certainly wasn't going to lead them to her killer, but it was an unlikely meal unless you were anti-animal products entirely.

She followed the pathologist into the tent. Bryant had waited and stepped in behind her.

'Okay, Keats, what've we…'

She stopped speaking as he moved aside.

She took a second to appraise the sight before her.

The body of a young male dressed in jeans and tee shirt had been dragged up onto the side of the lake. One black and white trainer was on his foot and the other was missing.

Kim could see that his clothing was beginning to strain against the formation of adipocere – or grave wax as it was commonly known. She already knew that mere moments after death, body decomposition kicked in as bacterial enzymes started to break down the body's soft tissue. She had learned it was a process of putrefaction, bloat, purge and advanced decay, but she also knew that submersion in water slowed down the process.

Where the skin was visible she could see evidence of blistering and patches where the top layer of flesh had turned to a greyish-white colour. The smell of ammonia was unmistakeable.

The boy was lying on his side facing away from her. Weeds from the lake were tangled in his clothing and his hair. The bloated face was framed by light brown hair.

Kim guessed him to be late teens or early twenties.

'He's just a kid,' Bryant breathed behind her.

Mitch held up a clear evidence bag.

'Twenty years old and his name is Tyler Short.'

Kim reached for the bag and took a photo of the address on the driving licence as a noise sounded overhead.

'Bryant…' she said, looking to her colleague who was closest to the door.

He stepped outside and straight back in again.

'Yeah, it's a drone.'

Kim groaned. She'd known as soon as she'd received the call from Keats that this wouldn't avoid press attention for too long. Gone were the days when only the highest budget news outlets could get an overhead view of a crime scene by hiring helicopters and pilots.

Any bloody newspaper could buy a drone and send it overhead.

'Who found him?' she asked.

'One of the guys from the sailing club. Took out one of the boats to check a repair and felt something hit the side. The lace on his trainer got caught up, so the guy thought it'd be a good idea to drag whatever it was to the side. He had no idea.'

Bloody hell, Kim thought, trying to work out how many procedures had not been followed by that one act, and what potential valuable evidence had already been lost. Underwater forensics required special training, and although she didn't know much about it she knew that some factors remained the same across the board. It was infinitely better if the body remained as close to the resting place as possible.

Given that the only similarity between this body and Samantha Brown was the closeness in age, Kim wondered how the hell she was going to juggle two separate murder enquiries at the same time. The answer was that she couldn't.

'I'm wondering how long you think he's been in there, although I reckon he's gonna be handed over to another team.'

'I'm going to say a few weeks at least and I wouldn't be too sure about it being handed over. A body decomposing in water is slowed to approximately half the time of a body in open air. And grave wax can start forming anywhere from three weeks given the right temperature of the water.'

'Which is?'

Mitch stepped forward to answer. 'Below twenty-one degrees Celsius.'

Kim glanced at the body of water. 'But its early September. The temperature of the lake is surely warmer than...'

'Aah, the water has three distinct layers,' Mitch cut in.

'Mitch, I did not know that,' she said, raising one eyebrow. The techie loved to impart his knowledge and she had to admit she'd learned plenty from him over the years. 'Please feel free to educate me.'

He laughed before continuing. 'The top layer stays warm at around twenty degrees, the middle layer drops dramatically to somewhere between seven and eighteen degrees and the lowest layer is often between four and seven degrees.'

Those were not necessarily numbers she was going to remember but she got the general idea.

'But if he's been lying at the bottom of the lake surely that means he drowned?' She knew that drowning victims sank to the bottom due to the water in the lungs being heavier than oxygen which would cause them to float back up to the surface. 'This could be an accidental death or suicide. It's nothing to do with my current case so...'

'Oh, you'll want it, Inspector,' Keats said, knowingly.

She glanced at Bryant before answering.

'Keats, I know you think I'm superhuman but I think one murder investigation is enough...'

'Inspector, I barely think you're human never mind super- but there's something you haven't yet seen.'

He nodded to Mitch, who moved to the boy's feet while Keats put his hands on the boy's shoulders. Gently they turned him so he was on his back and Kim saw what the body position had been hiding.

The boy's throat had been cut.

CHAPTER 21

'For fuck's sake, how long has that bloody thing been up there now?' Kim asked, as they stepped out of the tent.

'About ten minutes,' Bryant answered as it hovered right above them.

The total lack of respect for privacy boiled her blood. Few reporters were able to put themselves in the position of family members who didn't need to be viewing this on bloody YouTube.

She turned and gave it the finger, hoping that shot made the evening news.

It dropped lower. Kim took out her phone, zoomed in and took a photo.

'Got ya.'

If she could identify which cheap rag was using it, she'd get Woody to pull some strings at a higher level.

'How long can a Proflight Orbit fly for?' Kim asked, reading the name on the side.

She began walking towards the car. Bryant did not.

'Hey, guv, I can't walk and type at the same time. I ain't Stacey, you know.'

She stopped walking, and waited.

'Okay, that particular model is totally for amateurs. It can stay in the air for twelve minutes tops and has a transmission range of two hundred metres.'

'You kidding?'

He shook his head.

The cheap bit didn't surprise her. This was probably *The Dudley Star* after all not Sky News.

'You're saying the operator is no more than two hundred metres away from here?'

'Looks like it,' Bryant answered.

She glanced backwards. Frost couldn't be anywhere on the park. It had been cleared.

'Come on,' she said, striding towards the car.

Frost had to be close by, probably sitting in her car somewhere along the road outside the park.

'Okay, go left,' she said as Bryant headed them towards the exit. A right turn took them towards traffic lights and a crossroad. Left took them to the small village of Himley. As he drove she looked for the white Audi TT that belonged to the reporter. As she searched she visualised ripping the controller out of her hand.

Bryant continued to drive until he said the words she was thinking.

'Guv, I'm pretty sure we're getting out of range.'

'Turn around and go back, slowly.'

The woman had to be somewhere close by to spy on events at the lake.

'Where the…' Kim stopped speaking as a movement on the left caught her eye. They were almost back at the park entrance. 'Stop the car.'

Bryant pulled in at the kerb.

She unclicked her seatbelt and headed back three houses. The property she wanted had a low privet hedge with a waist-high wooden fence.

The anger began to dissolve as she let herself into the front garden.

'Hey, buddy, wanna do me a favour and bring your drone back?'

The teenage boy looked terrified despite her gentle request.

She took a seat on the wooden bench beside his wheelchair and showed her ID.

His face reddened. 'I'm sorry, am I in...'

'Ricky, what have you done?' asked a woman from the open doorway.

Kim held up her hands. 'It's okay, Mrs...'

'Wilde,' she answered, still looking at her son.

'I'm sure Ricky didn't know but we've got an incident over at the park which needs to be kept private.'

'I heard sirens. Is everyone okay?'

'It's all being dealt with,' Kim answered as she heard the sound of the drone returning.

'I didn't mean any harm,' he said, as the drone came into view.

'I know but we just gotta keep stuff private.'

The drone hovered and then landed expertly at his feet.

'Pretty cool,' she said, getting to her feet.

'Not as cool as the Tello Drone Boost. Now that's a beauty.'

'You got a licence for that thing?' Kim asked. The recent law dictated that any user had to sit an online test and pay £9 to join a register if the drone weighed more than 250g, which was pretty much all of them. How it was going to be monitored and policed was another story.

Ricky shook his head as his mum stepped forward, her face reddening. 'We've been meaning to...'

'Tell you what, we'll waive that thousand-pound fine if you just delete the footage and keep it grounded until you're legal, okay?'

The relief that passed over his face was nothing compared to that of his mother.

Kim smiled as he nodded eagerly.

She offered her hand. 'Thanks for your co-operation, Ricky.'

She turned and left.

Because now she had a second body.

CHAPTER 22

Bryant felt the vibration of the phone in his pocket as the two of them entered the station.

'I'll get the coffee,' he said as the guv took the stairs two at a time to brief Woody on the second body.

He didn't particularly want to check his messages around her. He knew how she felt about his continued involvement in the old case and part of him knew she was right. And maybe the text message was the final part of the journey for him. He knew what it was going to say.

Perhaps if he witnessed the event himself he'd be able to accept that there really was nothing more he could do.

He stood in line and selected an assortment of plastic-wrapped sandwiches along with the drinks.

Three people before him were yet to be served.

Finally, he took out his phone and read the message.

Peter Drake was due to be released from prison at 6 p.m. that night.

And he for one would be there.

CHAPTER 23

Kim entered the squad room, pleased to see that their second victim had made it onto the board.

'Thanks, Penn,' she said, grabbing a triangle of chicken salad from one of the open containers. She nodded her acknowledgment to Bryant as she perched her bottom on the spare desk.

If not for Bryant's gentle prompts throughout the day, she'd forget to eat completely.

'Okay, guys, update from your field trips this morning?' she asked, after her first bite.

Penn brushed back an imaginary curl from his forehead. Something he tended to do when he was dissatisfied, she'd noticed.

'Little from me, I'm afraid. Two neighbours barely knew anyone had moved into Samantha's flat and thought it was still empty, and the one who did know saw the family visiting a lot and what he thought was a bailiff, because he was burly and dressed in black, but seeing as this guy sent me outside to bring in shopping from a car he no longer has, I'm not going to stake my house on everything he says.'

Penn opened his hands expressively, saying that's all folks, and Kim could understand his irritation. Not much for a morning's work, and maybe the neighbour's observations weren't completely believable, but they still needed to be checked.

'Penn, make some calls about Samantha's finances. Check with her landlord about her rent payments. If this guy was a bailiff we need to rule him out.'

'On it, boss.'

'Stace?' Kim asked, hopefully.

'Not much from Samantha's friend. A lot of what we already know about her being outgoing and confident. Apparently, that changed when a boyfriend dropped her. But there is one weird thing,' Stacey offered.

Kim straightened. She liked weird.

'Sammy's best friend had no knowledge of her running away. She said Sammy's withdrawal was more gradual than that. She just stopped going out, returning calls to all the friends that reminded her of Callum; but Carrie seemed to think she'd met some new people and she simply faded away from the circle. She also said she'd seen Sammy's parents, who, when asked, said their daughter was fine.'

Hmm… that wasn't the only weird thing, Kim thought. If Carrie was one of Sammy's best friends why was she not the first call from the parents when Sammy disappeared?

'Any…'

'No missing person's report filed any time in the last three years,' Stacey confirmed.

'Okay, neither of you have found a smoking gun but, on balance, someone give the plant to Stacey.'

Betty was the communal plant who got to grace the desk of the most productive member of the team.

'Err… boss, Betty died,' Stacey said, gravely.

'What?'

'Yeah, someone left her too close to the radiator,' Penn said, resting accusing eyes on Bryant, the one member of the team who had never won her fairly. 'She dried up and died.'

A smile tugged at Bryant's lips. 'I didn't do it, honest. I would not knowingly harm or injure another living thing. Especially one with a name.'

Kim smiled at his defence as her phone pinged a message.

She read it and turned to Penn.

'Post-mortem of Tyler Short is at three.'

'On it, boss.'

She turned to Stacey. 'Get me everything you can find on Tyler Short. Two young people turning up dead with the same manner of death is a bit too coincidental for my liking. Start with his next of kin.' She paused. 'And do a bit of checking on Sophie Brown. Apparently the sisters weren't close, and the girl is on her way back from Thailand.'

Something about Myles Brown's dismissal of the sibling relationship between the two had bothered her.

Stacey pushed aside the half-eaten cracker and set to work. Kim noted she hadn't touched any of the sandwiches that Bryant had bought.

'You okay, Stace?'

'Yeah, boss,' Stacey answered, without looking up.

Kim took her word for it and met Bryant's questioning glance. The jobs had been apportioned all except for them and Bryant had already guessed what they were going to do.

She nodded in response to his silent question.

Yes, as normal, they were going to the last known address of the victim to tell whichever family member was there that Tyler Short was dead.

CHAPTER 24

Bryant pulled the car to a stop in front of a row of houses on Wrights Lane in Old Hill.

Built around Heathfield High School in the early seventies, the small council estate had been an aspirational place to live for people needing social housing.

The new properties had included a mixture of two and three bed houses and a few flats. The roads had names like Cherry Orchard and Blossom Grove despite there being no orchard or grove in sight. The houses now appeared tired and unloved.

'Used to be a park up there,' Bryant said, nodding up the road. 'My dad would offer to take me from under mum's feet for a couple of hours on a Saturday afternoon before the wrestling started. He'd sit in the Prince of Wales pub opposite and watch me across the road.'

Kim marvelled at how parenting had changed in the years since.

She knocked on the door of the last known address for Tyler Short already forming her bad news face. Luckily the expression wasn't too distant a cousin from the look that shaped her features naturally.

She was surprised when the door was answered by a woman in her mid-twenties with a baby suckling at her breast. Did the lad already have a young family?

Bryant glanced away as the woman hitched the baby back into position. Kim got the impression she didn't care one bit. She liked that. Baby needed fed, baby got fed.

'Mrs… Miss… Err… Ms Short?' Kim asked.

She shook her head. 'None of the above.'

Kim checked the number on the plaque to the side of the door. Yep, definitely the address on the driver's licence.

'Are you any relation to Tyler Short?' Kim asked.

She shook her head and winced as the baby obviously got rough.

'Sorry, little bugger's got hard gums.'

'We have this as the last address for a twenty-year-old male who…'

'Hang on. There was a kid that lived here before us with his nan. She died, which of course we weren't told before we took the place, but I don't know what their names were. We've been here about two and a half years but it was empty for a while before that.'

'So, you'd have no idea where he would have gone after that?'

'None, sorry. I assume the council kicked him out when his nan died cos she was the tenant not him.'

'Okay, thanks,' Kim said, walking away.

She took out her phone right at the second it started to ring.

'Stace, tell me you've found…'

'Can't find any evidence of any friendship between our victims,' Stacey said, getting straight into it. 'But Tyler was at Dudley College too. Dropped out almost three years ago.'

'Around the time his nan died,' Kim observed.

'Apparently, cos his last post on social media was a poem to his grandmother.'

'His last?'

'Yep,' Stacey said. 'Just like Samantha his presence on social media came to an abrupt end on the last day he attended college.'

Two victims, both at the same college, Kim thought.

'Thanks, Stace, could be a coincidence but see if you can find any other missing persons linked to the college, maybe talk to a couple of tutors and…'

'Hang on, I'm not done yet, boss. Talking of social media I'm not too sure about what Myles Brown told you about Sophie.'

'That the sisters weren't close or that she's in Thailand?' Kim asked.

'Both, either,' Stacey answered. 'Sophie isn't a massive sharer but there are definitely old photos of the two sisters together having fun, but nothing that would indicate she's travelling abroad.'

'Okay, Stace, thanks,' Kim said, ending the call.

'That's a bit weird,' Bryant said, hearing most of what Stacey had said.

Kim sat in the car for a moment, chewing over the facts.

In two days they'd had two victims under the age of twenty-two. One male, one female. Both had had their throats cut. Both had been students at Dudley College. Both had suddenly stopped using social media three years ago. And both had been emotionally vulnerable.

Stacey's findings about Samantha and Sophie confirmed to her that Samantha's parents were holding something back, which was bad enough if they were trying to protect something that only affected their daughter, but now she had a second victim whose murder commanded the same level of attention.

Kim decided that the Browns had guarded their secret for long enough.

CHAPTER 25

Penn had chosen not to mention to the boss how much he enjoyed a good post-mortem for fear of appearing a bit weird, he thought, as he headed through Russells Hall Hospital.

It wasn't that he felt nothing for the person being dissected. It was quite the opposite. He was a firm believer in respect for any living thing. If you killed a chicken to eat, then give it the honour of using every last ounce of it. Don't just eat a breast or a drumstick; use it all and then boil the bones for a broth. The animal had died for it.

It was the same for the poor soul on the slab. If their bodies were going to be violated for clues then do it good; look everywhere, search every nook and cranny then find the bastard responsible.

The body had so much to reveal after death, he marvelled, entering the morgue bang on time.

'Good afternoon, Penn. Your boss still out in the field breaking everyone's b—'

'Yep, as well as trying to find the murderer of Samantha Brown,' he responded. If his boss was not so keen on breaking balls, the girl's death would still be a suicide.

'Yes, quite. Your garments are over there.'

Penn climbed into the folded paper suit and then placed the mask over his face. 'And the hat,' Keats said. 'With you, especially the hat.'

By this time of day, the grip of the holding gel was no longer as firm and curls were starting to fall onto his forehead. He forced them under the blue hairnet.

Satisfied, Keats turned on the tape recorder.

'Commencing the post-mortem examination of Tyler Short, male Caucasian, aged twenty…'

Penn stood away as Keats continued verbally recording the initial weights and measurements before reaching for the scalpel.

He paused the tape as he held the blade above the waxy, bloated flesh.

'You ready for this?'

Penn rubbed his hands. 'Oh yeah, let's get this party started.'

CHAPTER 26

There were some cases that Kim felt could be solved if she simply set up camp and waited long enough at one location. That's how she was beginning to feel about the home of Myles and Kate Brown.

She was surprised to see Kate Brown answer the door instead of her husband.

'Have you caught them?' she asked, wringing her hands.

Kim shook her head as she stepped inside. She was unsure what the woman expected in the few hours since they'd last been here.

'I'm afraid not, Mrs Brown. We're here for more information from you and your husband.'

Kate headed for the room they'd already graced on their two previous visits.

'Myles is trying to work,' she said, opening the door.

Kim immediately noticed that the computer behind which he sat wasn't even switched on. There was no attempt at work going on here.

As he turned in the captain's chair Kim could see his eyes were red-rimmed and a handkerchief corner peeped out of his trouser pocket. Kim felt a rush of sympathy. There was no doubt that this couple was grieving and that she was trampling on their grief every time she knocked on the door. It was also clear that they were hiding something. She had no choice but to put her sympathy aside.

'Mr Brown, we…'

'I'll go and make tea,' Kate said, heading towards the door.

'Mrs Brown, I'd rather you stay…'

'And I'd rather go and make tea,' she said shortly.

'I'll help,' Bryant said, seizing the opportunity to get her alone.

For a second she saw fear in the eyes of Myles Brown but he quickly realised there was little he could do. To forbid a police officer from helping his wife make a hot drink would require some kind of explanation.

'Mr Brown,' Kim said, taking a seat. 'I'm afraid to say that I don't think you and your wife are being completely honest with us.'

His face hardened as he opened his mouth to speak.

Kim held up her hand to quiet him. 'Before you speak, you should know that any omissions up to this point I will attribute to the shock and grief of losing your daughter, but if you withhold information beyond this conversation I will assume that you are obstructing a murder investigation and will act accordingly. Do we understand each other?'

He hesitated before nodding.

'Does the name Tyler Short mean anything to you?'

He considered for a moment before shaking his head. 'Should it?' he asked.

Kim left the question hanging in the air. If he didn't know the boy, she would not go into detail.

'But you do know a girl named Carrie?'

He nodded without hesitation. 'She was one of Sammy's best friends.'

'A while back, though, wasn't it?'

'Yes, they were friends in college.'

'Before Sammy ran away?'

He had the grace not to nod in agreement as they both knew that story was a lie.

'Mr Brown, we know that Sammy had a bad break-up with a boyfriend that hit her hard. We know that it caused her to withdraw from her normal social circle and from social media, but she didn't run away. So, tell me, Mr Brown, where was your daughter for the last two years?'

His body visibly deflated before her eyes as though the truth was trying to find a way out of him.

He took a deep breath. 'Sammy joined a cult.'

'A what?' Kim asked, sitting forward. She could be no more surprised if he'd said she'd joined a travelling circus.

'A cult,' he repeated. Seeing the expression on her face, he continued, 'And that's why we kept it secret. You don't believe me, do you? You think cults only exist in other countries. You think they all look like Charles Manson or David Koresh?'

Strangely enough both the insane murderer and the leader of the Branch Davidians in Waco had been two of the first faces that had popped into her head.

'Not all cults are based on religion, and not all are in the public eye or in any of the research books, but it makes them no less real or dangerous.'

Kim shook her head in disbelief. There were no cults in the area.

'I can see you don't believe me but you wanted the truth and here it is. Sammy was caught by a recruiter when she was at her most vulnerable. After Callum called it off once and for all, she was courted and flattered, and we saw her less and less. The more we tried to hold on to her, the harder she pulled away, until she stopped coming home completely. No conversation, no explanation, she just faded away.'

'To where?' Kim asked, trying to keep the doubt out of her voice.

'Unity Farm in Wolverley. That's what the place is called but it's not really a farm. It's a commune for people who want to step out of real life. Over time they're brainwashed until they can no longer think for themselves and everything they do is for the good of the group.'

Kim frowned. 'But she was out of it. Did she come back?'

'Y-Yes, she ran away. We didn't ask her too many questions because we were just pleased to have her back.'

Kim was trying to get that information to gel in her mind as Bryant re-entered the room with a tea tray. Mrs Brown did not follow him in.

There was something in Mr Brown's explanation that was not making sense to her. If Sammy had joined some kind of group and had been influenced enough to leave her family, what would have prompted her to suddenly leave?

'Surely Samantha must have offered some kind of explanation when she returned,' Kim said as her phone vibrated an incoming call in her pocket. She ignored it.

'She just said the group wasn't what they had pretended to be,' he answered.

'Was she any more forthcoming with her sister?' Kim asked.

He coloured and shook his head. 'I've told you they weren't close. Sophie can't tell you anything about her sister.'

Kim knew that the man was lying to prevent her talking to the girl. But why, what exactly did Sophie have to hide? Kim wondered as her phone pinged a text message.

'I'm sorry, excuse me,' she said, taking out her phone. Someone wanted her attention badly.

The text was from Mitch and said simply

Need you back at the lake. NOW

She held the curse on the other side of her lips. She really needed to pump Myles Brown for more information, but Mitch was the lead techie at the crime scene.

She stood up, and saw the relief instantly rest on his features.

'I'm sorry we have to go but we will need to speak to you further.'

He nodded his understanding and walked them to the door.

'Oh, Mr Brown,' she said, stepping outside, 'was Sammy a vegan?'

He shook his head. 'She wasn't a massive meat eater but she couldn't have survived without a bacon sandwich now and again.'

'Was she on any kind of health kick?' she tried again. Maybe she was detoxing.

He shook his head impatiently as though this level of triviality was beneath his time. She thanked him and allowed him to close the door.

'Get anything from the wife?' she asked Bryant as they headed towards the car.

'Not a bean. Wouldn't answer a thing. Made the tea in silence and then headed upstairs to prepare the bedroom for Sophie, who is due back any time soon.'

Kim seriously hoped so. She wanted to speak to this girl now more than ever.

As he left the driveway at speed, Bryant almost collided with a vehicle turning in – a white Range Rover being driven by a burly man who appeared to be dressed all in black.

Kim recalled the description Penn had been given by Samantha's neighbour but had no chance to get the registration number before it disappeared around the bend.

Damn it, she couldn't hang about. She was needed back at the crime scene.

She let out a long breath, trying to expel some of the tension in her body.

She had the feeling that Myles Brown had been telling the truth but not the whole truth. The man was still hiding something.

CHAPTER 27

Myles closed the front door on the police officers and stood in the middle of the hallway. He considered heading straight back to his study and closing the door on the wall of animosity that was building between himself and his wife. Ever since they'd returned from the morgue Kate had been unable to tolerate being in the same room with him for more than a couple of minutes.

He began to climb the stairs, recalling the quiet sobs that had escaped from the lips of his wife throughout the night as she'd tossed and turned beside him. His efforts to offer comfort had been rebuffed as she had moved closer to the edge of the bed.

His own tears threatened to break free every waking moment for the loss of his daughter and only the need to be strong for the rest of his family kept them at bay.

He stood for a moment in the doorway to Sophie's room, watching his wife shake the quilt into the quilt cover decorated with a New York skyline print: Sophie's favourite.

Sensing his presence, she stiffened but didn't turn.

'Did you tell her the truth?' Kate asked, forcing a plump pillow into a fresh, crisp pillow case.

'No,' he answered, leaning against the door frame.

She paused, mid-plump. 'I think you're making a mistake.'

'We can't risk it, sweetheart. It's too dangerous. We don't know what could happen if we involve the police now.'

Finally, she turned to look at him. 'I think we can trust her. She seems to know what she's doing.'

Myles hesitated, torn between wanting to bridge the gap between them and the gut instinct that told him he was doing the right thing.

'We can't trust that she'd understand how these things need to be handled.'

'And we've done a fantastic job so far, haven't we?' she accused, her eyes blazing.

He swallowed the emotion back down. He knew what this was costing his marriage, but the silence and distance lengthened between them because he couldn't tell her what she wanted to hear.

'You know, Myles, mistakes have been made and contrary to your belief I don't blame you for all of them.'

This admission tore at his heart. He stepped towards her, aching to take her into his arms.

She moved to the side, deftly avoiding his touch.

Her eyes were now cold and empty.

'But this mistake is completely yours and if it all goes wrong be sure you'll be facing it alone.'

CHAPTER 28

Stacey ended her call to Dudley College with no more information than she'd had before. It had taken Sammy's psychology professor a good few minutes to remember her former student, and even then had given her stock responses as though she was writing an end of year school report. She hadn't even noticed the change in the girl after her break-up with Callum. Tyler's mechanical engineering tutor had barely recalled him at all, leaving her hanging for ten minutes while he searched his records rather than his memory for the name.

Stacey reminded herself that these people saw thousands of students every year and couldn't be expected to remember everything about every one of them, but still there was a sense that they would be more noticeable for their deaths than their lives. Their names would now travel the halls of the facility on the lips of people who hadn't even known them.

Her search of missing persons had turned up two mentions of Dudley College but both teenage boys had returned home safe and sound and neither case had been reported in the years since Sammy and Tyler had been there. So far she had found no link to the college other than that they had both attended at the same time.

She sighed heavily and fought the urge to nip down to the canteen for a double chocolate muffin.

Rosie often put one aside for her at the beginning of the day, so sure was she that Stacey would find her way down at some stage for her favourite treat. She'd resisted for two days now but it felt much longer.

By her reckoning she had twelve weeks to lose the stone in weight that she'd like to shed before the wedding. Given that it had taken almost a month to lose two pounds, the odds were not on her side.

She'd never been a dieter and had always felt that all was well in moderation. If she had a few days where she felt she'd eaten plenty, she'd spend a couple of days just cutting back, which worked well for the odd pound or two that crept on while watching a bit of late-night TV with a chocolate bar, or two. But for shifting a chunk of weight she'd had to resort to more desperate measures.

She lifted the lid on her lunchbox to check that nothing appealing had found its way in. No, it was as she'd left it: two cracker breads covered thinly with a low fat spread, a tomato, an apple and banana. She closed the lid again wishing she liked healthy food more.

Devon told her every night that she didn't want Stacey to lose weight and Stacey explained every time that she was doing it for herself. And it was easy for Devon to say that with her five foot ten frame that somehow repelled excess fat. The woman's weight hadn't budged in the eighteen months they'd been together. Naturally athletic, her body burned calories like a furnace. If Stacey wasn't so ridiculously, emphatically, deliriously in love with the woman, she'd hate her bloody guts.

The extra stone she carried had been reconciled in her mind by the constant thought of 'I'll lose that when…'

She'd never been clear when the 'when' was going to be but it had always been for something that mattered. And what could be more important than her wedding day?

It was the photos that stuck in her mind. Those photos would hopefully be shown to children and grandchildren, and she really didn't want to look at them in years to come hating the way she looked on the most important day of her life.

No, she had to stick with it, she thought, shifting her attention from the reserved chocolate muffin to twenty-year-old Tyler Short.

His social media didn't show the outgoing personality of Samantha. His friends were not in the triple figures, so he was not a collector: how Stacey viewed people who amassed hundreds of Facebook friends that they'd never met. But what she couldn't find were any family members: brothers, sisters, cousins.

There were not many photos of him. One when he'd passed his driving test and a few with a small group of friends. She skipped over those and went to his posts. There were a couple of shared photos of cars and funny memes that seemed to be *Star Wars* related, but what really got her attention were the thoughtful posts. Mainly about mothers and posted around Mother's Day each year. His oldest photo was a selfie taken with his grandmother and a birthday cake. Just the two of them.

Stacey moved away from his social media with a feeling that she'd missed something, but she had to focus on his past, his background, which she wasn't going to get from social media.

Ten minutes later she'd written a half page of notes on Tyler Short and it didn't make for particularly happy reading.

Born to a troubled mother ridden with bouts of depression, he'd spent much of his childhood with his maternal grandmother. Stacey had found no evidence of a father. His mother had committed suicide when he was twelve years old, at which point he lived with his grandmother full time. From what Stacey could gather he had given her no trouble and had worked hard enough to get himself into college to study to be a mechanic.

The merging of the hard facts and his social media left Stacey with an overwhelming feeling of sadness. The boy had suffered uncertainty in his younger years with little to no stability and had lost his mother before he'd even reached his teens.

She went back to his Facebook page and in particular to that one photo with his nan.

It really had been just the two of them. She had been the only constant throughout his life and when he'd lost her he really had lost everything.

Her gaze moved across to the most recent photo of Tyler amongst a group of friends and realised what it was that she'd missed the first time.

Her eyes rested on the face of someone she already knew.

CHAPTER 29

It was almost four when Bryant drove them through the cordon at the gates to Himley Park. Small groups of employees littered the grass on the side of the road as they approached the car park at the lake.

Inspector Plant was being talked at by a sturdy woman with her arms folded across her chest. Kim looked away before either of them could catch her eye. She couldn't answer the question that was most probably on the woman's lips. She didn't know when the site could be handed back, and the fact she'd been recalled wasn't good news for anyone.

She looked up as she got out of the car. No drones; the boy had listened.

The tent was still in place, even though the body had been removed. Kim headed straight for it, guessing that was where Mitch would be collecting his samples.

Before she stepped inside she glanced around the lake. In all she was guessing there were fourteen or fifteen white suits around the perimeter. Some were staggered in singles, but there were two clutches of three or four. One clutch about twenty feet west of the tent and the other bunch opposite the tent on the other side of the lake.

'Hey, Mitch,' she said, entering the tent.

'Inspector, sorry for having to call you back, and thank you for being prompt.'

Oh, the forensic tech was a breath of fresh air compared to the pathologist. He had manners. He used nice words like sorry and thank you.

'What you got?' she asked, approaching the small pop-up table that was serving as a work space. Clear storage boxes were open beneath it. She guessed they contained samples of soil and vegetation.

He reached for a clear bag from the box on the left. She recognised it as the matching trainer from the body of Tyler Short.

She took the bag and turned it. The shoe was more muddy than wet.

'Found just along the edge there,' he said, nodding towards the first group of techs she'd seen.

'Dislodged during a struggle before he went into the water?' she asked.

He nodded. 'Buried down with only the laces showing.'

'Good spot,' she acknowledged.

He smiled. 'We don't have a plant to hand around but I'll be sure to tell the guy you said so.'

'We don't have it any more,' Kim said, glancing at her colleague, who whistled and looked away. 'It died.'

'Sorry to hear that,' Mitch said, placing the shoe into the clear box.

The ironies of police work never failed to amaze her. They were standing at the site where a young man had lost his life and she was being offered condolences for a plant.

'So, what…'

'There's something…'

They said together. Of course there was something else. There were two groups of techs stationed around the lake. She rarely got called back to a crime scene for an item the forensic team expected to find.

He reached under the table into the right-hand box and took out an evidence bag similar in size to the other.

'Found over the other side of the lake. Maybe something. Maybe nothing but I thought you'd like to know.'

Kim took the bag from him and turned it.

Another shoe.

But this one had belonged to a woman.

CHAPTER 30

Penn removed the gown and mask when instructed to do so by Keats.

He had remained silent as the pathologist had worked steadily and methodically through the process of examining the body externally before turning his attention to the brain, heart, lungs, liver, kidneys, intestines, blood vessels and small glands. As he'd worked Penn had been surprised at the respect and reverence he had shown the body of Tyler Short. Every organ that was measured and weighed had been treated with the care of a newborn baby, as though he wished to cause no further damage. His only surprise had been when Keats had removed the stomach contents with a ladle.

Keats had not spoken during the process except into his Dictaphone as he worked, seemingly forgetting that Penn was in the room.

'So, we have established that this poor fellow didn't die from the laceration to his throat. Your killer cut him and then forced his head underwater so that he drowned.'

Penn assumed this was Keats's way of giving him permission to speak.

'Wanted to make sure?'

'Your question to answer. Not mine,' Keats said, pulling the sheet over the head of Tyler Short.

'Is that to help establish time of death?' Penn asked, as Keats took the contents he'd ladled out of the stomach over to the microscope.

Keats shook his head. 'In this case the placement of the contents within the digestive system will assist with knowing the time between his last meal and death, which I would estimate to be approximately three hours, but it's not going to help establish when he died, which I would estimate to have been four to six weeks.'

'You can't…'

'No,' Keats said. 'I can't be more specific than that, and your boss will get the same answer when she reads my full report.'

Penn hid his smile. They both knew she'd push for a more specific time frame than that.

Penn balled up his paper outfit and placed the items into the bin. 'Okay, I'll…'

'Did I say we were done?' Keats asked, without turning.

'Not sure what else…'

'This,' Keats said, motioning for him to look through the microscope.

'Okay,' Penn said, not really sure what he was looking at.

Keats pulled up a photo on his computer screen.

Penn rolled his eyes. 'Why didn't you just show me the bigger picture first? I still don't know what I'm looking at but…'

'What you're looking at is the stomach contents of…'

'Tyler Short. I know that,' Penn said, pleased he'd had at least one chance to interrupt the pathologist.

Keats peered at him over his gold-rimmed glasses. 'These are the stomach contents of Samantha Brown. Exactly the same.'

Penn looked into the microscope and back to the screen.

'So, if your boss needs any further proof that these cases are linked you can tell her that Tyler Short's last meal was also nothing more than rice and beans.'

CHAPTER 31

Callum Towney was not what Kim expected.

The photo Stacey had sent showed a reasonably good-looking lad with a healthy tan and a head full of untidy blonde hair. The boy collecting trolleys in the Asda car park had shaved his head and collected a couple of piercings on his face.

'Got a minute?' she asked, showing her ID.

'Sure,' he said, without changing expression.

In Kim's experience the majority of people underwent some kind of emotional change, however subtle, when approached by a police officer. Often she saw fear, anticipation, guilt, irritation, superiority but she rarely saw no change at all. For her that indicated a person who hadn't ever done a thing wrong or someone who didn't care if they got caught. It remained to be seen into which category Callum Towney fell.

'We'd like to talk to you about Samantha Brown,' she explained.

A knowing look flashed onto his face. 'Yeah, thought you might.'

Samantha's name had been plastered all over the press, so he knew the girl was dead. She detected no hint of sadness, regret, nothing.

'Why's that then?'

He opened his arms expansively as though it was obvious. 'Cos I was the love of her life, innit?'

Oh, the innit. A phrase she despised.

'Allegedly,' Kim offered, wondering already what the hell Sammy had seen in this guy.

'You dated at college?'

'Dated?' he guffawed, as though she'd used some ancient term. 'We did a lot of f—'

'I think the answer is yes,' Bryant interrupted.

Callum nodded.

'And you were studying what at Dudley College?' Kim asked, pointedly looking at the trolleys as he pushed his line into a stray one beside a Ford Fiesta.

'Not much,' he said. 'Only went so my parents wouldn't throw me out. And this?' he said, looking at his trolleys, 'Just to get me by. I'm claiming Jobseeker's at a different address so it's decent until I can get investors for an idea I've got.'

Kim heard the pride in his voice that he was swindling the government. She idly wondered if she had actually shown him her ID.

'Splendid,' she said. His grand plan was not something she needed to hear. Nor was the admission he was fiddling benefits. A quick call to the benefits office later would soon put paid to that.

'Callum, we're far more interested in your relationship with Sammy Brown.'

He looked at his trolleys and beckoned for them to follow him. His charges were left blocking a line of six cars.

'Err… shouldn't you?…'

'Nah, Bert'll be out in a minute. He'll move 'em.'

He stopped at the side of the building and took a pouch from his jacket pocket.

He paused. 'Look, she was a great girl to start with – she was a laugh and sexy as f— Well, you know what I mean. We had a lot of fun but then she got all serious. Started pulling a face if I forgot to meet her or if I changed my mind. And other girls…'

'Is it fair to say you had different ideas of how the relationship was?' Kim asked as politely as she could. This little rodent had used her for sex and strung her along.

'Yeah, yeah. I didn't want the hassle, so I finished it. Never really spoke to her again.'

'And you also knew a guy called Tyler Short?'

He frowned as he opened the pouch. 'Nah, didn't have no mates by that name.'

Kim took out her phone and scrolled to the photo.

Kim noted a smile as his eyes first fell on himself.

'This guy,' she said, tapping the screen.

He looked closer. The frown dissolved as recognition dawned.

'Oh him, my mate Spuddy knew him. Brought him along a couple of times. Never knew his name.'

Or bothered to remember it, Kim thought, as Callum opened up his pouch and took out a spliff.

'You do realise we're police officers?' Kim queried, just to be sure. So far, he'd admitted to benefit fraud and was now about to light weed right in front of them.

'I figure we're in deep shit if you ain't got bigger fish to fry than me, so what you gonna do, innit?' he asked, lighting the roll-up.

Before she could stop herself she reached out, whipped the joint from his mouth and stamped it on the ground. She ground it around the tarmac so he wouldn't be tempted to try and retrieve it.

'What we're gonna do about it is whip your ass down to the station to discuss in more detail your connection to both these people.' She paused. 'Innit?'

The lad's eyes were wide as he glanced down at her shoe. She ground it back and forth a few times more to make her point.

Callum looked up. 'Hang on. You saying this dude is dead too?'

She didn't answer the question.

'So, your recollection any clearer?' she asked.

A memory seemed to dawn on him. He rolled his eyes. 'Yeah, the kid kept asking me questions about Sammy. Pathetic it was. Obviously, she didn't want to know.'

'Because he was younger?' Kim asked. There was only one year between them.

'Nah, cos she couldn't stop thinking about me.'

'Of course,' Kim said. Obviously.

'Had it bad, poor kid, couldn't take his eyes off her.' He shook his head with derision. 'Dopey bastard would have followed her anywhere.'

CHAPTER 32

'You reckon they were both in this cult thingy?' Bryant asked after she ended her conversation with Penn. That both of their victims had the same stomach contents was not something she had encountered before unless they had shared the same last meal, which would have been impossible for Sammy and Tyler, as the boy had died weeks before.

'Is the disbelief in your voice at them both being members or that there is actually some kind of cult in Wolverley?'

'Both but probably more the latter,' he said honestly.

She couldn't really offer anything in disagreement.

Wolverley was a village two miles north of Kidderminster, lying on the River Stour. With a population of approximately two thousand people, it was usually peaceful, with a low crime rate, except for a gruesome murder somewhere in the village back in the nineties. She knew the area boasted thirteen listed buildings and caves cut into the sandstone cliffs behind some of the dwellings. Surrounding the sleepy village were rolling fields and wooded areas, and, they now knew, a place called Unity Farm.

'His face was a picture,' Bryant said, heading out of Wordsley.

'Huh?'

'Callum when you ripped the spliff from his mouth. Classic. And the benefits office was very pleased to take my call.'

'It's been a good day for that lad,' she agreed. While Bryant had been busy grassing up Callum to the authorities, she had tried to place a second call to Woody, to update him on the shoe found at the lake. The fact that he was unavailable in a quarterly budget meeting did not bode well for the request she was going to be making when she got back to the station.

'He was a bit of a dick, wasn't he? Should be interesting to see what he comes up with for his whereabouts when Sammy was murdered.'

'Smoking too much of that stuff and he'll barely remember what he did an hour ago,' she answered.

'What's your feeling?'

She shrugged. 'He's not out of the woods yet. I think there's more to his personality than we've seen. Perhaps a quick temper. So, he's staying on the radar for now.'

'Satnav says we're a quarter-mile away from the destination,' Bryant said as the fields either side opened up around them.

'Okay, slow down and…'

'Oh, the irony of you telling me to slow down.'

She chuckled. She only ever told him to speed up.

'There,' she called out as they passed an open gate with a small brass plate screwed in to the top.

Bryant steered the car quickly onto the single track road that turned into a dirt path as it rounded a bend that skirted a small wooded area.

'Hear that?' Bryant asked, winding down his window as he drove slowly.

'I can't hear a thing.'

'Exactly,' he said.

As they moved further away from the road the silence deepened. Something that always put Kim on edge. She liked the noise, the activity, the impatience and misery of people rushing from one place to another. Tranquillity unnerved her.

Bryant pulled to a halt on a gravel patch in front of a shack with a hand-painted sign that said 'Farm Shop'.

'Aspirational, eh, guv?' Bryant asked, switching off the engine.

Kim had to agree. The farm shop was a garden shed with a table out front. A bowl of eggs sat between a few clutches of carrots and a pile of misshaped potatoes.

The girl behind the table stood, her face alight with the prospect of making a sale. Not surprising as she was hardly on the high street.

'Buy some carrots, Bryant,' Kim whispered as they approached.

'You call them c—'

'Just do it,' she growled, fixing a smile to her face as Bryant picked up the best of a bad limp bunch.

'Two pounds,' the girl said, holding out her hand.

She heard Bryant's sharp intake of breath, but he fished in his pocket anyway.

Now was not the time to arrest her for extortion.

'Hi,' Kim said, holding up her ID. 'May we speak to the person in charge?'

The girl's delight quickly turned to alarm.

'There's nothing to worry about,' Kim reassured her. 'We're here about a girl named Samantha Brown, did you know her?'

Colour seeped into her cheeks as she stepped back into the shed mumbling something about waiting a minute.

Kim stepped to the side and watched as she retrieved a mobile phone and turned her back.

Kim took a quick look around and realised that going through the shed on foot to the other side was the only way to access the property. The farm shop itself was stationed between metal fencing that travelled off in either direction further than she could see.

Farm shop or gate keeper? Kim thought idly, wondering where vehicle access to the site was located.

She was about to ask when the girl finished on the phone.

'Jake is on his way,' she said, wringing her hands and looking around.

Kim detected both excitement and trepidation.

'If you just show us where we can drive through, we can…'

'He'll be just a minute,' she said, definitely.

Kim got the impression that without throwing her to the ground and overpowering her, they were not getting through that shed.

'So, did you know Samantha?' Kim asked again.

She nodded slowly. 'But she's gone.'

Kim was unsure if she meant gone or dead. Either way she was biting her bottom lip.

'Did she have any trouble with…'

'Oh, that's Jake now,' she said, turning away as some kind of engine sounded behind the shed. A man in his mid-fifties appeared behind her. His hair was completely white but thick and cut well. His shoulders were broad beneath an open-neck pale blue shirt. His skin was smooth with enough colour to radiate good health. His eyes were the purest blue she had ever seen. Once your gaze met those, the rest of his face was forgotten.

'DI Stone,' Kim said, showing her ID. 'We'd like to talk to you about Samantha Brown.'

The man moved closer to the girl and offered his hand in Kim's direction.

'Jake Black and is Sammy okay?'

Oh great. They didn't even know she was dead.

'Mr Black, we really need to go somewhere and talk.'

He moved towards the table. 'Of course, come through.'

'If you just show us where to bring the car through…'

'It's no bother. Please, this way,' he said, pointing to the gap he'd made.

Kim hesitated but followed. She needed to be on the other side of that shed.

Bryant walked in behind her, and Jake closed the gap. He surveyed the table and squeezed the girl's shoulder.

'Good work, Maisie, keep it up.'

Kim couldn't help the frisson of discomfort that swept up her spine at the physical contact. Maisie was clearly over the age of eighteen, but there was something that didn't sit right.

Maisie's blush deepened and she squeezed her hands together as though she might explode. A suspicious person might think that was the exact response he'd intended. Good job Bryant was the suspicious person in their partnership.

She followed Jake Black out of the shed and saw the golf buggy in which he'd travelled. To her left were fields and to her right was a dirt track that disappeared around a wooded area.

'Hop on and I'll…'

'Mr Black, I'd rather…'

'I insist. I'd love for you to come and see the house.'

Kim hopped on beside him and Bryant sat behind. It wouldn't hurt to put all this cult nonsense to bed and learn the whole truth about Sammy Brown.

'So, is everything okay with Sammy? And please call me Jake.'

'Thank you… Jake and no I'm afraid she isn't okay.' Had he not seen the news? she thought and then wondered if this vehicle could go any quicker. She had a meeting with Woody sometime today.

'I have to get me one of these,' Bryant said.

Not surprising, she thought, given the speed he liked to drive.

'We miss her,' Jake said, and she detected genuine emotion in his voice.

'As will her parents now because unfortunately Sammy Brown is dead.'

The golf cart came to a sudden halt just as a house came into view.

The property appeared to be an old farmhouse that had been extended in all directions.

'Please tell me what happened,' he said, turning towards her.

'Sammy was murdered by someone she knew and allowed into her new flat.'

'She had a flat?' he asked, re-starting the golf cart. There was an edge to his voice that she tried to fathom.

'Yes, she'd recently set up home on her own.' Although home was a stretch for the cold, impersonal space where she'd lived.

Kim decided to keep the news of Tyler Short to herself for now, as she wanted to monitor his emotional reaction to the news of Sammy's demise.

And right now, she thought, as she glanced at the tense jawline that shaped the handsome face, there was a lot of emotion indeed.

CHAPTER 33

'Really?' Stacey said aloud as she stared at the hastily scrawled note from her last conversation with the boss. Only once you've exhausted Samantha's and Tyler's friends the boss had said. Well, that was a given. Other friends of Sammy's had offered her no further information than what she'd learned from Cassie, and a few messages to Tyler's Facebook friends had been met with responses of 'Tyler who?'.

'I suppose I've got you to thank for this,' Stacey greeted Penn as he walked in the door.

'Probably but I'm not gonna commit right away. What's up?' he asked, taking a plain blue bandana from his top drawer.

'Big burly man in black in a white Range Rover, that's what your neighbour guy said, wasn't it?' she snapped.

'Yeah, but like I said, I don't totally trust what...'

'Well, guess who's gotta try and track him down,' she said, ending with a big sigh.

'You okay?' he asked, logging into his workstation.

'Peachy,' she answered. 'How the hell am I gonna find out who this guy is?'

'Search the internet,' he said, shrugging.

'Penn, are you taking the piss out of me?'

'Jeez, Stace, eat something already. You're pretty hangry right now.'

She took a breath before speaking. 'It's got nothing to do with that. I had a banana an hour ago. I'm pissed off because this is an impossible task.'

'No it's not.'

Stacey pushed herself back in her chair and stared up at the ceiling. And damn him, her stomach was making all kinds of noises at her, but she'd got through the majority of the day and she wasn't going to weaken now. She had a chicken salad to look forward to when she got home.

'Trust in Google,' he said, removing the Tupperware container from the middle of their desks.

She sat forward. 'What?'

'Put in a ridiculous search. I do it all the time. Say I'm looking for an easy to follow recipe for Jasper. He gets overwhelmed by too many lines of text. I'll put in a search for "easy to follow recipe for making tiramisu with less than ten instructions". I tell Google exactly what I want. It likes the challenge.'

Stacey couldn't help but smile at the picture of him downloading simplified instructions for his brother to do his favourite thing.

'Penn, you're an idiot but I'll give it a whirl,' she said, typing in exactly what the boss had said.

Big burly man dressed in black driving a white Range Rover.

There were no results containing all her words, but she scrolled down anyway, taking note of the words Google had put a line through to say 'not contained'.

Three hits from the bottom of the page she came to an item that had omitted the words 'big' and 'burly' but contained the rest. It was a news article from *The Dudley Star* dated three weeks earlier.

'Penn, you're a genius.'

He shrugged. 'Idiot, genius. All the same to me.'

She read through the piece written by none other than Tracy Frost. Her eyes scanned to the area that had been highlighted as being a match for her criteria.

*…Police are appealing for the help of a **man dressed in black driving a white Range Rover** who was seen just*

metres away from the site of the burglary that took place in
Cavendish Road last night…

'Looks like your unreliable witness was reliable after all,' Stacey
said, typing a search into Google Earth.

Cavendish Road was one street away from where Samantha
Brown had lived.

CHAPTER 34

Jake pulled the cart to a stop at the west side of the house. As she looked forward from the front of the property, Kim could see a collection of converted barns all set around a paved courtyard holding picnic tables, benches, colourful plant pots and hanging baskets. Some of the tables were occupied by groups of men and women soaking up the weak early September sunshine. Everyone she met the gaze of waved and smiled in their direction.

Kim followed Jake along the hallway, passing rooms as they went. The farmhouse appeared to have been renovated and as many walls as possible removed. To her left was a dining room ready for at least fifty people. To her right was a vast open space filled with sofas and easy chairs, footstools, woollen throws, bookcases and a huge fireplace.

They passed notice boards that listed activities like Meditation, Crystal Therapy, Massage, Reiki and a couple of things she couldn't pronounce.

And yet there was a stillness to the place that intrigued her. As they passed people in the hallway, greetings consisted of a smile and a nod. No words were exchanged. She heard no televisions or radios or raucous laughter. Everything was calm and sedate. She made more noise at home with her dog.

'Please, come in,' he said, opening a heavy oak door marked 'Private'.

This room wasn't huge. Probably the size of her kitchen and lounge combined but it was immaculately designed. Floor-to-ceiling bookcases filled most of the wall space, with a library ladder that slid along in front. An antique oak desk sat in front of the window. A plush sofa with a tartan throw occupied one side of the room, facing two high-backed leather chairs with an antique chess board on a coffee table between. Another easy chair and footstool were positioned before a well-stocked fireplace. Occasional tables and reading lamps completed the look.

'Nice,' Bryant murmured, and she could understand what he meant.

'We like to think of it as home,' Jake said, closing the door behind them.

The only thing missing was a computer of any kind, Kim realised, lowering herself onto the sofa.

Jake sat opposite.

'So, you own all of this property?' Kim asked, making no apology for her directness.

'We do,' he answered. 'The house, the barns and the surrounding seventeen acres.'

She whistled. 'Very nice. Who is we?'

'There are twelve of us that put capital in at the beginning and…'

'Equal amounts?' Kim asked.

'…we shared a vision,' he continued as though she hadn't spoken. 'We've been very lucky that murder helped us to achieve…'

'Excuse me,' Kim said, narrowing her eyes.

Amusement pulled at his lips. 'My apologies for my poor phraseology there, Inspector. The house and land was being sold way under market value due to the family slaying here in the early nineties. A nephew murdered his aunt and uncle and their two daughters and tried to make it look like a burglary gone wrong. No one wanted to buy the place after that.'

Clearly Jake Black was never one to look the misfortune gift horse in the mouth, Kim surmised.

'And how many people are here now?'

'One hundred and one,' he answered promptly.

'And they've all put capital into the Farm?' Kim probed.

'Every single person here contributes in some way, Inspector,' he said without missing a beat. 'We have to survive.'

'Sammy's death has been all over the news,' Kim said, broaching the subject that had brought her here and still unable to believe he hadn't known.

He smiled, revealing even white teeth. 'We don't much care for the news here. It's rarely good.'

'And what exactly is here, Jake, and why was Sammy here for two and a half years before she left?'

'We're a retreat, a spiritual safe place if you like. People join us for a number of reasons.'

'Like what?' Kim asked, bluntly.

'As I said, there are many reasons,' he answered, unfazed. 'But I suppose many have become disillusioned with the world and often their place within it.'

'So, they're running away?'

'Or choosing a different path,' he countered. 'People come here searching for many things but mainly they come to search for themselves, and no I'm not offended by the nature of your questions, Inspector,' he said with a mischievous smile.

'Good, and did Tyler Short come looking for himself?' she asked, thinking of the sad and lonely young man. The sudden insertion of Tyler's name was intentional. She wanted to gauge his initial response to the name.

'No, Tyler came searching for love,' he answered easily, as though he'd been sent her list of questions in advance.

'Sorry?' Kim asked, not wanting to divulge too much about her knowledge of Tyler and his feelings for Sammy.

'Tyler joined us to get closer to Samantha. It's not a way of life that suits everyone; if you're not committed to living a cleaner, freer kind of life you won't last. He wasn't interested in our philosophies and especially one in particular.'

'Which was?'

'No personal relationships between family members.'

'Family?'

He nodded. 'Of course. That's what we are, and physical relationships bring too many negative emotions and complications into the mix.'

'But surely you can't control that,' Kim said. Put a group of people together and sexual tension would appear somewhere.

'It's not about control. The people who are here want to follow our way of life. Many have been hurt beyond repair by abusive relationships.'

'Including Samantha?' Kim asked, still not convinced that feelings could be governed and controlled quite so easily as making them into a rule to be followed.

'It is my understanding that Samantha had been recently hurt by someone before joining us.'

'And that convinced her to give up her complete way of life?' Kim queried. 'One bad relationship?'

'Inspector, some people don't even realise what's missing in their lives until they find it. Sammy came here broken. She had no hope. She was depressed and had been abandoned by all her friends. Even her parents didn't understand the depth of pain she was feeling. With our help she blossomed into a warm, kind, enthusiastic...'

'But however well you put her back together and mended her broken heart you were asking her to give up the chance of finding love by keeping her here,' Kim stated.

'Now hang on,' he said, holding up his hands and leaning back in his seat. 'First of all, no one who joins us is forced to stay any longer than they want to. Unity Farm is not a prison and everyone is free to leave any time they want. Samantha found something here that was right for her right now. That's not to say she wouldn't have changed her mind eventually when she felt…'

'But she did,' Kim said, confused. 'She did change her mind and left this place a few months ago.'

Jake regarded her for a moment. 'Let me explain something, Inspector. Samantha had become a different person to the one who had arrived. Living a simpler life without some of the pressures of outside life enabled her to open up and discover the person she really was. Over time she became involved in many parts of Farm life. She enjoyed time in the garden, in the kitchen and had just signed up other members to form an art class. She wanted to teach. But more importantly her best friend here was due into hospital for minor surgery the day after Sammy disappeared and Sammy was due to go with her.'

'So, what are you saying?' Kim asked, to be clear.

'That Samantha had no wish to leave us. She was, without a doubt, taken by force.'

CHAPTER 35

'And that's all he'd say?' Woody asked as Kim relayed the conversation she'd had with Jake Black.

Kim nodded. 'Wouldn't say by whom or what made him so sure, just that Sammy wouldn't have left of her own accord. To be honest, he kind of dried up a little bit after that and offered to return us to our car.'

'Your thoughts on Unity Farm?' he asked.

'Place appears to be nice enough, everyone I saw seemed happy, a bit quiet but content. A lot of money has gone into the place. I'm not sure whose money as he evaded questions about the financial set-up pretty well.'

'Any suspects for the murders?'

Kim shook her head.

'Then leave it alone for now. We don't want to appear to be harassing a group of people who have chosen to live an alternative lifestyle.'

And that's why he was in charge, she reasoned.

'I'll need to speak to Myles Brown again, sir, and I may have to roll my sleeves up just a little bit. I know he's not telling me everything.'

'Okay, but don't roll them up too far,' he warned. 'And keep Bryant with you at all times.'

Bryant had dropped her off at the entrance and then shot off, and the rest of her team were waiting to be sent home too. She chose not to share that information.

She continued. 'Myles Brown claims Samantha left of her own accord and Jake Black says she didn't.' She shook her head. 'But that's not why I requested the meeting.'

He eyed her suspiciously.

She took a breath, 'Sir, we need to drag the lake at Himley Park.'

'On what grounds?'

'The shoe.'

'And?'

'Just the shoe, sir.'

'Oh, Stone, and here was me thinking you were making a serious request.'

This response was not good. Irritation, disbelief and scepticism she could work with, but instant dismissal of her request was a harder nut to crack.

'It is.'

'Rarely has my day ended positively because of you, Stone,' he said, standing and reaching for his briefcase. 'But today…'

'We need to see if there's another body in there,' she said, continuing to plead her corner as he placed files into the case. If necessary she'd follow him down to the car, wittering in his ear until he drove away.

'You have anything other than one rogue shoe buried in the mud? Other clothing?'

'No.'

'A suspicion of a missing person who might be in there?'

'No.'

He stopped packing his case. 'Then you know my answer.'

Kim understood the massive considerations involved in dragging a lake. In addition, the lost revenue and inconvenience to the property owners were factors to be considered. She knew he had spent the afternoon in a budget meeting, but he was a police officer at heart not a paper pusher, which made him an exceptionally good boss. Except when he was saying no to her.

'Sir, this case is…'

'Stone, anything further on this subject is a waste of breath for you and a waste of time for me. The answer is no.'

Kim growled on the inside. It didn't matter if she followed him all the way home and sat on his bedside table while he drank his cocoa. He wasn't going to change his mind unless she could give him something more.

She just didn't know what that something more was.

CHAPTER 36

Bryant knew he was doing himself no favours but it was something he had to see for himself.

All day he'd waited for a text message or call to say they'd changed their mind, that they'd realised they'd made a huge mistake and that Peter Drake was not going to be released after all.

He'd fought through the evening traffic after dropping off the guv at the station and had made it with just minutes to spare. He wasn't surprised to see Richard Harrison's car already parked. He pulled up, leaving one space in between.

'It's really going to happen, isn't it?' Richard asked, leaning against Bryant's rear door. 'That bastard is going to be free any minute now?'

Bryant said nothing as he appraised the man who appeared even more gaunt than the day before. Yesterday his suit had been clean, his shirt pressed and his hair combed tidily. Today, the creased clothing, the greasy hair and black shadows beneath his eyes told Bryant Richard hadn't had a moment of peace since the decision had been made. The man was in decline and there was nothing Bryant could do to stop it.

'You know he's going to do it again, don't you?' Richard asked.

Bryant heard the crack in the man's voice and thought about what the guv had said about *Minority Report* and not being able to predict future crimes, but damn it, his gut told him the same thing.

'Another girl is going to suffer just like Wendy did,' he said as the doors began to open.

Richard straightened up and moved away from the car.

And then suddenly there he was.

Peter Drake was standing on the wrong side of the prison doors for the first time in over a quarter of a century.

Richard leaned against the car as his legs appeared to weaken beneath him at the sight of the man who had viciously ended his daughter's life.

The prison officer beside him finished speaking and then offered his hand. The gesture annoyed Bryant immensely. How anyone could shake the man's hand was beyond him. But of course, Peter Drake had lived a whole other lifetime behind those walls.

The guard stepped back into the prison leaving Peter Drake alone. Bryant could feel the tension in the man beside him as they both stared in silence.

This Peter Drake bore little resemblance to the slim, dark-haired man Bryant had watched being taken away all those years ago.

The man's face had slackened beneath the grey hair and beard. His stomach now spilled over the waistband of his dark blue jeans. His neck thicker and his hands meatier, Bryant noticed as Drake took a roll-up from a tin and lit it.

They both watched as he stood, looking around as though trying to process everything he was seeing. His gaze passed over them, but it didn't linger and there was no recognition.

Bryant guessed that they too had changed significantly in the intervening years.

A taxi pulled into the car park and moved slowly towards the entrance. Peter Drake puffed heavily on the cigarette before the taxi came to rest before him.

'Part of me wishes he'd died in that place,' Bryant admitted to the only man he could.

'Not yet,' Richard said. 'He can't die yet.'

Bryant turned to look at the man. Richard had lost everything. He hated Drake for what he'd done to his daughter and yet he didn't wish him dead.

Richard returned his gaze but Bryant got the feeling he was looking through him instead of at him. 'If there's an afterlife and he gets there before me, how will I protect her? She'll be alone and I can't let her down again. I won't fail her twice.'

Bryant could feel the man's despair and opened his mouth to offer reassurance when he heard an urgent response request over his police radio; something he'd never stopped carrying.

He listened more closely. Squad cars were racing to the scene of an attempted murder. And it was an address he recognised.

CHAPTER 37

Kim tapped the door lightly and entered. Stacey followed with her notebook and pen and closed the door of Interview Room 1 behind her.

Myles Brown had arrived ten minutes earlier, which should have given him enough time to consider the starkness of his surroundings and contemplate giving them the whole truth.

He looked almost relieved to see her.

She didn't smile as she took a seat opposite.

'Have I done something wrong, Inspector?' he asked, looking from her to her colleague.

'Mr Brown, I think...'

'Myles, please,' he interrupted, wishing to bring their rapport back to the informal tone they'd enjoyed at his home.

This was a different kind of conversation and she had to make sure he knew that.

'Mr Brown, I understand that you've suffered a tragic loss; however, I feel that you've failed to be honest about all of the circumstances surrounding the murder of your daughter, which is not helping us find the person responsible.'

'Have you been to Unity Farm? Have you questioned anyone there?'

Kim nodded. 'I was there earlier today and I have to say that your description of a cult seems overly dramatic and far-fetched.'

'Yeah, and Jonestown was just a village in South America,' he replied.

'Sorry?'

'When Jim Jones moved his religious sect to Guyana it wasn't to enjoy the weather. It was to escape prying eyes into the practices of The Peoples Temple. And look what happened when those prying eyes followed him.'

'Wasn't there an American governor that visited that group?' Stacey asked.

'Leo Ryan; a congressman who went to investigate mistreatment. He and his party were shot dead as they were about to board the plane to go home. Within hours nine hundred people were dead when Jones ordered a mass suicide. But it was just a nice peace-loving church,' he added sarcastically.

'We met Jake Black,' Kim offered. 'Seemed a nice enough…'

'Well of course he did. Very few people will follow someone who looks like the Elephant Man.'

'Are you saying people go to Unity Farm because the top guy is good-looking?' she asked with disbelief.

He shook his head. 'It's not about good looks. You've only to look at Charles Manson to know that, though being handsome didn't hurt David Koresh. It's about charisma. Every group leader must possess that charisma, that something that makes you want to believe every word they say and follow them anywhere.'

Kim had no clue what her colleague was scribbling down because for her the man had yet to say something of interest.

'Mr Brown, you're talking about famous, well-documented cases of brainwashing and mind control that happened many miles from here. This is the Black Country in the West Midlands. Nothing like that—'

'Inspector, how many families of crime victims have you visited that thought things like this could never happen to them, that gun crime, even knife crime happened somewhere else.'

She silently conceded his point. But still, she couldn't believe what he was saying.

'I'm sorry but there's no murderous cult right here on our doorstep.'

'You can be sure of that?'

She nodded. Pretty sure.

'How long did you spend at Unity Farm?'

'About an hour?'

He leaned forward, resting his forearms on the table.

'And do you think you saw anything that Jake Black didn't want you to see in that time?'

She'd seen his office and a golf buggy.

'Wouldn't your job be so much easier if murderers looked like monsters, if they all had horns and they didn't appear as normal people? Cults very rarely look like cults, Inspector. They always dress up as something else.'

'Go on,' Kim said. She didn't believe him but she was keen to know how the man had convinced himself.

'They look like religious groups, political, racial, psychotherapeutic, even outer space. The fastest growing are the ones that centre around New Age thinking and personal improvement training, like Unity Farm.'

'So, you're saying that Sammy was lured to this evil place and brainwashed somehow because she was at a low point due to being dumped?'

He shook his head with frustration.

'You're not going to believe anything I say, are you?'

'It's hard, Myles,' she said, thinking about the girl selling vegetables in the shed. The girl hadn't looked brainwashed, apprehensive perhaps but certainly not brainwashed. 'Look, we're getting off track here. Jake told us something that disputes your story about your daughter. He says that Sammy didn't leave Unity Farm of her own accord. He states that she was taken by force. Is that true?'

His face fell into despair, and Kim knew that Jake was telling the truth.

'But why, Myles? Why would you do that to her?'

His watery gaze met hers but he held back the tears. He was teetering on the edge of letting go. She could tell he wanted to free himself of the burden.

'I need the truth now, Myles. All of it.'

CHAPTER 38

Bryant made it to the Crossley house in record time. The guv would have been proud.

Outside the house was an ambulance, two squad cars and a group of people bathed in the flashing blue lights.

Bryant pushed his way through and flashed his badge at the door.

He spied Sergeant Teagen from the station.

'You been assigned?' he asked, doubtfully. He was clearly waiting for CID and he expected an inspector.

Bryant shook his head. 'I know these people.'

Teagen eyed him suspiciously while he tried to see what was going on in the property.

He could see Tina's wheelchair in the lounge. Her body appeared to be slumped forward. Police officers surrounded her.

'Is she?…'

'She's fine. She's the one that carried out the assault. The victim is in there,' he said, nodding to the first bedroom.

Bryant tried to process the scene. Only this morning he'd spoken to them both, and although they weren't the happiest couple he'd ever seen, he could never have imagined this.

'May I?' Bryant asked, nodding towards the door.

Teagen gave him a look that he understood. He was to say or do nothing that would affect the investigation.

Bryant slipped into the room as Damon Crossley let out a cry of pain.

Two paramedics were tending a wound to his right side. A blood-soaked cloth lay on the floor beside the bed but the bleeding appeared to have stopped.

'What the fuck you want?' he asked, forgetting his pain for the moment.

Bryant ignored his anger, as one of the paramedics turned towards him. 'Be quick, mate, we need to take him in for assessment.'

So, his injury wasn't life threatening.

'What the hell happened?' he asked.

'It's your fault,' he accused, wincing. 'Fucking bitch didn't speak a word after you left. Just stared out the window. Relived the whole bloody thing after seeing you.'

'Damon, I never…'

'Did her fucking tea like I do every night. She never touched it. Wouldn't even look at it. Fucking years I've looked after the bitch,' he raged. 'Gave my life to take care of her and this is how she fucking thanks me.'

'But, how, I mean…'

The woman was confined to a wheelchair.

'Went to get her plate. Didn't realise she had the knife. Leaned over her and in it went. She's fucking lost it. Bitch tried to kill me, after all I've done,' he shouted as the rage produced droplets of spittle.

'Hey, mate, calm down,' one of the paramedics warned as a spot of blood appeared on the fresh dressing. He turned and shot Bryant a warning look. 'Enough,' he said, getting to his feet.

Damon stood but looked at Bryant.

'So, if you wanna do your job right this time get her the fuck out of here, cos I'm pressing charges against the loony bitch, so she'd best be gone by the time I get back.'

CHAPTER 39

'Okay, talk,' Kim said, as Stacey removed drinks for them all from a tray. 'And I want the truth this time, Myles, all of it.'

He nodded his understanding. 'It's true that Sammy was heartbroken after her split with Callum. If I'm honest I didn't pay too much attention. Par for the course of growing up and, truth be known, I was relieved. Didn't like the guy one bit.'

And after meeting him that was certainly something she could understand.

'So, I didn't get too involved in the upset. I left the tea and sympathy to my wife and waited for it to pass. But it didn't. It all seemed to get worse. She withdrew from her friends, stopped going out. Stopped showering and taking care of herself.'

'College?' Kim asked.

'Occasionally but she'd see Callum there so that didn't help, but we had to do something.'

'Like what?'

He looked uncomfortable with what he was about to say.

'We tried to shock her out of it. We showered her, we dressed her and I walked her into her first college class of the day. I felt sure that once she was back amongst her friends and her studies everything would snap back into place. It was a break-up, for God's sake.'

Kim felt her stomach react unfavourably to how he had treated his daughter, but she wasn't here to judge his parenting style. He had wanted to bring her back to herself. Yet a part of her felt there had to have been another way.

'Worst mistake I ever made,' he said, staring down into his drink. 'Although I didn't know it at the time.'

'What happened?'

'She came home with a smile on her face. Still retreated to her room and stayed there but there was a smile. It was a triumph. Next morning, she went to college of her own accord. I didn't question it. I was just relieved that she seemed more herself.'

'So, why the regret?' Kim asked, wondering how they'd got from that stage to where they were now.

'Because what I didn't know then that I know now was that was the day everything changed.' He paused. 'That was the day she met Britney.'

'Who the hell is Britney?' Kim asked.

'A recruiter for Unity Farm.'

'Are you joking me?'

He shook his head. 'They have them all over the place: colleges, homeless shelters, even AA meetings; anywhere they might find people open and vulnerable to the process.'

'Go on,' Kim said. Tyler Short had attended Dudley College too.

'A cult has two objectives: to recruit and to make money.'

'Did Samantha have money?' Kim asked, wondering if there was a trust fund she didn't know about.

Myles shook his head. 'No, we had some savings but I'm getting ahead here. You have to understand how it works. Sammy wasn't taken to a dark room and indoctrinated with the group's ideology. There was no instant injection. It was much more gradual than that. She mentioned this girl's name a few times. We were sad she hadn't reconnected with Cassie or any more of her old friends but pleased that she was spending time with someone.

'Eventually, she started staying over at Britney's and that's when we noticed the subtle changes. It started with small criticisms of our lifestyle: the waste, the greed, our lack of concern for the bigger picture. She began meditating and spent hours in her room in silence. Then my wife started to notice money going missing from her purse. She didn't take it too seriously at first but she started keeping track and the amounts were getting higher. At first five pounds, ten pounds, twenty until it was everything that was in there.' He paused. 'And then we got the statement.'

'What statement?'

'Credit card. She'd opened a new card in my name and accrued a bill of almost ten thousand pounds, in one month.'

Kim couldn't help her surprise at the way the girl appeared to have changed.

'We confronted her about it and there was a huge row. There was no remorse. She'd found a deserving cause to which she could distribute our obscene wealth as she called it.'

The view seemed extreme to Kim. They had a nice house and nice cars and it looked like they'd worked for it, but they certainly weren't ostentatious or obscene.

'And that was the last night Sammy spent under our roof. She moved to Unity Farm and came back to the house one more time.'

'For what?' Kim asked.

'Her stuff. I was away, at a meeting in Glasgow. She turned up with two guys and a van. She told her mother she was here to take all her things. Kate called me in tears not knowing what to do. I told her to let them. It was her stuff after all. And take it they did. Her furniture, clothes, jewellery, everything that wasn't nailed to the wall. But that wasn't the worst thing. When I got back hours later, Kate was still crying hysterically. Sammy had been cool and distant, as though they were strangers. She barely spoke until she handed back her door key and told her mother that one day she'd realise just how much of a zombie she was.'

'Zombie?' Stacey asked.

He nodded, took a sip of his drink and pushed it away.

'It's their term for the unenlightened. We're not alive, you see, we're just existing.'

'Carry on,' she urged. So far, this was only half of the story.

'Obviously I tried to call her, but her phone was off. As far as I know it was never switched back on again. We called the police but…'

'She was an adult who could make her own decisions.'

He nodded. 'So, I began researching the whole thing; learned everything I could about cults and sects. Reading books, articles, websites, joining chat rooms. I was beside myself. I felt powerless. I tried to visit and couldn't get in the place. I was at my wit's end when I suddenly received a call from a man named Kane Devlin.'

'Big man, dresses in black?' Kim asked, hazarding a guess. The man had not been a bailiff after all.

Myles nodded as Kim frowned.

'He made contact with you?'

'Yes.'

'How did he know you needed help?'

'I don't know and I don't care. I think he might lurk in some of these chat rooms to see who needs help and approaches them. He's very secretive about what he does. He doesn't get his business via a website.'

'And what exactly is his business?' Kim asked, wishing for Myles to spell it out.

'He helped us perform the intervention. His team watched the compound for weeks, got to know Sammy's movements and took her back.'

'By force?'

He looked shocked. 'Of course, it was the only way.'

Kim thought about his actions in forcing the girl into the shower. He clearly felt the ends justified the means.

'We knew that if we could just get her away from the group we'd be able to change her mind back. Get her to see what they were. Kane and his team run a programme. The first week was hell while she was being unfrozen. We weren't allowed to see…'

'Sorry?' Kim asked. 'Unfreezing?'

He sighed as though realising just how clueless she was.

'There are three steps to gaining control of the mind: unfreezing, changing, refreezing. It's the same for getting someone into and out of a cult. The first stage is to strip away the current belief system. It involves sleep deprivation, disorientation, privacy deprivation and being told that your values and relationships are all wrong.

'Next comes the changing. Given new beliefs, new ideals, repetitively, encouraged to accept without question and then refreezing.'

'Which is?'

'Being built back up, paired with older members of the group to enforce new ideals. Kane explained it was like taking a shower. You get undressed, wash yourself clean and then dress in different clothes.'

Kim appreciated the simplistic analogy but this was not about getting clean. This was the human mind.

'So, you're saying this Kane guy kind of deprogrammed her?'

'He started the process and we continued it once we got her home.'

'And, how was she?'

'Unresponsive at first. Other than swearing and calling us names she barely spoke to us. She hated us for what we'd done, but she started to come around as she settled back into the real world. Eventually she said she needed her own space and we trusted that she wasn't going to slip backwards.

'We found her that flat where we could keep a close eye on her, and Kane checked on her too.' He shook his head. 'I still can't believe that someone would kill her.'

'And you think someone at Unity Farm is responsible?'

'I don't know who else it could be. She had no enemies.'

'But why when she's been gone for months. Why wait so long?'

He shrugged. 'Maybe they're angry because she left. Maybe she knew something about someone. I just don't know,' he said, as his grief caught up with him. While he'd been talking about the mechanics of the group his mind had been occupied but now his loss was back at the forefront of his mind.

Kim pushed back her chair. 'Okay, Myles, that'll be all for now. If we need anything…'

'So, what are you going to do, about the cult, I mean?'

His hands were clasped together on the table before him. The pose seemed relaxed, but she could see the whites of his knuckles.

A shiver crept up her spine. The tension still surging through his body, despite his admissions, troubled her. Even now he was not being completely truthful.

'Myles, I swear to God I am considering charging you with every obstruction…'

She stopped speaking as her phone rang. It was Jack at the front desk.

'Stone,' she answered.

'Got a woman here who is insisting on speaking to you straight away,' he said.

'Bit busy at the minute,' she said, glancing at Myles who was rubbing the back of his neck. 'Get someone else to…'

'Yeah, she says her husband is here and that he's not telling the truth, whatever that means.'

Kim glanced again at the troubled man before her who for whatever reason was still not being completely honest about his daughter's murder.

'Bring her through, Jack,' she said, ending the call.

Both Stacey and Myles glanced at her questioningly as she remained silent and took a sip of her drink. It was stone cold and she pushed it away as a knock sounded at the door.

'Come in,' she called, watching Myles's reaction as the door opened and his wife stood behind the constable.

His expression turned to one of tenderness mixed with fear. 'Kate, what the…'

'I'm sorry, Myles, but I can't do this any more,' she said, pushing past the constable and entering the room.

'Please take a seat,' Kim invited.

'Kate, we agreed that—'

'No Myles,' she shot back. 'You decided and I went along with it but I don't think we're doing the right thing. I think she needs to know.'

Kim leaned forward. 'Mrs Brown, what the hell is going on here?'

Kate glanced at her husband. 'Has he told you all about Kane and what he did for us?'

Kim nodded.

Kate glanced at her husband, appearing to soften as she saw the anguish in his face.

'Please understand that he was only doing what he thought was best. He didn't mean to deceive you or impede the investigation by not sharing everything. We're frightened,' she said, reaching for her husband's hand.

He held on to her tightly as a tear rolled over his cheek.

Kim looked from one to the other wondering what the hell they had left to lose.

Kate took a breath. 'You see, we still need Kane's help.'

The pieces began to fall into place. Their secrecy, their continued tension about Unity Farm, the closeness of Sammy and Sophie, the absence of their younger daughter.

'Oh no,' Kim said, as the couple held on to each other tightly.

Kate nodded and when she spoke her words were no more than a whisper.

'Yes, our youngest daughter, Sophie, is still in there.'

CHAPTER 40

Penn slid back into his seat at 10.15 p.m.

He had been dismissed as the boss and Stacey had headed down to question Myles Brown, but something the boss had said earlier, following her meeting with Woody, had stayed with him. The idea had stuck in his mind while he and Jasper had visited their mother in the hospice and since.

Part of him was glad that his brother was having his first overnight stay at Billy's house. It had been a difficult visit and hard for them all. The knowledge that the lung cancer finally had the upper hand was evident. She had barely spoken but the silence had been filled by Jasper recounting every detail of his day, causing their mother's lips to lift in a brief smile on a couple of occasions.

Penn had wondered sometimes if Jasper truly understood the gravity of her illness and that she would not be coming home again.

He swallowed the emotion in his throat and remembered how his brother's motor mouth had shut down once they were back in the car. He'd spoken the odd word but had been keen to get out of the car and into Billy's house.

He understood.

Penn turned on his computer and took out his phone. He scrolled and hit his brother's name.

'Hey, bud, you okay?' he asked when Jasper answered.

A pause.

'Yeah, me and Billy're playing Xbox. It's the decider.'

'Okay, mate, not too late, eh?'

'Allllll righty,' he said.

'You sure you're okay, bud?' he asked again.

'Err… yeah. Waiting to kick Billy's a— bum again.'

Penn couldn't help the smile that turned up his lips. Down's syndrome or not, the kid was still a teenager.

'Okay, love you bud.'

'Yeah, oooooookay,' Jasper said, refusing to return the sentiment in front of his buddy. Yep, definitely a teenager.

'Goodnight,' Penn said, ending the call.

He logged into the network as his phone dinged a message.

He opened it and laughed out loud. The text message was from his brother and read simply

Love you 2 Ozzy

Followed by a tongue-out emoji.

But he was a good teenager, Penn marvelled, putting away his phone.

He took some scrap paper from his drawer and wrote down the only information he had.

The shoe found at the side of the lake was a women's leather shoe made by Bergen.

Woody had said to the boss that they had no idea or suspicion of who that shoe belonged to.

Well, he'd had an idea that might just help them narrow that down a bit.

He logged into Amazon and typed in the manufacturer's name. A shoe matching the description and the photo was called a 'ballet flat', and judging by the number of reviews it was a popular choice. He had a quick look at the reviews but that wasn't the information he was after. He didn't care if the heel was slightly smaller than it appeared on the photo. He didn't care that the stitching rubbed an area of one woman's little toe.

He scrolled down to the 'also bought' section which detailed other purchases made by people who had bought this item.

He started to make a list of similar items that appeared more than once.

Five minutes later he surveyed his list.

High-waisted pants
Night cream
Spanx
Shape wear
Socks
Concealer
Body tape

Okay, he thought, if he was building a profile of this particular shoe buyer he'd guess the woman was beyond her prime years but was sensible and still liked to look good. He'd wager between the ages of forty-five and sixty.

And that right there gave him somewhere to start.

He logged into COMPACT, the missing persons' database.

He entered the sparse information he had but hesitated over the date and age parameters.

He settled on females who had been reported missing over the last three years aged between forty and sixty-five. He waited for just a couple of seconds before the search engine returned fourteen results. Of these fourteen he could see that seven had been closed within forty-eight hours; four more had been closed up to one month following the official report.

That left three open cases of his target profile female missing in the last three years.

He clicked into the first. It was a homeless woman from Dudley reported missing by a concerned shelter worker who hadn't seen her for a while. Penn disregarded this. There was every chance that Lola Bedola, clearly her stage name, had moved on to pastures new.

The second he read with more interest until he reached the narrative at the bottom stating that Jeanie Riches had done this a dozen times before and would come back when she was good and ready.

The third report seeped under his skin immediately.

Fifty-five-year-old Sheila Thorpe had disappeared from her home eighteen months earlier, as reported by her married twenty-nine-year-old daughter, Josie Finch, who claimed her mother had never done anything like this before and was still grieving the sudden and unexpected death of her husband.

The narrative further explained that officers had been made aware that Sheila's bank account had been emptied. Enquires had revealed that Sheila herself had withdrawn the money, proving she was alive and well and that she was a grown adult able to make her own decisions. Little else could be done, but that had been twelve months earlier and she hadn't been seen since.

He opened a tab for social media and spoke to an empty room.

'Okay, Josie Finch, let's see what we can learn from you.'

CHAPTER 41

It was almost midnight when Kim took the lead from Barney's collar after their late-night walk.

Although his social skills had improved significantly since she'd rescued him, he still didn't respond well to total strangers and especially other dogs when they were out of the house. He'd formed relationships with Charley from down the road, who collected him for a walk and a bit of pampering back at his house when Kim was working, and he responded well to Dawn, his groomer, and most people who visited the house providing they bore gifts.

As ever he positioned himself in the kitchen, his tail whooshing to and fro across the floor, his big brown eyes staring up at her expectantly.

'Yeah, but I know your tricks now, don't I, boy?' she said, reaching for his post-walk treat. He took his carrot and headed back to the rug in the lounge, his favourite chewing spot.

She remembered what the vet had told her when Barney had had his last injections. Scientists had discovered that dogs appeared to have developed an extra muscle above their eyes that served no purpose to their physicality except to offer their owners a puppy-dog look when they wanted something.

So, she no longer felt as guilty for giving in to the majority of his requests.

Science was science.

She poured a coffee from the pot she'd left brewing before the walk that she'd hoped would help clear her head. It hadn't and she didn't see restful sleep anywhere in her near future.

Myles and Kate Brown were still on her mind. Her emotions had been mixed as she'd watched them leave the interview room, clutching each other for support. Part of her had been angry at them for keeping the information to themselves, and the other half understood their need to try and protect the only child they had left.

Myles's explanation that an intervention was planned this week to remove Sophie from Unity Farm had clarified why Kate had been busy preparing the bedroom for her arrival.

Kim couldn't help wondering if Sammy would still be alive if they'd left her alone. She had been an adult and the choices were hers to make. Who had she been hurting exactly? And the same question could be asked of Sophie. The girl had followed her sister to Unity Farm but had not followed her out. Didn't that mean she was happy where she was? As Sophie was a grown adult, Kim was powerless to forcibly remove Sophie from the Farm if she didn't want to leave, and yet they'd instructed Kane to snatch her in the same manner he had taken Sammy. *But what if she doesn't want to leave?* a quiet voice said in her head. Surely she wasn't being held there by force and could leave any time she chose. Kim suddenly remembered Myles mentioning a girl who had recruited Sammy into the group. Maybe she knew Sophie and could vouch for her state of mind and happiness. She made a mental note to track the girl down and find out more. Were Kane's services really needed again?

Given that this Kane guy had been spotted at Sammy's flat by both a neighbour and a news report, Kim had demanded that Myles arrange a meeting when he had flatly refused to hand over Kane's number. He had promised he would speak to Kane Devlin and contact her the following day.

Right now, Tyler's death was a complete mystery to her. It appeared that the boy had followed Sammy to Unity Farm, where he had continued to not matter to anyone. Jake Black had barely recognised the name. There was a deep sadness that struck her when she thought of the boy. He had mattered greatly to his grandmother and he would matter to them. And they would find the person responsible for his murder.

She knew beyond a shadow of a doubt that she needed to find out more about Unity Farm. It wasn't that she believed everything Myles said, but she didn't believe everything Jake Black said either.

If she visited the place again, she was sure she'd be given another tourist-guide insight. With no direct link to Sammy's death, given that she'd left months ago, Kim knew she wasn't going to get a search warrant. So, how the hell was she going to learn more about the place?

Kim had the feeling of being a lab rat in a maze. She was moving around but every corner she turned led to another dead end, not helped by Woody's refusal to consider dragging the lake. She understood the cost involved versus the chances of finding anything based on one bloody shoe, but what if there was another victim down there? What if...

Her thoughts were interrupted by the ringing of her phone.

It was Penn. Her heart leaped. His mother.

'Penn?' she answered, quickly.

'I think I've got her, boss,' he said, breathlessly.

'Sorry... what?'

'The shoe at Himley. I reckon we're looking for a woman named Sheila Thorpe, and I think we'll find her at the bottom of the lake.'

CHAPTER 42

'Okay, guys, thanks to Penn's great work last night Woody is now making the necessary arrangements to drag the lake at Himley Park.'

Woody had told them that without even an identity of a missing person to go on, his hands were tied. Penn's late-night project had untied her boss's hands and they had been given the all-clear.

Stacey offered her colleague a cheeky wink, and Bryant called out a genuine 'Well done'. She marvelled at the lack of competitiveness within her team. If one of them did good, they all did good.

Penn looked away, embarrassed. He didn't welcome public praise.

But Kim had been pretty impressed when he'd explained how he'd formed a basic profile form on Amazon to use on the Mispers which took him to Facebook and a photo of Sheila Thorpe at her thirtieth wedding anniversary two years ago. But the man had always liked a puzzle, she thought, remembering the word puzzle he'd solved which had saved Stacey's life.

'So, while we wait for the dive team to get here from Nottingham we need to carry on pushing this investigation forward. Myles Brown has a lot to say about Unity Farm. Most of which is pretty off the wall, and given that his younger daughter is still there I think his rational brain may be somewhat impaired. He believes that Sophie has also been brainwashed and that she's being held against her will, especially after Sammy was taken;

but both parents insist that they want Kane Devlin to repeat the intervention he performed with Sammy.' She turned to Stacey. 'I want to know all about Unity Farm and whatever you can find out about Jake Black, and when you're done with that start looking up Kane Devlin.'

Stacey nodded.

'Penn, I want you to go see Sheila Thorpe's daughter without giving anything away. Make something up but we need to know more about her disappearance.'

'Got it, boss,' he answered, removing the bandana from his head and reaching for the magic cream in his drawer that was used to tame his curls while out in the field.

Bryant leaned back in his chair and laced his fingers behind his head. 'Sounds like everything's covered, so I'll just put my feet up.'

'Ha, you wish,' she scoffed, reaching for her jacket. 'You and me are going back to college, my friend.'

CHAPTER 43

'Go on, Stace,' Penn said, pushing the Tupperware container forward to cover the hairline crack that separated their two desks. 'He made them before he went to Billy's last night.'

Stacey stared longingly at the chocolate brownies Jasper had baked. She had no idea what the lad did to them but they were the best brownies she'd ever tasted.

'I dare not,' she said, pushing them back towards him. 'Because I can't have just one of anything your brother cooks.'

Penn smiled and took them out of sight. 'Never let it be said that I'm not a supportive friend,' he said. 'Even though I think you're fine as you are.'

'Thanks, Penn,' she said, as he reached for his jacket.

Once he was gone she groaned out loud. Just the sight of those perfect little squares had transferred their devilishness to her taste buds. She could feel that velvety sweetness on her tongue, and if she could survive the day without nipping behind Penn's desk she could survive anything. Jeez, that boy could cook.

She shook away the temptation and typed 'Unity Farm' into a search engine.

She got fewer hits than she'd expected. The place only came up in mentions in local news. Most of the articles were a rehash of the murder that the boss had mentioned, where the name of the place was referred to along the lines of 'now known as', but direct references seemed to be non-existent. The boss had said they grew and sold things but there was no website or

Facebook page. Looked like all of their business was done by word of mouth.

She carried on scrolling and was a couple of hits from the bottom of the page when one news article screamed for her attention.

Teenage Girl Falls from Third Floor Window

Stacey frowned and clicked into the piece.
How the hell was Unity Farm involved with that?

CHAPTER 44

'That's her,' Kim said, nodding towards the directional board at the far end of the car park.

Dudley College of Technology dated back to 1862 and consistently received 'outstanding provider' awards. Over the years it had spread its wings and now operated from six or seven other buildings and included an all-weather football complex used by the college and the wider community.

But it was the main complex on The Broadway where she'd been told she'd find Britney Murray, and the girl fitted the description from Myles perfectly: five feet three, slim but with long red curls that reminded Kim of a cartoon character she couldn't name. Kim guessed her to be mid-twenties but she appeared younger when she smiled, as she did at everyone who walked past her.

She held out her right hand, which was clutching a leaflet. Most people carried on past without even an acknowledgment. Kim got the impression folks were used to seeing her around.

'She's keen,' Kim observed, just watching for a moment.

'And has the skin of a rhino,' Bryant added as people continued to rebuff her open, friendly smile. 'You know those guys who jump in front of you when you're out shopping, selling some kind of new phone tariff or satellite package?'

'Yeah,' Kim answered, as a student took a leaflet then immediately dropped it.

'I've always wondered why they do it, cos I've never seen anyone accompany them over to the kiosk or shop, but they must be having some kind of success or they wouldn't keep doing it.'

'So?'

'Well, if Britney's been here doing this since Sammy joined, we're looking at three years or more.'

'You're wondering just how many she's recruited in that time?'

'All I'm saying is that she must be having some success or she wouldn't still be here.'

'That's approximately fifteen thousand students per year multiplied by three years gives us a total of forty-five thousand students, so if you wanna call Stacey and ask her to start checking their whereabouts, be my guest,' Kim said, moving towards their target.

'Value my nuts too much, guv,' he whispered as they approached.

The girl turned and smiled before a small frown settled on her face. Not the kind of people she was expecting to see.

'Britney Murray?' Kim asked, to be sure.

She nodded, slowly. 'I've got permission to be on the car park. I just can't go past...'

'We're not from the college,' Kim said, showing her ID.

'Oh my god,' she exclaimed, covering her mouth with her hand. 'Is everything okay? Is the Farm...'

'I'm sure it's all as you left it. We want to talk to you about Samantha Brown.'

Panic shot into her eyes before she began to shake her head.

'I don't know anyone called...'

'Sammy Brown, twenty-one years old. You met her here on this site,' Kim clarified. Britney couldn't have forgotten her quite so soon. She'd only left Unity Farm a few months earlier.

'I'm sorry but I meet a lot of people,' she said, gesturing towards the groups that continued to surge past after another bus had pulled in.

'Well, you did more than meet her, Britney. You took her to the Farm and…'

'Oh, I take many people to a meditation class or reiki session,' she said, appearing relieved. 'But I don't remember all their names.'

Kim caught Bryant's eye and thankfully he looked as bewildered as she felt. There was no fathomable reason for Britney to deny knowing Samantha.

'Sammy didn't attend one class, Britney, she stayed for more than two years.'

'Sorry, I didn't know her, it's a big place. We might not have…'

'There are only one hundred people there, so I'm not sure how you could have missed her, especially as you introduced her to the Farm in the first place.'

Colour appeared to be building in her cheeks but she still shook her head resolutely. 'No, still not…'

'Her sister, Sophie, is still there?'

'There's no specific rel— I mean, I don't know anyone who has a blood relative at the Farm.'

Kim found the term 'blood relative' a little strange but she let it pass.

'What I mean is that everyone is like family at Unity Farm.' The smile was back on her face. 'Everyone just gets along.'

'But not too well,' Kim said. 'I hear you're not allowed a boyfriend… or a girlfriend at Unity Farm.'

A shadow passed over her face before she chuckled. 'Don't want either, thank you very much. I'm happy now just to focus on me. We all feel that friendship is much more valuable.'

'And yet you can't even recall the name of one of your family members?' Kim observed, bringing the tension back to Britney's face. 'But I agree with you,' Kim said, changing topic again. 'Romance and sexual attraction just muddy the waters, but I'd imagine keeping those feelings hidden can be quite...'

'I don't have feelings for anyone,' she protested, as the colour once again filled her cheeks. Britney had a complexion that was not on her side.

'Was Sammy having any kind of relationship?'

'Sammy who?'

'Britney, I don't know why you're lying to us,' Kim said. Her mouth could lie but her cheeks would be controlled by no one.

'I swear... I don't...'

'We just want to know more about her time at the Farm.'

'But I didn't know her.'

'Was she happy?' Kim pushed.

'Everyone at the farm is happy.'

'Did she upset anyone?' Kim asked, firing the questions to unnerve her.

'I couldn't say but...'

'You didn't know her?' Bryant said, stepping forward.

Britney said nothing.

'You used the word "didn't" know her. Past tense, indicating you know that she's gone from the Farm or that you know she's dead, but either way you know who we're talking about.'

For a moment, she looked stricken.

'Britney, why won't you talk to us about Sammy?'

Her gaze dropped to the floor before she mumbled, 'I'm sorry; I've been told I can't.'

'By whom?'

The girl just shook her head.

'You know, Britney, we could always have this chat down at the station,' Kim threatened. 'Maybe then you'll remember more about your old friend, Sammy.'

Britney raised her head and met Kim's gaze. Her expression was resolute. 'You can say what you want but I'm not talking and I'm not scared of you.'

No, she wasn't, Kim realised. But she was certainly scared of someone.

CHAPTER 45

Penn smoothed back his hair one last time before knocking the door to the home of Josie Finch, the daughter of Sheila Thorpe.

The semi-detached house lay at the arc of a cul-de-sac in Coseley that he hadn't even known was here.

Lie, the boss had instructed him, until they had something more concrete, but he intended to stay as close to the truth as he could.

He cleared his throat as the door began to open.

He recognised the blonde bob hairstyle from her Facebook photos. She wore less make-up and was dressed in jeans and a shirt.

'Josie Finch?' he asked.

She nodded as she appraised him, wondering who or what the hell he was. He got that a lot.

'DS Penn,' he said, holding up his ID.

The normal expression of alarm registered on her face.

'There's nothing wrong,' he assured her quickly before she did a quick mental inventory of all family members and their whereabouts. 'I'd like to chat about your mum if that's okay.'

He saw a flash of anger but she stood aside and pointed towards the room on the right.

He stepped into a comfortable lounge just as Holly and Phil were coming onto the screen.

'Is she dead?' Josie asked, as though preparing herself for the worst.

'Why would you ask that?' Penn hedged, taking a seat.

'Because you lot didn't want to know before.'

Penn got the impression that the words were not filled with as much anger as she'd have liked them to be, almost as though she understood that they'd been unable to do more but she was pissed off anyway.

'Mrs Finch, I'm new to my current team and I've been looking through our current list of missing persons. I've been tasked with refreshing the file, noting any new developments.'

Not too far from the truth, he consoled himself. He didn't do outright lying very easily. Not least because if their suspicions about the lake at Himley were correct, this woman was shortly going to receive some very unwelcome news.

'As I'm new to this case, could you take me through it from the very beginning?'

From experience, he knew that details could be overlooked or omitted from statements, especially by an overworked detective who already knew there was little he could do to help.

'Three years ago, my father died unexpectedly. A massive heart attack while driving to work. He was fifty-six years old. It left my mum totally devastated. My dad had always worked long hours and Mum had often joked about not being able to wait until he retired so they could spend more time together. Well, they never did get that time. She didn't have many friends and they were one of those couples that seemed to exist in a bubble. They didn't need anyone else and sometimes I felt that even meant me. I didn't mind because they were happy as long as they had each other.

'When Dad died my mum went completely into herself. She didn't eat or drink properly, she didn't cook, clean or wash herself.'

Penn thought briefly of his own mother, unable to do any of those things but for completely different reasons. He pushed the thoughts away.

'I had no idea what to do to help her. Her sole purpose for years had been to take care of my dad. She cooked for him, cleaned and never let him lift a finger. About two months after he died I came round and she was out. She told me she'd bumped into an old friend who had also been recently widowed. I was relieved. She seemed brighter, happier and I could stop worrying, or so I thought. Until it went to the other extreme. She was never in. She had excuse after excuse until I realised I hadn't seen her for almost three months. I called and we arranged to meet for coffee. She never turned up and her phone was switched off after that.'

'What did you do?' Penn asked, thinking it sounded very much like the gradual withdrawal of Sammy Brown from her family.

'I went round to the house and let myself in. Everything seemed fine. There were things I probably should have noticed but my only concern was for her. I checked with the neighbours, who had barely seen her for months. I reported her missing that day, which was the day after that last phone call where she didn't answer.'

'The statements say the team made no contact with her at all.'

Josie shook her head. 'They did little more than I did myself. Tried her phone, spoke to a couple of neighbours just like I did.

'There was nothing until two weeks later when the police told me they had CCTV footage of her clearing out her bank account. I was relieved that she'd finally showed up somewhere. I thought it was the start of the trail to getting her back. I thought the police would be able to use CCTV to see who she was with, where she went.'

Penn could understand her disappointment but the CCTV footage would only have served to convince the team that she was alive and well and functioning. They would not have committed hours of manpower to gathering and viewing CCTV to trail her from the bank. She was a woman in her fifties with no history of mental illness, appearing to make her own decisions.

'Part of me wants her back so I can give her a piece of my mind, tell her I never want to see her again. I know how that…'

'I get it. You're…'

'You can't get it, not unless your own mother abandoned you.'

He said nothing. His own mother was about to leave him but by a totally different route.

'I mean, how can she not be missing me as much as I'm missing her? But she has the power to come back. She knows where I am. A miscarriage and a failed marriage while she's been gone and I'm not sure I can ever forgive her for that.' She wiped a tear from her eye. 'I needed her.'

Only yesterday Penn had been hoping that the shoe belonged to Sheila Thorpe. Now he was praying it didn't. If she was alive and well somewhere, there was hope for this relationship to be saved.

From his memory of the report, it was up to date and there was nothing new for him to note.

He pushed himself to his feet. 'Thank you for your…'

'That's not the only reason I'm angry with her,' Josie said, as her jaw set into a hard line.

'Sorry?' he said, pausing.

'It's all gone, everything.'

He sat back down.

She continued. 'A few weeks after the CCTV footage, I went round to the house. I'm not sure why but it was a particularly bad day. I think some part of me hoped that miraculously she'd be there, cooking lunch or tending her plants. Another part of me just wanted the familiarity of the home. Picture both my mum and dad there as they'd always been.'

'And?'

'My key no longer fit the door. I looked inside. Thank God there was no one home. The house and contents had already been sold.'

Penn sat back, surprised.

'So, whoever she's with, officer, has taken her for all that she's worth.'

Now that hadn't been on the report.

CHAPTER 46

Kim approached the lake at Himley Park, already feeling the change in energy from the day before.

The tent had been removed from the spot where Tyler's body had been found but it remained cordoned off. There were still approximately ten white suits around the perimeter of the lake and a collection of five more where the shoe had been.

To the right was the diving crew, which consisted of a team of nine.

'You feel it?' Bryant asked, as they approached the team.

There was an energy, an air of expectation, as though the arrival of the diving crew had galvanised everyone.

'That was a quick turnaround,' Mitch said, approaching from the left. 'Last I heard your boss refused the request to drag the lake.'

'I've got a creative team,' she responded.

If it hadn't been for Penn, they wouldn't be here at all. Clearly the techies had found nothing so far that would have strengthened their case.

Mitch nodded towards the divers. 'Head guy, named Guy, says they should be ready to go in about ten minutes.'

'Cheers, Mitch,' she said as he went back to his business.

She watched the new arrivals for a moment as they prepared for the task at hand away from everyone else like a well-oiled machine. These guys relied on each other to stay alive.

She knew from experience that underwater teams were normally called in for recovery of bodies, vehicles or evidence.

It was an unenviable task, not to mention physically demanding and mentally taxing. It could get disgusting down there.

Scuba divers scoured the bottom of a body of water by hand, moving back and forth in straight lines, like mowing a lawn. Working in pairs, they held on to a rope while sifting through silt, mud, rubbish and foliage.

Had the divers been called in the previous day, before the sailing guy tugged Tyler Short back to the bank, the body would have been placed into a body bag underwater to preserve any evidence but also to avoid family members or press seeing the body being removed from the water.

Kim approached the diver who had been pointed out to her. He was already fully kitted out in his dry suit; unlike wet suits, they were designed to prevent water reaching the skin to guard against polluted water.

Three other divers were busy hoisting oxygen tanks onto their backs. Five divers were not suited at all. For safety more divers stayed out of the water in case of problems.

'Thanks for getting here so quickly,' Kim offered.

He smiled. 'Hey, it's a day search. We're good with that,' he said, attaching a yellow safety line to one of the divers.

Kim knew these guys undertook an intensive eight-week training course followed by regular refreshers for the privilege of being submerged in near-freezing conditions with zero visibility and for the pleasure of being on the police dive team. Not a job for the claustrophobic or faint-hearted.

'We're gonna do a quick whizz round on the boat with the sonar first and then send the guys in.'

Kim knew that the sonar equipment used sound propagation to detect objects underwater, which would then be explored more thoroughly by the divers.

'You really think there's a body down there?' he asked, as one of the divers called him towards the shored dinghy.

Kim nodded. 'I do,' she said, as a familiar sound could be heard in the distance.

Guy headed back to his colleagues as Bryant reached her.

They both looked up into the sky.

'Jeez, we asked that kid…'

'It's not his,' Bryant said, shielding his eyes.

Kim followed his gaze and could immediately see that this one was bigger.

Everyone else looked up too as the drone hovered overhead. This one definitely belonged to a news crew somewhere.

'Fuck it,' she said to Bryant, who was watching it thoughtfully. If she had a gun she'd shoot the bloody thing down.

'I'll be back,' her colleague said.

'Bryant, it's bound to have a much longer range. You've got no chance of finding…'

'Yeah, yeah,' he said, continuing to move away at speed.

Damn it, did no one listen to her any more?

The people around her had all gone back to what they were doing, she noted, as she took out her phone.

Her boss answered on the second ring.

'Sir, we've got a drone overhead and the divers are about to go in.'

'Damn it. Okay, leave it with me.'

It was one of the shortest calls they'd ever had and she didn't hold out much hope of success. Even if he was lucky enough to find out which press outlet it belonged to, he had to convince them to take it down.

Maybe Bryant's wild goose chase would be more successful.

She was about to head back over to Mitch when her phone rang from her pocket. She'd already keyed in the number of Myles Brown.

'Inspector?'

'Go ahead,' she said, watching the drone as it moved west and hovered above the dive team.

'Kane has agreed to a meeting.'

How very nice of him, Kim thought, aware they could have done it her way down at the station, seeing as he'd been witnessed loitering around the victim's home.

'When?'

'Twelve, at Rosie's café in Brierley Hill. He's happy to talk one-on-one informally or he won't speak at all.'

'Really?' she asked, wondering why he thought he could make conditions to a meeting with the police.

'Sorry, but if it's more than one he'll just walk out.'

Despite the irritation that burned within her, she agreed. This man was intrinsically involved in the lives of the Brown family and was planning another snatch. She had to find out more about him and what had occurred.

First meeting was on his terms and if there was a second, it would be on hers.

She gave her agreement and ended the call as two things happened around her: the sound of a second drone could be heard in the distance and Bryant pulled up on the car park.

What the hell was going on? she wondered as both the second drone and Bryant headed towards her.

She watched as the second drone hovered above the lake, turning and then ducking and diving. It paused in mid-air as it seemed to find the bigger drone. The bigger drone was paying no attention to it as it circled the area above the dive team.

Bryant arrived beside her as the little drone moved east towards the bigger one. It picked up speed, climbing until it was level with the other one. It found another speed as it flew into the other drone. A mid-air fight seemed to ensue before propellers were entwined and both drones fell to the ground.

Everyone who had stopped to look gave a small cheer.

She turned to her colleague with a smile.

'You know, Bryant, if you hadn't already killed Betty, she'd be winging her way to your desk right now.'

'Good to know,' he said, looking around distractedly.

'Hope you promised the kid something good.'

'Oh yeah. I'll be on Amazon as soon as I get home.'

Now for the bad news. Something he wasn't gonna like one bit. She'd break it to him as gently as she could.

'Look, Bryant, I've got a meeting with Kane but you can't come,' she said, heading towards the car. The words had sounded much more diplomatic in her head.

He didn't much like being left out of conversations but she really needed to talk to this guy.

'No probs, guv. That suits me just fine.'

Although she was grateful for his understanding, it was not the response she'd expected.

CHAPTER 47

The guv entered the café a few minutes early saying she wanted to get in first.

Normally he would have minded being excluded from any conversation related to the case, but on this occasion, he was relieved. He needed a minute to himself.

He took out his phone and read the message again. Richard had tried to call him twice and Bryant had purposefully ignored the calls. He knew he had to let the case go. After visiting the home of Tina and Damon Crossley he had fought the urge to get involved. He could understand the rage and frustration that had built up in Tina after finding out about Peter Drake's release, and there was no one else to take it out on. But he'd forced himself to step away. A team was handling the case, and although Damon wanted the book thrown at her, CID would decide the charges.

Despite him ignoring the calls, Richard had sent him a text message. Just three little words.

Have you heard?

He dialled Richard's number, as he watched the guv take a seat at an empty table.

The man answered on the second ring, already shouting at him.

'Fucking hell, Bryant. Where've you been. What the fuck is going on, Stone?'

'Richard, slow down. What are you talking about? I'm out here doing my job.'

Despite everything, cursing was something he'd rarely heard from Harrison. He barely recognised the man's voice.

Silence. 'You haven't heard?'

'Heard what?' he snapped. He wasn't going to sit here playing guessing games.

'It's all over the fucking net, man. Exactly what we feared. He's gone and done it again.'

CHAPTER 48

Kim could see her colleague in animated conversation with someone. She checked her phone. No missed calls or messages. If it was anything to do with the case, she was sure he'd let her know.

She took a sip of her latte as the door opened.

There was no mistaking the man who entered. Dressed from head to toe in black, his combat trousers and plain tee shirt did little to hide his muscled physique. Immediately she thought ex-forces, probably army.

She raised her hand to indicate she was the person he was looking for. He offered no acknowledgment but approached the counter and placed an order. The girl appraised him appreciatively before advising him to take a seat.

He nodded towards her before pulling out the opposite chair. 'Inspector?'

'Good to meet you, Kane,' she said, noting that neither offered their hand. 'You know why I'm here?'

'To talk about Samantha Brown,' he replied.

Kim noted that his dark-featured handsome face remained completely neutral at all times. There was neither a frown nor a smile lurking anywhere.

'You were seen loitering close to her home,' she said without preamble.

'Absolutely, but I wasn't loitering and I wasn't hiding. I can give you the exact dates and times if it'll help.'

Kim hadn't expected him to admit his presence at Sammy's home quite so easily.

'Why were you there?'

'Because I knew she wasn't ready.'

'For what?'

'To be left alone. She needed much longer at home with her parents, readjusting to normal life before getting a place of her own. Just because she understood what the cult was didn't mean she didn't want to go back to it.'

'But isn't that what you do?' Kim asked. 'Deprogram cult members?'

'I start the process, Inspector. It's up to the family to do the rest.'

'And the process. I'd like to know more about what you do.'

'Why?'

She liked dealing with people who didn't waste words.

'Because I'm told you're about to do it again, this week.'

'We don't actually tell the family when we're going to do it.'

'Well, they seem to think Sophie is coming home soon.'

He shrugged without emotion. 'They're given an idea of time but we don't give exact dates and times. We don't know when they'll be ready.'

'To snatch?' she asked, confused.

He remained silent as the waitress placed his cup of black coffee before him.

He thanked her without looking her way. She appeared disappointed.

'Getting them is the easy part. That's not what we do. The Browns could have done that themselves.'

'So, why didn't they?'

'Because they knew that the first time Samantha saw an open door she'd be right back at Unity Farm.'

'So, what exactly do you do?'

'We take the person out of the cult and then the cult out of the person.'

'Is that the company strapline?' Kim asked, unable to help herself. She could see it now on glossy brochures.

'No, it's what we do,' he repeated without humour.

'So, you're saying you snatch someone and keep them until you think they're ready to go home?'

He nodded. 'There's no point otherwise. What's your favourite food?' he asked, surprising her, but she decided to play along, and although she didn't really have a favourite food, she did enjoy the occasional pizza.

She answered him.

'If I took you away from the pizza shop and told you never to eat another pizza, you'd completely ignore me and go get one. If I get the chance to show you the fat content and additives and explain the effect it's having on your body, you might think twice. It's not as simple as me getting you away from the pizza shop – that doesn't change your mindset. Few people are kept in a cult against their will. They want to be there. They've been persuaded.'

'And you dissuade them?'

He took a sip of coffee. 'There's a technique used by cults called freezing…'

'Yeah, thawing and refreezing. Myles told me about that.'

'In effect, we use the same technique to undo the damage.'

Kim pictured a piece of meat. 'But surely once something has been thawed you can't refreeze it again. It's not safe.'

'It is if you change its structural composition. If a chicken is frozen you can defrost it, cook it and refreeze it again. It has been changed.'

'But it's still the same chicken,' Kim said, wondering how many times the mind could take being frozen and thawed.

He held her gaze but said nothing.

'And you're an expert on this?'

'Yes,' he said, simply.

'Why?'

'Because I am.'

'So, how long does the process take?'

'It varies.'

'From what to what?' she asked.

'Five days is the shortest. Thirteen days is the longest.'

'Sammy Brown?'

'Thirteen.'

So, she'd been his biggest challenge yet.

'Let me get this right. You can undo months of brainwashing in less than two weeks?'

'First of all, cults don't brainwash – that's a term when a victim knows they're in the hands of the enemy. Thought reform is a type of influence and persuasion which is like gaining weight. It happens gradually and like weight the slower it goes on the harder it is to lose.'

'Thought reform?' she asked. It wasn't a term she'd heard before.

He studied her for a minute before necking his coffee.

'Myles told me you had some kind of understanding, but if I need to educate you to this degree you're going to have to buy me another drink.'

From the article and subsequent research, Stacey learned two things. The girl, named at the inquest as Helen Deere, had spent seven months at Unity Farm and she had not fallen from the window of her parents' town house. She had broken the window and jumped. A verdict of suicide had been recorded.

Stacey sat back and thought for a moment. Two murders and now a suicide all linked to Unity Farm. The inquest had confirmed that no one other than the girl's mother had been present at the home at the time Helen Deere took her own life, so Stacey knew that her death was not connected to their murderer, but why the mention at all? Why was the place involved in the narrative of her suicide?

A couple of quick searches and she had a landline for the home of Helen Deere's parents.

The phone was answered on the second ring.

'Mrs Deere?' Stacey asked.

'Who's calling?'

Check before committing. Stacey liked that.

Stacey introduced herself and her position.

The woman offered no response and simply waited for the purpose of the call.

'Mrs Deere, may I ask you a couple of questions about your daughter, Helen?'

'I know my daughter's name, Officer, and I assume you know she died, so how can I possibly help you?'

The woman's tone hovered around unfriendly with the threat of outright hostility if Stacey said the wrong thing or took too long.

'Unity Farm has come to our attention and I understand that your daughter spent some time there before her death.'

'My daughter was a normal sixteen-year-old before she met those people, Officer. They changed her. They brainwashed her until I didn't even recognise my own child. The place is evil and destructive and they took my daughter from me,' she spat.

'You feel that Unity Farm was somehow related to your daughter's suicide?'

There was a pause. 'If you need to ask me that question, you don't know as much about the place as you should.'

'I'm sorry, I didn't mean…'

'Never mind. You're a police officer. If someone isn't physically assaulting someone in front of your face, you're not interested. There are other types of crime.'

Stacey had no idea what she meant but she felt compelled to make her understand. 'Mrs Deere, we're just trying to find out more about the place.'

She snorted. 'Good luck with that.'

Stacey wanted to assure her that they were committed to learning more. 'We have visited Unity…'

'Visit as many times as you want and you'll see the facade but you're never going to find out what truly goes on in that place,' she said, before she hung up the phone.

CHAPTER 50

'Right,' Kane continued. 'There are no secret drugs or potions involved in thought reform. There's no violence and we're all subjected to it in various forms every day through advertising and marketing, but there are other tactics involved that are employed by a cult.'

Kim opened her mouth to speak, but he held up his hand.

'Please, Inspector, if you take nothing else away from this meeting then please accept that a cult does not look like a cult. It always appears as something else.'

'Okay, please continue,' she advised. In the absence of getting back in there to see what was going on, she was going to have to get information from him. For now.

'Language, not physical force, is the key to manipulating minds. The first thing a cult does is destabilise someone's sense of themselves. They get someone to drastically reinterpret their life history and alter their view. Sammy was convinced that she had suffered psychologically as a child because her younger sister had been prone to health problems as a baby. Sophie became the favourite child and Sammy was loved less. Her parents had made her less of a person through their neglect of her needs.

'The next step is to develop a dependence on the cult. Initially they're kept unaware of what is going on and the changes taking place. They control the person's time and environment. They're not left alone; they're given activities that reinforce the changes. Eventually the cult introduces a "them and us" philosophy. It separates the person from anyone not in the cult. Outsiders are given an identity.'

'Zombies?' Kim asked, remembering what Sammy had called her parents.

He nodded. 'Similar to tactics used by the army. Give the enemy a name. Eventually the cult creates a sense of powerlessness, fear and dependency.'

Kim remembered the girl selling the vegetables. Her anxiety and then her joy when Jake appeared.

'They suppress much of the old behaviour and attitudes while instilling new ones. Finally, they offer a closed system of logic, allowing no real input or criticism. Esteem and affection from peers is important to new recruits. Initially, a new member will be showered with praise, affection to make them feel safe and loved. The changes happen over time. Newbies are cut off from families, friends and love bombed.'

Kim raised an eyebrow.

'Flattery, compliments, always in the company of a long-term member who is affectionate, kept busy so there is no room for doubts. Sometimes kept awake for long periods so they're sleep deficient, phones will be broken to prevent contact. Once you change someone's surroundings to that degree, you're halfway there.' He thought for a moment. 'Have you ever spent time in hospital, Inspector?'

She shook her head.

'Attended a team-building course for a few days?'

She nodded.

'The few people around you take on more importance. Cut off from everything you know, a new reality forms. You become dependent. A cult will tap into any unresolved feelings and exploit them. Eventually the only people a newbie will care about are the people in the group. Their new family.'

Kim recalled Britney's allusion to family.

'Is that what newbies want?'

'Everyone wants to belong: to a team, a group. Take someone's family away and they're ripe to become part of another one. You have to remember that these groups are highly cohesive. They are controlled by a shared system of beliefs.'

'Do they target vulnerable people?'

He sipped and nodded. 'In most cases they do. People who are emotionally unstable are prime targets – they're easier to coerce – but most people are susceptible to flattery and being told what they want to hear.'

'And do you use the same techniques when you break them out?'

'That subject isn't up for discussion,' he said, finishing his drink. 'But what I can tell you is that people who aren't extracted properly may never recover from the experience.'

'Why not?' Kim asked. Surely the influence of the group was like a drug. If you no longer took it, it wore off.

'Remember my pizza example. It's not enough to take the person out of the cult. You also…'

'Have to take the cult out of the person,' she finished for him.

Kim sensed their meeting was coming to an end but there was more she wanted to ask.

'Did Sammy recruit Sophie into the group?'

He shook his head and pointedly looked at his watch.

'My understanding of their dynamic is that Sophie wanted everything her sister had and she went of her own accord. As children they were very close and Sophie looked up to her sister. Sophie wasn't as bright, academically, as Sammy. She had to work harder to do well at school but Sammy never made fun of her and would help her revise for exams and tests. Sophie is more artistic, more of a dreamer, from what her parents have said.'

'But why would Sophie follow her sister into—'

'My understanding,' he said, cutting her off and glancing at his watch again, 'is that when Sammy pulled away she shunned everyone, even Sophie. Myles and Kate think she followed to try and get that connection back. Basically, Sophie missed her sister.'

And now to what Kim had to say before she ran out of time. There was a meter running in his watch or in his brain.

'Look, I understand the wishes of the Browns with regard to their younger daughter, but I must ask that you hold off on any plan to snatch her while we're investigating exactly how Unity Farm is involved in Samantha's murder.'

'You're not paying me,' he said, pushing his chair away from the table.

'No, but I can throw your ass in prison.'

For the first time, she saw the promise of a change in expression but it quickly disappeared.

'On what charges, I'd be very interested to know.'

'Yeah, if we can't find any we make 'em up,' she said, drily. 'Especially if it'll stop you potentially hampering a murder investigation by snatching another girl.'

He leaned down as he passed by her chair. His voice was a whisper as it sounded in her ear.

'Who says we don't have her already?'

CHAPTER 51

Kim took a second before pushing back her chair and tried to analyse her feelings towards the man who had just left. Strangely, she had remained neutral throughout the exchange.

There was no doubt in her mind that he was knowledgeable on the subject of cults and mind control, and yet she still struggled to equate the information with Unity Farm. Damn it, she needed to get back in there. Everything about him was controlled and measured. His facial expression had barely changed, just like his tone, which had remained tempered and calm. She had studied him for ticks and tells to indicate if he was lying and she'd found nothing, not even when she'd asked him about his reasons for being at Sammy's flat.

His parting words about Sophie had almost propelled her to run after him, cuff him and haul him down to the station, but Woody's potential wrath at her actions had played through her mind before Kane had even closed the door behind him.

Is Sophie Brown a legal adult?
Yes.
Is Sophie Brown a missing person?
No.
Have her parents asked for your involvement?
No.
Do you have any physical evidence to suggest Sophie Brown is at risk?
No.

She sighed. Right now, every lead was drying up before her eyes. It was time to get back to the station and see how they could move this on.

Her phone rang as she stood. Surprised to see Travis's name, she answered straight away.

'Hey.'

'What the fuck is going on, Stone?'

'Excuse me?' she said, trying to think of any part of their case that had impinged on the jurisdiction of West Mercia. There was nothing but their chequered past, and her knowledge of her old partner told her that he was seriously pissed off.

'What's with Bryant calling and giving me the third degree?'

Kim turned away from the café window, confused.

'About what?'

'A particularly horrific crime scene I was called to this morning.'

'You gotta give me a bit more than that, Travis.'

'A young girl, butchered and raped.'

Kim got it. Peter Drake had been released yesterday.

'I don't fucking appreciate the Spanish Inquisition by an officer from another force.'

Kim felt her own anger rise in line with Travis's temper. What the hell was Bryant doing going behind her back to another force about an investigation he had no part in? Right now it looked like she couldn't control her own damn team.

Bryant had stepped way out of line. It was both unprofessional and unethical to try and involve yourself in another force's case. Travis was right to be pissed off. Had it been her she wouldn't have been content with going to the officer's DI. She would have gone higher, and Travis was doing Bryant a favour by coming directly to her. She could cap it right here and that would be the end of it.

She opened her mouth to speak as she turned back towards the window.

Her colleague was staring forward, a set expression on his face. His fingers tapped on the steering wheel.

She realised that over the years he'd supported every decision she'd made both as a colleague and a friend even when he didn't agree with her. He had always given her the benefit of the doubt. She thought back to their conversation in her kitchen. She had told him to drop it and then dismissed it. She felt a sliver of shame roll into her stomach. Was their friendship just a one-way street?

'Stone, what the?…'

'Travis, I'll talk to you more later because there are things here you don't understand, but do me a huge favour just this once, eh?' she said, heading towards the door.

'Go on.'

'Give Bryant whatever he wants.'

CHAPTER 52

Bryant looked on confused as his boss and colleagues left the office. The guv had offered to shout them lunch.

'But not you,' she'd said, placing a hand on his shoulder to sit him back down. 'Take a nap, make some calls, whatever. I'll grab you something.'

He tried to put the pieces of the puzzle together. He was no Penn but even he knew something had gone on that he was unaware of.

Damn it, Travis must have called her. It was the only thing that made sense.

So, right now he should be receiving an almighty bollocking in the privacy of the Bowl. Instead he'd been given some privacy and some time.

His mouth lifted in a smile. The guv never wasted words. Make some calls, she'd said.

He took out his phone and dialled. He was being given an opportunity to repair the damage.

The DI answered on the third ring.

'Hey, Travis. Listen, I just want to apologise about…'

'Forget it,' Travis said. 'Went over the old case files of Peter Drake. Didn't realise you'd been on watch duty with that poor kid.'

Travis's understanding made him feel even worse about ringing up to demand information about a crime scene that had absolutely nothing to do with him.

'Listen,' Travis continued, 'we've got the techies over at the scene and the post-mortem later this afternoon. We're debriefing around seven if you can make it.'

Bryant was speechless. What the hell had the boss said to him? Regardless, he was grateful. He knew he wouldn't be able to offer Richard Harrison detail of the briefing but he hoped to be in a position to assure him that everything possible was being done. The man needed something. He was unravelling before Bryant's eyes.

'This ain't charity,' Travis continued. 'You might be able to offer something useful, that's all.'

'Thanks, Travis. I'll be there.'

Silence filled the line between them.

'Go on, ask,' Travis said.

Travis had already combed the reports of Wendy Harrison and Tina Crossley, so he had to know the answer.

'Is it the same?'

A slight pause before the DI answered.

'Yeah, Bryant. It's the same.'

CHAPTER 53

Kim headed for a table by the window and laid down her tray. She hadn't even looked at the plastic triangle she'd selected for herself, but had chosen a prawn triple for her colleague back in the office.

Penn had opted for a plate of chips and gravy, and Stacey was the proud owner of an egg salad bowl. She had valiantly refused the muffin that had been produced from behind the counter, although Kim had thought she was going to burst into tears.

'Okay, Penn, continue,' she said. He had started to talk about Josie Finch in the canteen queue.

'So, according to Josie, whoever Sheila was with took her for everything. She withdrew every penny she'd saved and then sold the house as well. Mortgage was clear so it was £150k that went somewhere.'

'Okay, try and find the estate agent and solicitor who handled the sale and see where the money went.'

'You think she was at Unity Farm?' Penn asked, wiping a blob of gravy from his chin.

Kim shrugged. It was a leap from finding a shoe that might or might not belong to the missing woman, but it had to have been more than a fleeting affair with some kind of con man for the woman to have completely exited her daughter's life.

Kim turned to Stacey, who appeared to be trying to eat the salad while avoiding the lettuce. Penn caught her eye and shook his head. Kim silently agreed. For a woman about to marry the love of her life she'd never been so miserable.

'Stace, you find out anything?'

She put down her fork for a minute. 'So far I can find no mention of anyone named Kane Devlin. I've got a few more places to check, but I did see a few mentions on Facebook about Unity Farm but it's from a closed group. I've tried to join and was refused immediately, so I was about to set up a fake profile and try again.'

'Ooh, devious, Stace, you have been spending way too much time with me.'

'And I spoke to the mother of a girl named Helen Deere who threw herself out of a window after spending time at Unity Farm. There was no one else involved, so there's no direct link but the mother blames that place for brainwashing her.'

'Damn, Stace, great work. Did she say anything else?'

'Just that we're never going to find out exactly what goes on in there.'

Yes, that's what Kim was starting to fear herself.

'How was the meeting with Kane?' Stacey asked, pushing away her bowl completely. Only the egg had been eaten.

'Informative about cult culture in general but not so much about Unity Farm. It's bloody frustrating. With no clear links from our victims to the place, we can't get a search warrant and we can't get in to have a damn good look.'

Yes, Sammy had lived there but that had been months ago. No judge would sign a warrant giving them full access on that. Right now, they couldn't even prove that Tyler had lived there and they didn't know for sure if Sheila Thorpe was even dead.

'Aaaargh,' Kim groaned, dropping her head into her hands. Stacey was tapping her fingers on the table while Penn finished off his lunch.

'What we need…' Stacey began.

'Is someone on the inside,' Kim finished.

'Innocent looking…'

'But intelligent,' Kim said.

Their eyes met as Penn speared his last chip and mopped up the remaining gravy.

'You thinking what I'm thinking?' Kim asked the constable.

Stacey smiled. 'Yeah, pretty sure I am, boss.'

CHAPTER 54

'Hiya teeeeam,' Tiffany called from the doorway.

'Come on in, Tink,' Kim said from the top of the office.

Tiffany Moore was a bright and committed twenty-four-year-old police constable who looked much younger than her years. She'd been called in to assist Stacey with some of the desk work on their last major case due to Penn being seconded back to West Mercia.

Kim had nicknamed her Tinkerbell not only because she wore her blonde hair up in a bun at the back of her head but because she truly had walked off the pages of a fairy tale book. Kim would not have been surprised to see butterflies and rabbits entering the squad room behind her.

'Close the door,' Kim instructed.

The girl did so and then stood in front of it.

'Sit down,' Kim told her. 'So, what has Wood... I mean DCI Woodward told you?'

She sat and shrugged. 'He asked me if I'd like to book the afternoon as annual leave and pop up here to give you a hand with something.' She rolled her eyes. 'I was like, err... yeah.'

Kim hid her smile. On paper this girl should have annoyed the hell out of her. She was bright, chirpy, cheerful, innocent and she whistled show tunes when she was concentrating. And yet Kim didn't find her irritating because she had allowed neither life nor the police force to knock that joy of life out of her.

'Okay, we need you to go undercover, which sounds a lot more exciting than it is.'

Tiff clapped her hands together. 'Cool.'

Kim almost said it did not include going to Disneyland but held her tongue. It was that youthful innocence they were counting on.

When she'd shot upstairs to see Woody straight from the cafeteria, she had known immediately what his response would be.

Organising an official undercover operation took weeks, even months, of planning. Officers were vetted and analysed. Operational Orders and Risk Assessments were formulated by experts, checked and double-checked to cover everyone's behind. It was a process they didn't have time for. With two bodies in two days they had to be creative.

'Okay, Tink, here's the issue. There's a place called Unity Farm that's linked to two murders. Bryant and I have visited briefly and got the shortest of tours; the tourist view if you like. We need to get someone who is not a police officer in there for a few hours. Get a better look around, a feel for what's really going on and if it's as innocent as it seems. Make sense so far?'

She nodded, eyes wide.

'They seem to favour young, vulnerable kids who are in a state of emotional turmoil, upset about something.' Kim frowned. 'I mean, you do get upset, don't you?' she asked, to be sure.

'Well, not often but I'm sure I can if I try.'

'Go on then,' Kim said, folding her arms and praying Tiffany had been chosen as a kid for the school play.

Tiffany threw her head back and began wailing. Her eyes were tightly closed and her face scrunched into some kind of constipated grimace.

Kim's jaw dropped to the ground. Bryant looked away. Penn covered his eyes and shook his head while Stacey groaned out loud.

Kim's bewilderment was interrupted by the ringing of her phone. Mitch at the lake.

She watched as Tiffany's performance reached its climax and realised they were in all kinds of trouble.

CHAPTER 55

Kim checked her watch again as Bryant pulled up behind the college building.

'You ready, Tink?' she asked, turning around in her seat.

Tiff nodded.

She'd been fully briefed on the murders, the names, the layout of the site and had been given strict instructions about leaving.

'So, there'll be a car waiting on the main road at ten o'clock tonight. You call me the second you're out, got it?'

'Yep, got it, boss,' Tiff said, getting out of the car.

Kim felt there was something more she needed to say, but didn't know what it was.

'Speak later,' Tiff said, heading across the road.

Kim watched silently as she fell into step behind a group of four boys. Changed into jeans and trainers and with a backpack borrowed from a colleague, she really didn't look out of place.

'You okay, guv?' Bryant asked, following her gaze.

'Yeah, yeah, she fits right in,' Kim said, as she went out of view.

Ever since she'd witnessed Tiff's attempt at crying, a feeling of unease had started to build in her stomach. What had seemed like a good idea at the time was rapidly losing its appeal. It had seemed so simple: get her in there, do a little digging and leave, but as they'd briefed her, Kim had begun to realise they had no idea what kind of people they were dealing with. Tiffany had never been undercover before. Officers undertook extensive training before embarking on this level of deceit.

'She'll be fine,' Bryant said, starting the car. 'It's just a few hours.'

'I'd forgotten how bloody young and naïve she…'

'Guv, she's many things. She's also a fully trained police officer.'

Kim nodded. Easy to forget sometimes.

'It's only a few hours. She'll be back later and we really need to get to the lake.'

'Yeah, you're right,' Kim said, as he pulled away from the kerb.

Kim glanced back once more to the spot where Tiffany had disappeared into the crowd and realised what had been on the tip of her tongue.

She had wanted to tell the girl to stay safe.

CHAPTER 56

Tiffany spotted the girl Britney as soon as she turned the corner. She was speaking animatedly to three girls having a smoke, looking bored and trying to edge away.

Tiff looked around and saw a great spot on a wall not too far away from the red-haired girl.

The boss had told her not to cry but to look upset instead. She didn't have much experience with crying because it wasn't something she chose to do. She never had.

The boss had also given her a cover story of a bad boyfriend break-up, but Tiff had chosen her own. She knew she wasn't good at outright lying. Her brain just didn't work that way. Her plan was to stay as close to the truth as she could.

She lowered her head and remembered the conversation she'd had with her mother before she'd left for work.

Tiff knew that still living at home at her age was uncommon. She was a police officer and could easily afford a small place of her own. She didn't stay for financial reasons.

As the youngest of five children, Tiff had been born when all four of her brothers had needed their parents' attention more than her. Three weeks after her fourth birthday, her father had been killed in a motorway accident, leaving even lesss attention to go around.

Largely ignored by her brothers, she had invented her own world where everyone was happy, and she convinced herself that her day would come. One by one her brothers had left home to start their own lives and the day had finally come that she had her mum all to herself.

It was not the picture she'd dreamed of. Her mum still spent the majority of her time running around after 'her boys'; going to their houses to clean, to accept deliveries, pick up shopping, tend their gardens, anything to make their lives easier. A year ago, her mum had downsized to a three bed end terrace. Perfect for the two of them, or so she'd thought until this morning.

'Ryan's coming home,' her mother had said.

Hardly a shocker, Tiff thought. She'd heard the conversations. He'd been caught cheating and his wife had thrown him out.

'So, you'll have to move into the box room,' she'd continued.

'Why do I have to move?' Tiff asked, surely as the incumbent child she should be able to stay where she was. Ryan had spent a couple of nights in a hotel hoping Sasha would relent. She hadn't and he was clearly missing his home comforts.

'Because boys need more room,' was the answer that explained everything.

The reasoning had taken her back to her whole childhood. Move over so the boys can sit down. What are you upset for, it's only a doll? Put that down, it's for the boys.

'Hey, are you okay?' asked a voice from above. Tiffany had been so lost in the memories she'd almost forgotten why she was here. And the reason was now right in front of her. Close up Tiff noticed a smattering of freckles that crossed the bridge of her nose beneath friendly green eyes filled with concern. She wore no make-up or jewellery except for a necklace with a butterfly resting in the hollow of her throat.

'Yeah, I'm fine, thanks,' she answered. 'Just had a huge row with my mum this morning.'

Not strictly true. She had accepted the news as she always did, with silence.

'Oh no,' Britney said, sitting beside her. 'Families can be so difficult, can't they?'

Tiff nodded. 'We both said some pretty nasty things.'

Britney nodded. 'We all do when we're angry.'

Tiff nodded and wiped at her dry eye.

'I'm Britney, by the way,' the girl said, offering her hand and a friendly smile.

'Tiffany – Tiff,' she responded as she always did.

'So, what was it about, the argument?'

'My brother,' she answered, and gave a very brief summary.

'Oh, that doesn't seem very fair,' Britney offered.

'I'm sure it'll all be fine. We just need a bit of cooling-off time. I just don't want to see her quite yet, but I've got no money and no place to go,' she said, shrugging.

Britney tapped her arm reassuringly.

'Don't worry. I know a place you can go.'

CHAPTER 57

It was almost four by the time Bryant pulled up at the Himley Park lake.

'Shit,' Kim said, as Bryant parked next to Keats's van. He would have been Mitch's second call.

She wasted no time in hurrying to the nucleus of the action.

She arrived and looked around.

'Where is it, then?' she asked, in the absence of a body.

'Stuck,' Keats said, as a head bobbed up out of the water, and he called out an instruction to his colleagues in the boat.

'What do we know?' Kim asked, turning to Mitch.

He shrugged. 'That there's an unidentified mass attached to some foliage in the water.'

'But they're sure it's a body?'

Mitch raised an eyebrow. 'Pretty sure they wouldn't have told us to summon everyone if it was a discarded shopping trolley.'

'Mitch, you have been spending way too much time with Keats,' she said, as Inspector Plant approached.

'Stone, the manager here is gonna pop a blood vessel if she doesn't get some information soon. She's seeing all kinds of vehicles arrive and her anxiety is going through the roof. She's desperate to know when she's going to get her site back.'

Kim opened her mouth to answer. She felt sorry for Plant having to try and keep the staff calm and, more importantly, out of the way.

She was prevented from answering by a shout from the boat on the lake.

The guy in the water was giving the thumbs up to the crew in the boat as she saw the bottom end of a body bag break the surface of the water.

She turned to Plant. 'Tell her it's gonna be a little while yet.'

She didn't wait for an answer as she headed closer to the lake to get a better look.

'Looks like Penn might have had something after all,' Bryant said, standing beside her.

Perhaps, Kim thought, keeping her gaze on the boat.

She approached the bank as the dinghy pulled in.

'Let me help,' Keats said, taking two steps down. The divers said nothing as the pathologist helped lift the body bag out of the boat.

Kim craned her neck to get a better look as they carried it gently up the bank and onto Keats's waiting trolley.

'We're going back down,' Guy said, as he passed her.

'For what?' Kim asked.

'One hand and one foot missing.'

She looked to Mitch.

'Perfectly normal.'

Keats brought the trolley to rest beside her. 'You ready?'

She nodded as he slowly began to unzip the bag.

'Bloody hell,' she said, covering her nose as the stench of death mixed with dirty water filled her nostrils.

What she saw could only be described as a skeleton wrapped in wet brown paper bags.

'This one doesn't look bloated and waxy,' she observed to Mitch, remembering how Tyler had looked.

'Temperature of the water,' Mitch answered. 'If the water was warmer when the body went in, adipocere wouldn't have started forming.'

'You think this one has been in there longer than Tyler Short?'

Both Keats and Mitch nodded, but it was Keats who spoke. 'How much longer is difficult to say right now.'

Keats continued to pull down the zipper.

Kim followed the motion while continuing to assess the body, unsure whether or not it was Sheila until her gaze reached the foot that had remained attached.

Bryant's sharp intake of breath told her he'd clocked the same thing as she had.

This poor soul was wearing a large, man-size trainer and was definitely not Sheila Thorpe.

CHAPTER 58

Tiff found herself already confused. The taxi had dropped them off at the main road. Britney had laughingly helped her climb a gate as she'd explained they were taking the scenic route.

This was not where Stacey had shown her on Google Earth and it wasn't where the car would be waiting at ten.

She walked alongside Britney as they crossed two fields, circled a small wooded area and climbed a steep hill. It wasn't a journey she'd care to make in the dark.

'There it is,' Britney said, breathlessly, as they reached the top of the mound.

Tiff forced herself to remember that Britney had said very little about where they were going except that she'd love it.

'That's your house?' Tiff asked, as she looked down on Unity Farm.

'Ha, I wish, but it is my home.'

'What is it?' Tiff asked as she looked down into a small valley.

'It's a retreat,' she explained, simply. 'And you'll be made very welcome.'

Tiff tried to take in everything from the vantage point.

To the left was a stone farmhouse building that looked out on to a collection of barns that had all been refurbished. Beyond the barn at the end were slabs of concrete that looked like foundations for more buildings. Immediately at the bottom of the hill were polytunnels and fenced-off planting areas.

Tiff took a step forward, but Britney touched her arm lightly.

'Just one minute.'

Tiffany wondered why they were standing at the top of the hill as the light began to fade.

Britney looked at her watch and held up her hand.

'Any second…'

Before the word now could leave her mouth, the whole site below suddenly came alive with light as uplighters fitted into the ground illuminated, bathing all the buildings in a warm orange glow showing the beauty of the stone structures.

Delicate warm fairy lights adorned the guttering of each of the barns and in surrounding trees. Waist-high lamps illuminated the paths to all of the buildings. In the corner of her eye, a tree branch moved, and Tiff thought she saw a light in the wooded area.

'Never gets old,' Britney said, taking a step to head down the hill.

Tiffany took another good look as she followed Britney down and she really had to agree.

She'd never seen anything so pretty in her life.

CHAPTER 59

Stacey put down the phone and returned to her fake profile. The boss was on her way back and she hoped to have something to show for her time. She'd been told to focus on Jake Black and Unity Farm. So far she'd had little luck with either.

Her searches on the cult leader had revealed that he had been an only child born into a family of inherited wealth from his paternal great-grandfather, who had made his money buying cheap clutches of land and selling to developers at the right time for both housing and expansion.

Jake's grandfather had managed to squander most of the family fortune on dubious overseas investments leaving just enough to give Jake a decent private education at the best schools in the country.

When Jake had graduated from Cambridge, unable to sustain their lavish lifestyle further, his parents sold the family estate to pay off debts and emigrated to Australia, leaving Jake Black used to a lifestyle that he now had to fund himself.

So far she'd been unable to find anything more on his activities, and Stacey knew that nothing she'd learned so far was going to ignite any excitement in her boss, but what had been more interesting to her, after speaking to the mother of Helen Deere, was the veil of secrecy that seemed to surround Unity Farm and that was where she had now turned her attention.

Even to her own eyes, the fake profile of Janey Taylor looked a little bit suspect.

She had done all she could to make it seem legit: she'd posted photos stolen, or borrowed, from other profiles and had shared posts about Scientology, meditation and yoga. She was hoping that the moderator of the group wouldn't look too closely before allowing her to join.

It had taken longer than she'd thought, and Penn had offered to do the digging on the financials of Sheila Thorpe.

'Okay, here goes,' Stacey said, pressing the request to join button.

She sat back in her chair. All she could do now was wait.

'Yeah, doing a fair bit of waiting, myself,' Penn said. 'Estate agents wouldn't consider giving me any information except for the name of the purchaser's solicitors. They've given me the name of Sheila's solicitors, who are now debating whether they'll tell me anything at all. Even given the situation they're seeking advice.'

'And you're sure the money from the house sale didn't go into Sheila's account?'

Penn shook his head. Just about the only people who had been helpful were the bank, who had confirmed that no money had been transferred in after Sheila had emptied the account.

Stacey saw his pensive expression.

'You really want to give Josie Finch something, don't you?'

He nodded. 'And yet, I don't know how anything I have to offer can help. She's either lost her mother or lost her mother.'

Stacey saw the sadness that crossed his face. She knew the time for his own mother was close but he didn't mention it, so neither did she.

'Hey, Penn, if you ever…'

'Did you just ding?' he asked, glancing at her phone.

She wasn't sure but the message she'd got from her colleague was loud and clear.

She picked up her phone and sure enough, a message had popped up in the mail box of her fake profile.

Before pressing on it she noted she'd had no notification to say she'd been allowed into the group.

As soon as she opened the message it was clear the sender was shouting.

It read:

If this is you Eric Leland trying to get in with another fake profile Fuck Off

Stacey read the message again, which had been sent from someone called Penny Hicks.

Oh well, she hadn't made it into the group but she now had two names for the price of one.

CHAPTER 60

As they reached the bottom of the hill, two minibuses pulled up to the side of the farmhouse.

'Who are they?' Tiff asked, as men and women piled off chatting animatedly with each other.

Everyone smiled and waved in their direction.

'Some of the guys coming back from work. Everyone here contributes something.'

Tiff noted the vehicles were both just a couple of years old. She wondered who had contributed those.

'Come on, there's someone I'd like you to meet,' Britney said, grabbing her hand and holding it tight. Tiff suddenly had the feeling of being back at junior school, about to skip around the playground with her new best friend.

Tiffany tried to take note of where they were going, but the farmhouse was bigger than she'd thought and filled with people coming and going to somewhere.

Tiffany realised they were heading towards the most delicious smell she could imagine.

Her stomach grumbled in appreciation. She'd been about to eat lunch when she'd been summoned to see the DCI.

'Aah, there you are,' Britney said, brightly, as an attractive white-haired man headed towards them. She was immediately struck by the light blue eyes that stared straight at her. She was unsure if she saw a hint of suspicion in those eyes before he smiled widely and offered his hand.

'Jake Black, pleased to meet you.'

'Tiffany – Tiff,' she answered, unable to look away.

'He's not just Jake Black,' Britney said. 'He founded this place and welcomed us all to share in it.'

Jake smiled fondly as he placed a hand on Britney's shoulder. The girl glanced up at him with unconcealed admiration.

He leaned down closer and spoke intimately into Britney's ear. 'If you make it back quickly I'll save you both a place at my table.'

Britney coloured and grabbed her hand again as Jake wandered away.

'First sitting *and* Jake's table, come on,' she said, heading back out the front door.

Britney guided her through the beautifully lit courtyard to the first barn.

'I'm in here,' she said, taking the second door on the left.

The room was small, basic and not unpleasant. A single bed, dressing table and bedside cabinet were the only items of furniture in the room.

'Just drop your bag here before the food gets cold.'

Tiffany reached into the side pocket and took out her phone.

Britney shook her head. 'You need to leave that here. Really, you need to switch it off. We don't have phones here.'

Reluctantly Tiff did as she was asked and put the phone back in her bag. She could live without it while she ate. She'd grab it afterwards.

Time to get to what she was here for.

'So, sittings?' she asked Britney as she followed her out of the door.

'Yeah, there are about one hundred of us and the dining room only holds fifty, so there's two sittings for every meal. Always best if you can get on the first; food's hotter and you get first choice. Second sitting it's warmish but all the good stuff is gone.'

Didn't seem very fair to Tiffany. The force canteen at Hale-sowen wasn't great but it was consistently average if you were at the front or the end of the queue.

'So, is it oldest, youngest or...'

Britney laughed as they re-entered the farmhouse. 'Nah, it's performance based. The more you contribute dictates which sitting.'

Tiffany noted the framed motivational posters that seemed to hang on every wall. Pebbles, sunrises, beaches, meadows, forests and shouty words like 'peace', 'fulfilment' and 'motivation'.

'But, do you get?...'

'Shush, we eat in silence, appreciate the food,' Britney said, entering the dining room.

To the left were tables holding hot plates with three women behind serving portions to the queue. The rest of the space was taken up with five tables seating ten people each. Jake Black was already sitting at the top table with two spare seats to his left.

The queue moved quickly, and Tiffany was suddenly in front of the source of the delicious smell from earlier.

'Yummy, my favourite: pork chop in onion gravy with mashed potato.'

Tiffany couldn't help her disappointment. The aroma had promised so much more than basic chops and smash.

'You just wait,' Britney whispered with a smile.

Tiff followed Britney through the tables to where Jake Black sat. Everyone she passed smiled and nodded in her direction.

Without speaking, Jake indicated that Tiffany was to sit next to him. Tiff caught the quick look of disappointment that crossed Britney's features before she took the other seat.

She sat, trying not to be unnerved by the lack of noise other than the scrapings of cutlery on plates. It was a stark difference to how mealtimes had played out in her own home. With four broth-ers it had been like feeding time at the zoo; her mother cooking different things for the boys, the boys changing their minds and wanting each other's; tantrums, complaining, food throwing. Oh yes, she could see the value in silence at the dinner table.

She cut a piece of pork and added a little mashed potato. It was like heaven in her mouth. The pork was tender and tasty, seasoned with something she'd never tasted before. The onions were tasty little slivers that accented the taste of the pork. Simple mashed potato had been elevated with lashings of real butter, garlic, cream cheese and chives.

She glanced at Britney, who offered her a conspiratorial smile, which said, I did tell you. And she had been right, Tiff admitted, taking another mouthful. Her stomach grumbled in appreciation, and if anyone noticed they made no indication. She took another bite vowing not to leave even a mouthful on her plate.

Jake finished his meal, save for a line of pork fat pushed to the side.

He glanced towards the door and the sound of panpipes filtered into the room.

The silence faded away as people began to speak to each other while they ate.

So, Jake Black preferred to eat in silence, she suspected, as she speared another piece of pork.

'So, Tiffany, what brings you to Unity Farm?' he asked, turning towards her.

She chewed the pork in her mouth while he waited for an answer.

'Britney offered me a place to come for a few hours. I didn't want to go home.'

She was telling the truth.

'Why not?' he asked, leaning closer as the volume of chatter at their own table increased.

Regretfully, Tiff put down her knife and fork. She couldn't continue eating when he clearly wanted to engage her in conversation.

'Had a row with my mum.'

He nodded his understanding.

'Families are complicated. We place high expectations on blood relatives to do the right thing.'

Yes, telling Ryan he could have the box room would have been the right thing for her mother to do.

'They often let us down, but do you know why that is?'

Tiffany had the sudden feeling that they were the only two people in the room. The chatter fell away as he continued.

'There is an expectation on family members to love equally and they don't. Parents do have favourites, maybe one child is prettier, funnier or more intelligent. They get favoured and it's hard for the kids who get left behind. Not feeling good enough for your parents can lead to a whole lifetime of misery. Unloved kids seek approval until the day they die.'

Tiff listened carefully. He was right. She was still seeking approval now.

He touched her hand lightly. 'There comes a time that you have to take control. Decide enough is enough and that the approval is no longer important to you.' He paused and tipped his head, a smile playing on his lips. 'If your family don't appreciate just how special you are, they're idiots and it is definitely more their loss than yours.'

Tiffany felt emotion gather at the back of her throat.

Jake squeezed her hand once more before standing.

'People, listen up,' he called out. Everyone turned.

'This is Tiffany, or Tiff. Please take care of her and make her feel welcome. She is a special friend of Britney's.'

Everyone nodded and smiled. Jake gave her one last smile as he left the table and walked away.

Tiff would have liked to have listened to him some more.

'He likes you,' Britney said, finishing her plate of food. Tiff looked sadly at her own which had now gone cold.

At the exact second Jake went out of sight the three women began to remove the hot plates.

'Where are they going with that?' Tiff asked. There was the second sitting still to eat.

'To get the rest of the food.'

'But there was plenty left,' Tiff observed as the last of the pork and mash was removed. They'd been at the back of the queue and the third hotplate of food had been almost full.

'Don't worry about that,' Britney said, standing. 'I want to show you around.'

Tiffany followed her out of the room as the women brought in two huge saucepans and placed them down. The lids of the pots were uncovered.

Tiff noted they were filled with rice and beans.

CHAPTER 61

'Okay, guys, quick refresh,' Kim said, once she returned from briefing Woody. He'd been perturbed that the body found was not the person they were looking for but had agreed to keep the divers for another day.

'Can't believe it wasn't Sheila down there,' Penn said, running his hand through his loose curls.

'Hey, your work got us the dive team and a body that we weren't expecting. Which by the way is male,' Kim said. She'd received a text from Keats on her way up to see Woody.

'Wonder if his name is Eric Leland,' Stacey offered.

'Why?' Kim asked, folding her arms. It wasn't a name she recognised.

Stacey explained about the Facebook group and the two names she had.

'Get right on it tomorrow,' Kim advised. 'Anything on Jake Black and Kane Devlin?'

Kim watched the constable's expression turn to dissatisfaction. She knew by now that Stacey looked that way on days she didn't feel she'd earned her keep.

'Jake Black came from a family rich in reputation but piss poor. His parents sold their possessions to get him a decent education and then high-tailed it to Australia to start a new life. Jake stayed but then the trail runs cold, and Kane Devlin doesn't appear to exist at all,' she said, opening her hands.

'You come across this often?' she asked. Normally Stacey could get background on anyone.

Stacey shrugged. 'Some folks do manage to live completely offline, especially if they really want to. Staying out of trouble and away from social media can do it.'

Kim couldn't imagine Kane being the sort to share his evening meal on Instagram.

'Of course he could be using a false name,' Stacey offered. 'It's not like he has to show his passport to the Brown family, and they're the only link we've got.'

'Keep on it, Stace. I don't like using Myles Brown as the middleman.'

Stacey nodded.

Kim turned to Penn. 'Anything on the financials?'

'Still waiting, boss. Data protection block.'

Kim understood. Sometimes they hit a wall in an investigation where just about everyone was hiding behind that law.

'Get on it tomorrow but it's time to call it a night.'

It was almost seven and they had another twelve-hour shift under their belts.

'Boss?' Stacey said, nodding over at the empty desk. 'Is Bryant okay?'

She'd seen Penn glance questioningly behind her when Bryant hadn't followed her in.

'He's fine, just caught up in something from an old case.'

Kim saw the relief on both their faces and understood. In many ways Bryant was their glue. He was solid, dependable. He wasn't moody and his demeanour put people at ease. In one way or another they all relied on Bryant.

'Okay, enough. Get out.'

Kim had just enough time to get home, collect, feed and walk Barney before…

'Boss,' Stacey said. 'I've ordered a car. It'll be waiting for Tiff at the…'

'Cancel it,' Kim said, grabbing her coat.

'But, boss… we told her…'

'Stace, it's fine. Just cancel it,' she said, heading out of the office. She intended to go and collect Tiffany herself.

CHAPTER 62

It wasn't even seven and Tiff was already exhausted.

Britney had taken her on a whirlwind tour of the whole site.

She'd been in and out of all the buildings, except the small barn right at the end which apparently was not yet finished.

She'd seen the yoga room, the meditation room, the crystal therapy room, the massage room, the reading room, the inner reflection room, the colour therapy room and the reiki room.

'Is there a TV room?' Tiff asked. After a long shift as a police officer she often returned home and unwound during a couple of hours of mindless TV.

'Spoken like a true zombie,' Britney said, digging her in the ribs. Tiff laughed, unable to believe she had only known this girl for a few hours.

'What's a zombie?' she remembered to ask. It was getting difficult to keep track of the fact she was supposed to know nothing about the place.

'People out there,' Britney said, moving her head to signal outside. 'Do you know how the telly box has killed conversation? Why would you sit and watch other people doing stuff instead of doing it yourself?'

'So, you have no televisions on the premises?'

Britney shook her head. 'No computers, no smartphones, no tablets or…'

'But how do you survive?'

Britney turned to her laughing. 'You really think you need 3G to stay alive?'

'Well, there's 5G now,' Tiff corrected. 'And I didn't mean to physically survive but just get things done.'

'How old is your phone?' Britney asked, taking a seat amongst the fairy lights in the courtyard.

Tiff followed suit. 'About a year old,' she answered.

'And what do you use it for?'

'Social media, taking photos and sharing on Insta—'

'Photos of what?'

'Anything, really.'

'Why?'

'I like to share, I suppose.'

'How old were you when you got your first phone?'

'Eleven, I think.'

It was Ryan's old Nokia after her mother had bought him a new one.

'And you didn't die prior to getting one.'

'All my friends had one before…'

'Ah, so because they had phones you wanted one too?'

'I suppose so,' Tiff answered, not minding the conversation one bit.

Britney's tone was not judgemental or combative, just amused.

'Interesting. Okay, what else do you do with it?'

'I message people, use the maps to give me directions, order stuff from Amazon, research for college projects,' she added for good measure. 'Pretty much everything.'

'But what is it?' Britney asked, tipping her head.

'What do you mean, it's a phone.'

'And yet not once have you said you use it to make calls.'

Tiff opened her mouth to argue and then closed it again. She actually couldn't remember the last time she'd used it to make a call even though it was close by twenty-four hours a day.

'But, I have another question,' Britney continued. 'I asked you almost three hours ago to turn off and leave your phone in my room. You did and how much thought have you given it?'

Jeez, had it really been three hours? Surprisingly, she hadn't thought about it once. Normally she was checking it every ten to fifteen minutes.

'I want to ask you a question, but I don't want you to think about the answer. Just say the first word that comes into your head, okay?'

Tiff nodded.

'How have you felt for the last few hours?'

'Relaxed,' she said, without thinking. And it was true. Without her phone, she had known that no one, absolutely no one, could reach her. She was alone and independent. She was not checking what her friends were up to or responding to tagged comments and posts. She was sure her notifications were building up but she didn't care. She'd check later when she was good and ready.

'You see how you've become a slave to it?'

Tiff nodded. It was true. If she was away from her phone for longer than half an hour she began to panic: why?

She had no answer.

'Just take a breath,' Britney advised. 'See and enjoy what's right in front of you.'

Tiffany let out a long breath and looked around. The twinkling of the fairy lights was hypnotic and compelling.

'It really is beautiful,' Tiff said, watching the lights dance above Britney's head.

'It's my favourite spot,' Britney agreed. A smile spread on her face as a slight girl in her twenties approached, holding a chunky green cardigan. She smiled in Tiff's direction before holding the garment towards Britney.

'Thanks, Brit. Kept me warmer in the shop today.'

Britney made no effort to take it. 'You selling veg again tomorrow, Maisie?'

The girl nodded.

'Keep it for now, okay?'

Maisie leaned down and pecked the red-haired girl on the cheek. 'Cheers, Brit. You're the best.'

Britney coloured at the compliment and rolled her eyes as Maisie headed away.

'So, how did you find this place?' Tiff asked, feeling comfortable enough to ask her the question.

'It found me,' Britney answered, fixing her gaze on the hypnotic fairy lights. 'A girl here called Lorna found me bedding down for the night in the doorway of Greggs in town. She almost fell over me as I was breaking up my two cardboard boxes.'

The words immediately saddened Tiffany, who wondered not only how the girl had reached that point but how she recalled it so matter-of-factly. She tried to picture Britney alone on a cold dark night, hungry and tired; trying to sleep amongst predators. Suddenly, the box room at her own house didn't seem all that bad.

'Lorna wasn't like the other do-gooders who'd tried to speak to me,' Britney continued. 'She didn't probe, she didn't ask me how I'd come to be in this state and she offered me a bed for the night.'

'And you just never left?' Tiff asked.

Britney smiled and shrugged. 'Why would I? Lorna found me at the lowest point in my life. I had no family, I'd stolen from all my friends. I'd made some really bad decisions. I had nothing but the clothes on my back and I didn't know where the next meal was coming from. The Farm gave me everything I needed and changed my life for ever.'

Tiffany wanted to ask so many more questions about how Britney had reached that stage in her life, but a devilish smile was playing on the girl's lips.

'Hey, how about we nip back to my room, make hot chocolate, grab a blanket and come back and look up at the stars?'

Britney's excitement at such a simple pleasure was infectious, and Tiff couldn't help but agree.

They headed back to the room where Britney pulled out a travel kettle and a couple of small mugs. She produced a couple of sachets from her bedside cabinet.

'My last two,' she said, ripping the top off with her teeth.

Tiffany felt strangely touched that she was using her last two drinks. As she busied herself pouring the water, Tiff took the opportunity to check the messages on her phone.

She reached into the side pocket of the backpack. It was empty. She would have sworn she put it there, but it was so manic when they'd arrived she could be mistaken. She checked the zip section and then the main body of the bag. Twice.

No, there was absolutely no doubt in her mind.

Her mobile phone had gone.

CHAPTER 63

Bryant pulled into the grounds of Hindlip Hall, a stately home that had housed West Mercia Police since 1967.

As he walked towards the building he couldn't help compare the biscuit-coloured frontage with regal sash windows to the drab, grey concrete of their own station in Halesowen town centre. Since being rebuilt after a fire in 1820, the property had been a family home, a girls' school and during the Second World War was taken over by the Ministry of Works, and now accommodated both the police headquarters and the Hereford and Worcester Fire & Rescue service.

He remembered the way to the correct squad room from when the two teams had worked together on a hate crimes case. It had almost resulted in the death of one of his team mates, but thanks to Penn's input had not. And yet only months later they had indeed lost one of their own.

There were still days Bryant expected to see his old colleague sitting at the desk nearest the door and, in all honesty, he missed the detective's cocky arrogance, but if someone other than Dawson had to occupy that chair, he was glad it was Penn.

He placed the temporary ID left for him at the front desk around his neck and waited to be keyed in to the main body of the building. They trusted him to wander around the building but not enough to let himself in and out.

He headed to the third floor and knocked on the closed door before entering. The door to his own squad room was rarely closed, but as he stepped inside this one he immediately understood why. He nodded a greeting towards Travis, who stood at the top of the room, beside blown-up images of the victim.

He tore his eyes away for the moment and appraised the room. Lynne was the only officer he recognised. She gave him a small wave before returning her attention to Travis.

'For those of you who don't know, this is DS Bryant from West Mids, who was involved in the rape and murder case of Wendy Harrison over twenty-five years ago.'

A few turned and acknowledged his presence but most just wanted to be debriefed before going home. He understood. The first day of any murder investigation was the most harrowing. It involved details of the injury; sometimes brutal, horrific details that had to be processed, considered, analysed. The brain had to absorb all the specifics while looking for clues. Family members had to be notified, empathised with, questioned at the most godawful time. And this team sure looked like they'd been through the wringer today.

'Okay, initial findings are that the attack is exactly the same as that of Wendy Harrison. Our victim is named Alice Lennox. She was twenty-two years of age and a night worker. She kept herself to herself but other girls have confirmed that she went off to buy a pack of smokes and never came back. Her mutilated body was found at Spinners Corner at 9 a.m. this morning.

'The similarities to the earlier attack are not random, they are exact,' Travis said, pointing to the board. 'In addition to the rape, the inside of Alice's legs were cut in exactly the same way as Wendy's.'

Bryant forced himself to look at the cuts that reached from the girl's groin all the way down to her ankle as though the seams of her skin had been undone.

Bryant could see all the crisscross marks where the bastard had tortured her with smaller cuts. He also noted the blood staining on her legs. Blood had poured from the wound on her left leg from the top to the bottom. On the right leg the blood flow had slowed as he'd reached the knee.

He knew full well that meant the poor girl had been alive through most of the incision and had likely died from bleeding to death.

He tried to fight down the rage that was building inside him. Letting Peter Drake out of prison had been a huge mistake and this girl had paid the price.

'Full post-mortem is at nine in the morning. In the meantime you all need to go home and—'

'You're not arresting him tonight?' Bryant blurted out.

Travis gave him a warning look and Bryant held his tongue as the team began to file out the door. Lynne squeezed his arm as she passed.

'Travis, what the hell?'

'Bryant, calm down,' he said, closing the door.

'But you know who it is. He's pretty much left you his confession. The crime couldn't be any more similar.'

Another night, another death was all Bryant could see if they didn't haul him in right now.

'We're watching him. If he leaves the halfway house, we'll know, but right now we have a bit of a problem.'

'Which is?'

'This time he didn't rape her with his penis. There was something he used but it wasn't himself.'

Bryant closed his eyes in anticipation of what Travis was going to say.

'So, right now we have absolutely no physical evidence to link him to the case.'

CHAPTER 64

Kim checked her watch for what must have been the hundredth time. Two minutes to ten. She'd been parked up on the road, ready, since 9.35 p.m.

'She'll be here any minute, boss,' Stacey said, beside her.

As soon as she'd told Stacey she was picking Tiff up herself, Stacey had asked to tag along.

'Try her number, Stace,' Kim said. If she was to be here by ten, she had to be away from the building by now. It was a few minutes' walk down that dirt track.

'Switched off, boss,' Stacey said, trying to keep her tone light.

One minute to ten.

'I'll bloody kill her for that,' Kim said, checking her rear-view mirror.

'Probably just forgot to turn it back on, boss. She wouldn't want anyone calling her and giving the game away.'

'That's why we have a silent button, Stace,' Kim said. There was really no excuse at all for removing herself from the only communication channel they had.

She checked her watch again.

Exactly ten o'clock.

'Where is she, Stace?' Kim asked, tapping the steering wheel.

'I'll try her again, boss,' Stacey said, ringing her number again.

Kim waited.

'Nothing,' Stacey said.

Kim started the car. She'd drive up towards the dirt track, shine the headlights and see if Tiff was on her way down.

'Jeez, boss,' Stacey said as she did a three-point turn in the middle of the road.

What she hoped to see was a single figure walking along the grass verge towards her.

She drove slowly towards the dirt track and turned in.

The headlights illuminated the rough road right up until it disappeared around the wooded area. Tiff was not on her way down.

'Damn it,' she said. 'Where the hell is she?'

'What we gonna do, boss?' Stacey asked, unable to keep the alarm out of her voice, which did nothing to assure Kim she was overreacting to the whole situation.

No call and no show. There had to be something wrong. What the hell had she been thinking letting the girl go in there?

'Okay, Stace, if you want to get out you can but I'm gonna drive this car right up to that bloody shed and ram my...'

She stopped speaking as her phone rang.

The display said it was an unknown number.

She answered and put it on loudspeaker.

'Hey, Mom, it's Tiff,' said the cheery voice on the other end. The relief flooded through her.

But mom?

'Tiffany, where the bloody...'

'Sorry not to have called sooner, Mom, but I lost my phone. Listen, I'm sorry about the things I said earlier. I didn't mean them but I just didn't want to come straight home until we'd both calmed down.'

'Tiff, are you okay?' Kim asked.

'I'm fine, Mom. I'm with a friend... no, you don't know her. Her name is Britney Murray, we're at a retreat and, before you ask, I've eaten. We were lucky enough to get first sitting and, hang on… ooh, can't talk for long but I just wanted to let you know I'm with lots of nice people who are taking great care of me.'

'Tiff, are you sure you're okay?' Kim pressed, her foot still hovering over the accelerator pedal.

Tiff laughed. 'I promise I'm fine. You don't need to worry about me. We'll have a proper chat about things tomorrow.'

'Tomorrow?' Kim asked, looking at Stacey.

'Yes, Mom. These lovely people have invited me to spend the night.'

CHAPTER 65

Tiffany had been on Kim's mind all night and was still heavily present as she prepared to start the morning briefing.

She hadn't driven away from the site until Stacey had agreed that Tiff sounded completely okay and not as though she was being coerced into anything.

A part of her had wanted to smash through that shed and bring Tiffany out even after they'd spoken, but after replaying the conversation over and over in her mind she had to trust that the constable knew what she was doing.

Replaying the conversation had helped convince her that Tiff was not sending any cry for help. She was fine and she had sounded it. The only worrying part of the conversation had been about the phone. How had she lost their only source of communication? It had concerned Woody too and she had come up with an idea to put into action later that day.

'Okay, so Stacey has apprised you on the situation with Tiffany. Anyone got any thoughts?'

'Other than we should have pulled her out anyway,' Bryant said.

'Understood but as you said yourself yesterday, we also have to trust that she's a twenty-four-year-old woman playing the part of a teenager and that she knows what she's doing.'

Bryant's natural fatherly instincts were on overdrive given that he had a daughter of a similar age.

'She knew her time on the phone with you was limited so everything she said had to mean something,' Penn observed.

'She gave us Britney's full name and was sure to enforce that she was fine and being taken care of,' Kim said.

'And I've been thinking about the mention of food,' Stacey said. 'It was a random thing to say that they'd made it for the first sitting.'

'Perhaps the first is different to the second,' Penn offered.

Bryant looked thoughtful.

'You know, when I was a kid…'

'All your food was raw cos they hadn't invented fire yet?' Stacey joked.

Bryant smiled. 'Hey, Stace, you had some real food for breakfast cos your mood…'

'Continue, Bryant,' Kim advised, as the detective constable bobbed out her tongue.

'Well, my dad used to work long hours at the foundry. Mum cooked for him every night and we weren't allowed to touch the food until he'd filled his plate.'

'So, you're saying…'

'There may be a hierarchy of food. Best workers get fed first.'

'Not really earth-shattering, is it?' Kim asked.

'Tyler was found with a stomach full of rice and beans,' Penn offered.

Kim was still unimpressed.

'It's subtle, boss,' Penn continued. 'But control of the food supply is a very powerful tool. It's a basic need that…'

'Okay, okay, enough on that for now. We need to get moving. Stace, any address for Eric Leland?'

Kim was interested to know why he was persona non grata in the Facebook group.

'Yep, already sent to Bryant's phone. The guy is twenty-seven years old and has form with us for drugs and violence. Last arrest was four years ago. Heard nothing since.'

'Okay, that's our starting point for the day. Stace, I want to know more about Kane Devlin and Britney Murray. Do not deviate from that task.'

'Got it, boss.'

'Penn, I know how much you love a good post-mortem, so Keats is starting on our third body. Just after nine. After that I want you back on the money. Over a hundred and fifty grand is a lot to just disappear. I want to know where it went.'

'Okey dokey, boss,'

Kim headed into the Bowl to retrieve her jacket and paused.

Regardless of her own bravado and justification about Tiffany still being at Unity Farm, Kim still wished she'd gone in and got her back.

CHAPTER 66

Tiffany woke to a gentle shake of the arm.

'Come on, sleepy head, or we'll miss breakfast.'

Britney's smile was wide and infectious.

Miraculously, when they'd returned to Brit's room the night before, it had been rearranged to accommodate another bed.

Lying on the bed had been a brand new set of fleecy pyjamas, a dressing gown, slippers and a sealed pack of new underwear beneath which had been a small toiletry bag.

She remembered falling into bed and off to sleep immediately. She had no idea what time it had been but she hadn't woken once.

'And if you were wondering, you snore,' Brit said, as Tiff got out of bed.

'I do not.'

'Do so, not big snores but delicate little lady noises,' Brit said and began to impersonate her.

Tiff burst out laughing.

'Well, you've missed shower time so just throw your clothes on and let's head up for brekkie.'

Tiff went to reach for her phone and remembered it was missing. Britney had helped her go through all her things and had then gone to let Jake and someone called Lorna know that a phone had been lost. Britney was convinced it had fallen out of her bag and that someone would find it and hand it in.

Tiff knew there was nothing she could do about it right now. She was in no danger and was surprised to find that she was ravenous. If they were serving leftover chop and mash from the night before she wouldn't mind a bit.

She dressed hurriedly as Britney turned away and started preparing her backpack.

'Oh, Brit, can we check to see if my phone—'

'Yep, we'll check with Jake en route,' Britney said, heading for the door. 'Come on, we've got a busy day ahead.'

Tiff pulled on her second trainer and ran after her.

Britney checked the typed list on the wall and smiled. 'First sitting.'

Thank goodness for that, Tiffany thought. She was sure her insides were beginning to chew on themselves.

A quick appraisal confirmed that Jake was once again at the top table, which was full. Britney pretended not to notice but a brief look of disappointment was chased away with a clap of the hands as she surveyed the breakfast offering. Tiff had noted from the waves and smiles of the diners that most folks were the same as the previous night, but not all.

Another difference to the previous night was an extra table at the end of the line holding rows of sandwich boxes stacked high.

'What're those?' Tiff whispered, as the room was dining in silence.

'Packed lunches for the workers,' Brit whispered back as she took her plate laden with sausage, bacon, eggs, beans, hash browns and toast. Tiff indicated to the dark-haired woman that she'd have the same. She could feel the saliva gathering in her mouth as it was plated up.

She followed Britney to the last two seats at the bottom table. Quite honestly, she didn't care where she sat, she just wanted to eat.

Again, she was content with the silence. It gave her a chance to focus and savour the deliciousness of the food.

She realised that she hadn't once looked up from her plate when she felt a tap on her shoulder.

She looked up into the cool blue eyes of Jake Black, who was smiling down at her.

Oh no, not again.

'Tiffany, I understand you'll be returning home today but I've been thinking a lot about our conversation last night and I'd really like to talk to you some more. I think I can help, so if you do return with Britney, I'd love to continue our chat.'

Tiffany nodded as he smiled and walked away.

The panpipe music began to filter into the room and the chatter started up.

She wondered exactly what it was that Jake wanted to say to her.

She'd think about it later.

Right now, she just wanted to eat.

CHAPTER 67

'Not bad,' Kim said, as Bryant parked in front of a detached house on the outskirts of Kingswinford.

If this was Eric Leland's home, they were not looking at his criminal activities as a result of an underprivileged childhood.

A silver Lexus sat on the gravelled, low-maintenance drive.

Kim knocked the door, which was answered immediately.

The woman was in her late forties with a blunt fringe bob. Her face was fully made-up and she was dressed in a powder pink skirt suit. The heels were not something Kim would have attempted to walk in, in a million years.

'Mrs Leland?' Kim asked.

'Yes,' she said, reaching for an oversize handbag.

'Is Eric home?'

'No, I'm afraid he's not. Who wants him?'

They both held up their ID at the same time.

'May we come in?' Kim asked.

'Of course, but Eric isn't here right now.'

'When might he be back?'

'Officer, my son is twenty-seven years old. He really doesn't give me details of his plans.'

'Well, may we speak to you for a moment? Maybe he'll turn up while we chat.'

'No, he… umm… let me just make a call. I'm due in early for a meeting.'

'Thank you,' Kim said, entering the room she pointed to while she headed away, her phone in her hand.

Kim instantly felt out of place in the room, which was furnished in varying shades of white. Everything was focussed or pointed towards a piano that stood before the window.

Framed photographs of a handsome man, Mrs Leland and a young boy at varying ages stared back at her.

'Okay, meeting delayed,' Mrs Leland said, entering the room. 'We all like to think we're indispensable, don't we?'

Kim said nothing and the woman followed her gaze.

'Henry, my late husband, was a pianist.'

'Sorry for your loss, Mrs Leland,' Bryant offered.

'Martha, please, and it's almost six months now but thank you anyway.'

'May I ask how he…'

'Massive stroke. Died instantly. He didn't suffer, thank goodness; now how may I help you?' she asked, tucking her skirt behind her legs as she sat.

'Ideally, we'd like to speak to Eric.'

'Unfortunately, that's not possible so you'll have to make do with me.'

The words were not unpleasant but they were final.

'Mrs Leland, have you ever heard of a place called Unity Farm?'

Her face paled and her eyes hardened.

'Yes, I've heard of it. The damn place pretty much ruined my life.'

'Please, tell us about it,' Kim urged.

'Happy to. They got hold of my son and wouldn't let him go. Don't get me wrong. I was glad of his new friends at first. I was getting a lot less calls from you people but that didn't last long.'

'Go on.'

'Okay, I need to explain that Eric was not an easy child. We tried every form of parenting and nothing worked. He was extremely demanding and not happy unless he was the centre of attention all the time.

'He got expelled from three different schools and none of his friends ever visited twice. He was a bully who enjoyed negative attention more than positive. We tried everything: boundaries, no boundaries, tolerance and loving, firm. We tried two different counsellors and one of them refused to see him again after he touched her inappropriately. As parents, we totally failed and hoped he'd grow up. The behaviour followed him into his twenties and actually got worse. And then he met a man named Jake.'

She paused for breath and shook her head.

'This man became like God to him and after seeing the initial change in our son he became a God to us too for a while. It was as though we had the son we'd always hoped Eric would be. The violence stopped, the attitude went away and when we saw him he no longer called us names.'

Kim wondered just what it had been like to live with Eric.

'After about eighteen months, Eric started to ask for money. Small amounts at first. We knew he wasn't using it for drugs, so initially, we indulged him. I suppose it was relief or guilt that we hadn't been able to effect this change ourselves. Anyway, the requests got bigger and more often until his father said enough was enough. He would give no more money until he could see where it was going. When we sat down and did our sums, we saw that he'd spirited away almost twenty thousand pounds.'

'How did he react to your refusal?' Kim asked.

'Badly. We woke one night to find him trying to take our possessions from the house. Henry tried to stop him, but the van outside was already half full.'

Martha took a breath.

'Eric beat up his father, called him a zombie – that's their favourite name for non-cult members – and told him that the Farm needed the stuff more than we did. My husband never fully recovered physically or emotionally from the attack. That one action from Eric that night changed Henry's life completely.'

'What did he do?'

'Eric stamped on his hands, repeatedly. Broke seventeen bones and he was never able to play the piano professionally again.'

Kim tried to hide her horror but failed. There was a cruelty in that one action that said so much about their son.

'Exactly. That's when we knew Eric had been brainwashed. Old Eric, however bad he'd been, would never have done something so cruel.'

Kim couldn't have stopped listening even if she'd wanted to.

'We thought getting him back from Unity Farm would be the hard part. We were offered an opportunity and took it but our problems only increased. We thought if we could just get him away from Jake we'd be able to talk some sense into him. It just made him worse. He resisted every attempt we made to make him understand that he'd been lured into a cult. His loyalty to the Farm and the people there grew even stronger being forced away from them. He began to threaten our lives, saying that once he got back home to his family he would make a plan to come back in the night and kill us both. It was as though we were dealing with a stranger; a violent hate-filled unpredictable stranger, who was capable of murdering us while we slept. We really did fear for our lives.'

'So, what did you do?' Kim asked.

'The only thing we could do.'

'Which was?' Kim repeated, unable to join the dots.

'To save our son and to save ourselves we only had one option.' She paused and breathed deep. 'We had our son committed.'

CHAPTER 68

The boss had instructed her to get background on Kane Devlin and Britney Murray. After a quick search, Stacey had decided to start with the easiest first.

Sad as it was, Britney Murray's story was not unique. Born to a teenage mother in the late nineties, she'd been placed on the 'at risk' register when her unnamed father had walked out when she was five years old. Child Services had been alerted to her mother's neglect by neighbours who had feared the child was being left alone for long periods of time. Despite their best efforts to keep the family together, the girl had been taken into care when she was seven years old. Foster homes had followed until she dropped out of school and the care system when she was sixteen years old. She had no criminal record, and Stacey couldn't help but wonder at the girl's life in the intervening years before she'd found safety at Unity Farm.

A part of Stacey hoped that the place was not as dubious as it was beginning to appear and that Britney had found somewhere she could be happy amongst the family she'd never had.

Judging by the quick update she'd just received from the boss, Eric Leland had been happy there too. And yet the closed group on Facebook had not wanted Eric Leland to join. He was still loyal to Jake, so did that mean the people in that group were not?

The boss had told her earlier not to deviate from her tasks and she wasn't going to. Well, not for long, anyway.

She searched for the group again. No result. She tried again. Nothing. Damn, either the group had changed its setting to 'secret' or had been closed down completely.

She logged into the fake profile she'd made the day before and accessed her messages. The terse response from Penny Hicks was still there telling her, or Eric Leland, to fuck off.

Stacey stared at the screen and tapped her chin.

She'd tried every devious method she could think of to infiltrate this group to learn more about Unity Farm, except for one. Honesty.

She clicked on the bar at the bottom of Penny's response and typed.

May I be honest about who I am?

Stacey watched as the blue circle with a tick appeared. Message delivered.

The photo of a plain blue sky dropped down. Message read. Three dots. Typing.

Stacey readied herself to be told again to go away.

Yes

came the response.

I'm a police officer investigating the murder of two people linked to Unity Farm.

Three dots.

Names?

Stacey hesitated.

Samantha Brown and Tyler Short

Tyler's dead?

You know him?

Stacey asked, quickly.

Yes

Were you at Unity Farm at the same time?

Yes

Did Tyler follow Sammy into the cult?

Yes

Because he was in love with her?

Yes

Did he leave because she was gone?

Not straight away

Why not?

Because he'd made other friends.

Was he seeing someone else?

Not allowed

Who was…

I'm going now

Penny typed before Stacey had chance to finish her question. She backspaced and asked a different one.

Did you leave Unity Farm?

Yes

How long were you there?

12 years

What are you scared of?

Jake

Why?

He hates people who leave. Always has.

What does he do if he finds them?

Stacey asked, feeling the anxiety rise in her stomach.
Message delivered.
Message read.
No response.
Stacey wondered if her system was frozen. The responses up to now had been brief but immediate. She pressed refresh and returned to her message folder.

The message was still there but the profile had turned grey and was called 'Facebook User'.

She returned to the search bar and typed in the name but it was too late.

The profile of Penny Hicks was gone.

CHAPTER 69

'So, who were the other guys on the bus?' Tiff asked, as they were dropped at a housing estate just outside Netherton.

'Sam, Frankie and Enya work full-time at the Tesco Superstore and the others ask for donations.'

'You mean begging on the streets?' Tiff asked, surprised. Unity Farm seemed above that somehow.

'Jake doesn't like to call it that. Every member of the family has to contribute something. Some are illiterate and can't manage even the most basic work. Jerry even borrows a dog from an old mate sometimes. Beggars with dogs make more. Double whammy of social conscience and dog lovers,' Britney explained, heading deeper into the estate.

'Where are we going?'

'You'll see,' she said, turning a corner. 'You're going to meet one of my favourites, Hilda, she's a character.'

Britney pushed open the gate to an unremarkable semi-detached house with a box porch.

She stepped inside and retrieved the key from beneath a pot holding a dusty artificial plant.

She unlocked the door and pushed it open.

Hilda looked startled for a second until she saw who it was. She smiled widely at the red-haired girl and then transferred that smile across to Tiffany when she realised she was not alone.

'This is Tiff, she's my new friend. You're going to love her.'

The woman's face creased even more as she clutched Britney's hand. 'If she's anything like you, I will.'

Britney blushed. 'Has Liz been gone long?'

'Not long. She'll be back later.'

'Liz is her home help,' Britney said, taking the pillow from behind Hilda's back. 'Comes in twice a day to get her up, put her back to bed and prepare easily cooked meals for later. It's not enough,' Brit said, punching the pillow and sliding it back behind her.

Brit positioned herself back in front of the old woman.

'What shall I fetch today, Hilda?'

The woman reached for her purse, which was lodged between her thigh and the chair.

A short list was on the table on the other side.

Britney read it. '"Boiled ham, a tomato and a tub of Lurpak".'

Hilda nodded and handed Britney her purse.

Britney opened it and took out a five-pound note. 'This is all we need today, Hilda.'

Hilda nodded and put the purse back by her thigh.

Britney put the list in her back pocket.

'You wanna keep Hilda company and make us all a cup of tea?' Britney asked.

'Of course,' Tiff said, as Brit headed out.

She stood in front of the elderly lady. 'How do you like your tea, Hilda?'

'Strong with two sugars,' she answered with a smile. 'Cups not mugs.'

Tiff headed to the kitchen and filled the kettle. She retrieved three cups and opened the unmarked canisters. The first was wedged full of triangle tea bags. She placed one in each cup. The second held neither coffee nor sugar but a rolled-up stash of notes. Tiffany smiled as she replaced the lid. Her own grandmother had kept an envelope of money behind the bread bin. Some people didn't trust banks and building societies. The third canister contained the sugar.

She headed back into the lounge, pleased that she'd accompanied Britney. It warmed her heart seeing the help she gave this lady. She forced herself to remember what she was here to do.

'How often does Britney come to see you, Hilda?' Tiffany asked, taking a seat.

'Couple of times a week. She is an angel. Fetches me anything I want. Liz doesn't have the time.'

'No children?' Tiff queried. If there were they should be shot leaving this woman's care to total strangers.

She shook her head. 'Wasn't meant to be but Ernest was enough for me,' she said with a little sniff of emotion. 'I look forward to her visits, always smiling. She's a good girl.'

Yes, Tiff was beginning to see that.

'She brings her new friends now and again but mainly she's on her own.'

'How did you meet?' Tiff asked, sitting down.

'She just turned up one day saying she was doing some volunteer work in the area and asked if there was anything I needed from the shops.'

'And when was that?'

'Well Ernest had only been gone a couple of weeks so it was about four months ago.'

She leaned forward and winked. 'I think one time she brought her young man with her. I didn't say anything but I could tell the way she looked at him.'

Tiffany chuckled at the glint in the woman's eye. The woman must have been mistaken. They weren't allowed to form romantic attachments the boss had said.

She left Hilda for a few minutes to finish making the tea.

When she returned with the drinks on a tray, Britney was just coming back in the door.

'Ah, lovely,' she said, spying the steaming hot mugs.

Britney held her hand out for Hilda's purse and dropped the change back in.

'I'll just go and pop these in the fridge and you'll be able to make your nice little supper sandwich later.'

Hilda smiled as though Britney knew all her secrets.

'Yes, that fridge is making a strange buzzing noise. I think it's on its last legs,' she said. 'A bit like me.'

'Nonsense, Hilda,' Britney said, coming back into the room. 'You're just getting started.'

Britney sat and took a sip of tea. 'I've told you. You need to sell this place and come and live with me. I'd look after you.'

Hilda smiled fondly. 'I know you would, love.'

'Speaking of which, do your feet need doing? I'm happy to cut your nails and rub in some cream.'

'They're grand, love. Maybe next time.'

Britney finished her tea and Tiff followed suit.

'Okay, Hilda, best be off.'

Tiff collected both their cups and took them through to the kitchen. She rinsed them out, dried them and put them away.

She turned and hesitated before leaving.

For some reason, she reached over and picked up the middle canister.

She was surprised to find it empty.

CHAPTER 70

By the time Bryant approached Russells Hall Hospital Kim still wasn't sure how she felt about Mrs Leland's admission.

Further questioning had revealed that seven months ago Eric had been removed forcibly from the cult using the services of none other than Kane Devlin. And of those seven months Eric had been in Bushey Fields for six and a half of them. She had explained how Kane had advised her that Eric was so indoctrinated he feared for her life and that she had to make the choice to allow Eric to return to the Farm or ensure he could not hurt her or anyone else until he'd received professional treatment.

On one hand, Kim could understand that the ever present fear of your own son coming one night to kill you could only be terrifying. But was it believable? And even if it was, was sectioning your own son really the only option?

Bushey Fields was the Dudley Psychiatric Unit, built to accommodate the closing of mental health services at nearby Burton Road. It was attached to the hospital and consisted of five sections: three acute wards; male, female, and an admission ward. Two further wards were exclusively for older people.

'There,' Kim said, pointing to the building that held the Clent ward.

Each ward was housed in a separate single-storey building that looked like an oversized bungalow, and Eric Leland had been placed in the 'Acute Male' category.

Kim stepped into the foyer and tapped on a plate glass window. The man behind the glass slid it aside.

'May I help you?'

'Eric Leland, can we speak to him, please?'

'And you are?'

She looked to Bryant, who held up his identification.

'Wait a minute,' he said, closing the window.

He turned his back and spoke to three colleagues, who all glanced their way before giving him a response.

Still with his back to them, he placed a call to someone.

She turned to her colleague. 'You didn't have your thumb over the bit that says police, did you?'

'*He's* their priority not us,' Bryant said, easily.

'But we are investigating a murder,' she snapped. Surely that took priority over everything.

'Yeah and I'm sure they already know that Eric didn't do it.'

'You know, Bryant, sometimes you are so…'

'Right,' he said, moving towards the inner door. 'Sometimes I'm right.'

'What are you doing?' she asked, deciding to let that one pass.

'Filling out the visitor's book. I'd imagine they're gonna insist whether we're police or not.'

She followed suit and signed her name as the inner doors opened.

A woman with a shot of blonde hair wearing minimal make-up held out her hand.

'Susan Robinson, Administrator. How may I help?'

Even though Kim was sure the reason for their visit had been relayed to her, she repeated the request.

'May I ask why? I'm sorry but Eric doesn't get many visitors, so I have to ask.'

'We believe he can help us in our current investigation.'

She frowned and made no movement to let them through. 'He's been here for quite some time so I'm unsure how he can be involved in…'

'I didn't say involved, Ms Robinson. I said he may be able to help, and as we're police officers investigating murder, we're not in the habit of spending too much time talking to people who we don't think can help.'

'Does this have anything at all to do with his mother?' she asked, cautiously.

Kim shook her head.

'Because the last time she came to see him he damaged three tables, two chairs and had to be heavily medicated and restrained for twenty-seven hours.'

'And other than that?' Kim asked, as the woman swiped them into the ward.

'Follow me,' she instructed, heading through a spacious common area. 'And to answer your question, Eric is no trouble at all. In fact, we rarely see him. Eric doesn't like television, which is a popular pastime for most of our residents. He hasn't watched a programme since he got here. He leaves his room for meals and returns immediately afterwards. He spends hours in deep meditation and listens to gentle music on his iPod.

'Phone?'

She shook her head. 'Just iPod.'

'Is he heavily medicated?'

'Not heavily. We have him on mild antidepressants and any anxious spells are usually soothed by a gentle walk in the garden. He responds well to the peace and quiet out there.'

Kim stopped walking as Susan led them into the dining room.

'Does he really need to be here?'

There was no hesitation before she nodded yes. 'Until his therapy works, I'm afraid he does. Okay, wait here. I'm going to ask Eric if he wants to meet with you, but if he says no we'll respect his wishes.'

She waited a second to make sure they understood.

Once she'd left the room, Bryant turned towards her.

'You know, guv...'

'Yeah, okay, Bryant. You were right and gloating does not look good on you.'

'Jolly good but I was going to say that it sounds to me like Eric Leland is taking a place here that would be much better used by someone else.'

Exactly what she'd been thinking.

'Reckon he'll give us the time...'

Bryant stopped speaking as Eric Leland entered the room.

He wore jeans and a tee shirt with a pocket on the left-hand side. Earphones had been tucked in with a lead hanging and draping around to his back pocket.

'She didn't send you, did she?' he asked, before sitting down.

Kim didn't have to wonder for long who 'she' was.

She shook her head. 'We're here to talk about Unity Farm.'

He sat and glanced at Susan to tell her he was happy to stay.

'I'll be just outside,' she said.

Kim wondered why the woman felt she needed to stay in the area.

'Have you been?' Eric asked, crossing his legs. 'Have you seen Jake?'

Kim nodded. 'Seems very nice but we're here to talk about you. About your time at Unity Farm. Is that okay?'

'Sure,' he said, seemingly relaxed.

Right now, Kim was struggling to identify the man before her with the picture his mother had painted. He seemed calm, relaxed and co-operative. His sharp features were open and his long hair tucked behind his ears.

'Eric, did you know a girl named Samantha Brown?'

He shrugged. 'It's hard to know everyone.'

'Tyler Short?'

Again, he shrugged. 'Couldn't say.'

'How about She—'

'Yeah, I'm not gonna remember anyone. We don't talk about family members to zom— people not at the Farm.'

'But you're no longer there.'

He smiled. 'But I will be. As soon as I get the chance. I'll be right back where I belong.'

Kim was flummoxed. According to his mother Eric had been at the Farm for almost three years, but he'd been away from Jake and his influence for months. What the hell was it about the place?

'Did the Farm help you in some way, Eric?' she asked.

'Err… yeah. It's my home. Jake and the others helped me understand that I wasn't a freak, that I wasn't wrong.'

'About what?'

'My parents. See, I never liked them. Even as a kid I didn't want to be around them. The guilt I felt for my feelings ate away at me and made me hate them even more. Jake explained that I was normal.' He smiled. 'Jake called it Transfamily. He explained that I'd just been born into the wrong family. It wasn't my fault. I had no control. It was like a weight had been lifted. He told me it was time to break the chains, be my own person and start to take care of myself. He taught me how to meditate. We talked every night.'

'Eric, did people at the Farm ever want to leave? Go back to their old life?'

He laughed. 'Never, why would they?'

'But what if?…'

'They didn't. It's a family. You don't leave your family.'

'Did Jake ask you to steal from your parents?'

He wasn't offended by the question and shook his head.

'No, but look at it this way: if a couple divorces all the posses-sions are shared. Each party gets something of their own. They decide to leave the family and they walk away with items accrued during the marriage. What does a kid get if they decide to leave the family? Nothing. How is that fair? They've been a part of it too. They deserve something.'

Kim wondered who had planted that seed into his mind and left it to grow.

She wasn't going to argue that with divorce each parent had likely contributed financially throughout the marriage. Eric's argument had nothing to do with money.

'So, what's this Facebook group you've tried to join?'

He rolled his eyes. 'Haters, all of them. Just didn't get what the place was about.'

'So, you tried to join to abuse them?'

'Put 'em right. It's my home they're slating.'

'So, you didn't appreciate your mother instructing Kane Devlin to bring you home?' she asked.

'The Farm is my home and the man is an idiot.'

There was no anger, aggression or hostility in his tone as he spoke of the man, more an observational amusement.

'He didn't manage to change your opinion of the Farm or Jake?'

Eric laughed out loud. 'The twat needs to update his processes. I knew everything he was going to say and do. We talk about shit like that at home. He was never gonna get to me.'

Throughout their exchange Kim had wondered on what grounds this man was being kept here. Other than being biased in his devotion to the Farm he seemed perfectly balanced, rational and certainly able to lead a normal life. He seemed to be making no effort to regain control of his former life. A part of her wondered if there was something in him that needed the feeling of being institutionalised: the order, the routine.

'So, when you get out of here you'll go straight back to Jake and Unity Farm?'

He shook his head

'Nah, I'll head back to my other home first.'

Kim was surprised.

'To your mother?'

His face hardened and Kim saw a glimpse of the person Mrs Leland had described.

'Oh yeah, I'll be going to slit the old bitch's throat.'

CHAPTER 71

Both of them reached for their phones as they headed back to the car.

Bryant had felt his own vibrate three times during their meeting with Eric. A meeting that had confused the life out of him.

He was surprised to see that it was Travis who had been trying to reach him.

He indicated to the guv that he was going to make a call. She nodded, already speaking to someone.

He tried to call Travis back and got no answer. He tried again straight away. Travis had wanted to tell him something. Still nothing. He put the phone away. He'd try later.

'Hope you had better luck than me,' he said, as the guv finished her call.

'Remains to be seen,' she said, getting into the car. 'Asked Myles to arrange another meeting. Kane Devlin has too many tentacles in this case. You?'

'Travis but got no—'

The ringing of his phone cut off his words

'Aah, speak of the devil and he will appear,' he said, hitting the answer button.

'About bloody time, Bryant,' Travis said, affably.

Bryant could hear commotion in the background.

'What the hell's going on there?'

'We're celebrating and I wanted to give you the good news.'

'Go on,' Bryant said, feeling a knot of tension in his stomach.

'We got him. Forensics picked up every fag end in a twenty-metre radius and guess what?'

'Jesus,' he exclaimed as a rush of different emotions surged through him. Relief, disgust, more relief.

'Feel free to come by later. We're just on our way to pick him up so it looks like you were right all along.'

Bryant ended the call and after remembering the girl who had just lost her life, he really got no joy from being right at all.

CHAPTER 72

Kim spotted Britney before she saw Tiff. Both were giving out leaflets on the college car park.

As they approached Kim was careful not to glance in the direction of the police officer. She kept her focus only on the redhead.

'Hey, Britney, how are you doing?'

The girl looked surprised to see her but she wasn't the reason they were there.

'Just wanted to ask you another couple of… oh, excuse me,' Kim said, as Tiffany approached, looking concerned.

'This is my friend, Tiff,' Britney said, with a wide smile. 'She's my new friend, so there's no point asking her anything. She doesn't know anyone.'

Kim dismissed Tiff's presence with a glance that she made sure Britney saw.

'Just wondering if you'd remembered Sammy Brown yet or Tyler Short. Oh, and we have another name to run by you: Eric Leland?'

'Is he dead?' Britney asked before she could stop herself.

'Oh, so you do remember Eric?' Kim asked, stepping closer.

To her credit Tiff was adopting a decent bewildered expression as she looked from one to the other.

'The name rings a bell,' Britney said, backtracking.

Kim tipped her head. 'You see, Britney, what I don't understand is how you cannot know the names of your family members. I mean, clearly you're not as close as you think you are.'

'Oh yes we are,' Britney said as the colour flooded her cheeks. 'We all put family first. We take care of each other. We are loyal to…'

'But what if someone chooses to leave?' Kim asked. 'Are you still loyal then?'

'Well, of course not but no one really wants to leave.'

Yeah Kim was hearing that a lot.

'So you say. Okay, Britney, nice talking to you again. We'll be in touch.'

Kim didn't even glance in Tiff's direction as she turned to leave.

She just hoped Bryant had managed to get the girl's attention while she had been baiting Britney.

CHAPTER 73

Tiff had mixed feelings as the boss and Bryant walked away.

Part of her wanted to walk away with them but her friend was visibly shaken by the exchange.

For a few minutes, at least, she had to play along.

'Hey, Brit, don't let her get to you. You know what it's like at the Farm, so why would her opinion matter? Looks like a proper hard-faced cow anyway.'

Brit smiled.

'You get it, though, don't you, Tiff? You see how great it is? How we're lucky to have such a wonderful family? Outsiders just don't understand how bonded we are. Hurt one of us and you hurt us all.' She sighed. 'See that's what's missing out here. There's no love left, no cohesion. It's all take, take, take, all the time.'

Tiff couldn't help thinking about the money that had gone from the tin, but she pushed the thought away.

'I get it, Brit. It's a special place to be,' Tiff said, patting her on the arm.

Brit's smile widened as she took Tiff's hand and held it tightly. 'I knew you'd get it, Tiff. From the minute I saw you yesterday I knew you were special.'

Jeez, had it only been the day before that they'd met for the first time? She really felt that she'd known Brit for years.

'Of course, I get it,' Tiff placated, removing her hand. 'Now I need to pop inside to the loo, so I'll get us a drink from the vending machine while I'm there.'

'Want me to?…'

'No, Brit. You carry on spreading the word.'

This time she really needed to go alone.

CHAPTER 74

'Jeez, Tink, you took your time.'

'She was almost in tears, boss,' Tiff said, as they sidled to the far end of the loos.

Kim took out the smallest phone she'd been able to find and placed it in Tiffany's hand.

'Don't care where you keep it but have it on you at all times. If we lose communication again we'll just pull you out. Got it?'

'Got it, boss,' she said, slipping the phone down the front of her jeans.

'Just text, okay?'

She nodded. 'Listen, I've not got much time but the place is amazing. Everyone there seems happy, but food is controlled and seems to be both a punishment and a reward. Jake Black is held in godlike regard by everyone. He wants to talk to me when we get back.'

'About what?'

'Family and stuff,' she said, dismissively. 'But they send people out to do all kinds of things and the folks who have few skills go out and beg. They're dropped off and collected by minibus.'

'Do you have any names?'

Tiff shook her head. 'I've not been out of Britney's sight yet, and they get suspicious if you ask too many questions.'

'Have you met Sophie yet?'

Tiff shook her head. 'That's why I want to stay again tonight. I'm hoping to give Britney the slip and speak to some other people later.'

'Okay, but stay…'

'Hang on, that's not all. I think they target old folks with no family. We visited a lady this morning. Brit was dead helpful, did her shopping and offered to massage her feet. She was lovely, but I think she took some money too. There's great value on what you can bring to the Farm.'

Bryant made a note as Tiff recited the address and the woman's name.

'Look I've got to get back. I'll text more as I find it.'

'Tiff, are you okay?' Kim asked. 'They're not getting to you, are they?'

Part of her wanted to keep Tiff talking for as long as she could.

Tiff laughed. 'Of course not. I know what I'm there to do and I'm absolutely fine. I promise.'

She gave a small wave as she headed out the door.

Despite the words of reassurance Kim found herself unconvinced.

CHAPTER 75

Britney stood just outside the entrance doors to the college for two reasons: the first being that she'd been banned from going inside; the second was because there was a sensation in her tummy that wasn't feeling so good.

The visits from the police officer unnerved her. The woman kept asking about people who were once part of the family. She didn't seem to understand that once they were gone they were dead to the family and never spoken of again. To leave was the worst betrayal to Jake and everything he did for them.

But there was something else, a tension that had fallen around them once Tiffany approached. She suspected what they were trying to do. They wanted to take Tiffany away from them.

She watched as Tiff appeared and headed to the vending machine. Ten seconds later the police officer exited the toilets and left through the other door.

They'd been talking in there. Britney knew it.

She had no choice but to tell Jake.

And he was not going to like it one little bit.

CHAPTER 76

'Feel better now you've seen her?' Bryant asked, as they got in the car.

Kim had known that Britney wasn't going to reveal anything about Eric Leland or his time at the Farm. She'd used it only as a way to get the phone to Tiff.

And actually, yes, she did feel better knowing the girl now had a phone and could be contacted. More importantly, Tiffany could call her if she needed to.

She took out her phone and called Stacey.

'You got anything on Kane Devlin yet?'

For their second meeting, she wanted to be better prepared.

'Boss, there is absolutely nothing. No social media profiles, no mentions, no news reports. Absolutely bugger all.'

'Stace, this is not smelling so good. How is he completely off your radar?'

'I don't get it, boss, even searching for Bryant brings up a few results.'

'Thanks, Stace,' her colleague called out having heard her.

'I'm really starting to think we're not being given the right name.'

'Okay, Stace, leave it with me,' she said, ending the call.

Immediately, the phone rang again.

'Myles, I was just going to call you.'

'Kane has agreed to meet again. Same place at four o'clock. Same conditions.'

'Yeah, yeah, we'll see but I want to know something else. How did you make contact with Kane in the first place?'

'I'm sorry, I thought I told you. It was Kane that contacted me.'

CHAPTER 77

'You okay, Brit?' Tiff asked for the third time. She'd been quiet since the boss had left. Had it unnerved her being asked about Eric Leland?

'I'm fine,' Brit said, not looking at her. 'Just feel a bit sick. Must be something I ate.'

Tiff doubted it. They'd both eaten the same thing from the prepared sandwich box; a ham sandwich, a packet of crisps and a nutrition bar.

'You're not letting that copper bother you, are you?'

Britney shook her head. 'I just don't like being reminded of the folks who have left. Makes me sad.'

Tiff could understand it. Her own family drove her mad but there wasn't one of them that she didn't want to see again. Even Ryan.

Tiff looked around. Nothing made Brit smile more than a big group of students who might be receptive to her pitch.

'Hey, Brit, look at that group of…'

'Nah, not right now, Tiff. I'm not in the mood. I think, right now, I just wanna go home.'

CHAPTER 78

'Hey, Keats, shall I save these for the next one?' Penn asked, holding up his protective suit for the second time in as many days.

'Yes, you do appear to have moved in,' Keats answered. 'Although I'm not sure your presence here today was warranted.'

Penn had been thinking the same throughout the post-mortem of the victim retrieved from the lake the previous day.

The procedure had been completely different to the examination of Tyler Short. There had been much more of Tyler to examine.

Today there had been no removal or weighing of organs, no sawing of bones to access the inner workings of the human body. There had been no stomach contents to analyse. Instead, Keats had laboured silently and diligently to work around the tissue-paper skin to find clues underneath. He had been advised from the outset that, given the condition of the body, many of his findings would be approximate.

That hadn't stopped the pathologist examining every inch of what he had available to make determinations.

'So, there you have it,' Keats said, consulting his clipboard. 'We have a male victim aged between twenty-five and fifty who has been submerged anywhere from three months to three years. He was below average height at five feet four, with an old fracture to his right femur. There are no other obvious fractures, broken bones or serious injuries and in the absence of any soft tissue, no obvious cause of death.' He paused and looked over his notes once more. He frowned and Penn took a step closer. Had he missed something?

Keats shook his head. 'No. That's definitely it.'

'So, this death could have been accidental?' Penn confirmed.

Keats nodded. 'Or he could have been stabbed forty times, but if the knife didn't hit one bone I wouldn't know it. And when your boss makes that face she does when she's dissatisfied with the results please tell her that's all she's going to get.'

'Oh yeah, I'll be sure to pass that along,' he replied, drily.

'Joking aside, Penn. There is nothing more I can tell you about this poor fellow.'

Penn nodded and reached for his jacket. He understood. Sometimes the crime scene of the body yielded a plethora of clues and leads, but what amassed to little more than a bag of bones had very little left to say.

'Well, thanks for the…'

'Ah, Penn, just the man,' Mitch said, stepping into the morgue. 'The divers did one last sweep of the area. They found this.'

Mitch held out a plastic evidence bag.

Penn took it and turned it around. It was a burgundy velvet jewellery gift box.

'Not sure if it means anything.'

Penn was reminded of something his boss often said when it came to things uncovered at a crime scene.

Everything meant something.

CHAPTER 79

'Want me to stay in the car again?' Bryant asked, pulling up outside the Brierley Hill café.

'No, you're coming in,' she said, getting out of the car.

This time it was her rules and if Kane Devlin didn't like it he could walk right back out again.

'Looks like he beat you to it,' Bryant said, as they approached the door.

Kane sat in the far corner. Only one other table was occupied by a woman with a pushchair.

Kim noted there were two cups already on the table.

'I got you a latte,' he said, coolly, glancing at Bryant. 'I didn't realise we were going to have company.'

'That's fine, I'm not thirsty,' Bryant said, taking a seat.

Kim sat before the drink and took a sip. 'Thank you for agreeing to meet again. Could we start by finding out your real name?'

As before he was unruffled.

'No,' he said, simply.

Kim felt the frustration travelling along her nerve endings.

'You do realise we're police officers?'

'And you do realise that I know my rights and that I am presently assisting you with your enquiries with full co-operation which, of course, can change any minute I choose.'

Oh, how Kim would have loved to be having this conversation over a square metal table with a tape recorder whirring in the background. Without any shred of evidence to tie him to any murders the option to arrest him was not in her near future.

It had been worth a try and there was more than one way to skin a cat. She hadn't expected him to tell her but she did want him to know they'd been looking.

'So, what can you tell me about Eric Leland?'

'That he was the most indoctrinated individual I've ever come across,' he answered, without hesitation. Was there no question or statement she could make that would incite an ounce of surprise in this man?

'You were asked to snatch him by his mother?'

'That's who we worked for, yes.'

'Does it pay well?' Kim asked. Both families he'd helped were reasonably well off.

'None of your business.'

'Fair enough.'

She was beginning to feel that poor people caught up in a cult could just stay there and rot.

'Back to Eric. How long did you keep him?'

'Almost a month.'

'I thought Samantha was your longest?'

'She was.'

'But you lied. Eric took longer.'

'Your question was what was the longest it had taken to crack someone. We never cracked Eric, so I didn't lie.'

Kim swallowed her irritation at his semantics. 'So, one of your clients is dead and the other is in a psychiatric facility. Way to go on your success rate.'

'Yeah, cos that's why we do it.'

'Why do you?' Kim asked, pushing him as hard as she could.

'For the money,' he said, raising his eyebrows. It was a lie and he was just echoing her earlier comment.

'What made Eric such a challenge?'

He sat back and folded his arms. 'Have you bothered to research anything about cults since we last spoke?'

'Well, no, Kane, I've been a bit busy.'

For a second she thought she saw a hint of amusement in his eyes.

'Then I'll take a moment to explain a few things to you. People are more vulnerable to social influence when they are made to think, sense and feel differently than usual. The human affinity for close-knit groups is an innate trait. We don't even realise how much we want to belong to something that is bigger than ourselves, which is a simple trait to exploit. A new member is poised between reward for closeness and punishment for alienation. Each minor episode of reward and punishment, on moving closer to the group or further away, is a learning experience.'

'Like training a dog?' Kim asked.

'You're learning, Inspector. You see there are common mechanisms of group influence. Firstly, they have a shared belief system which comes from the leader of the group. They sustain a high level of social cohesiveness, and they impute a charismatic leader with divine knowledge or leadership.'

'Eric thinks of Jake as a god,' she stated.

'Which is a view we couldn't shake him from, regardless of what we told him. Jake Black could murder a whole classroom full of kids and Eric would think they deserved it.'

'Eric doesn't seem to like anyone except Jake. Even his own mother is the enemy,' she said, recalling the last words Eric said to her.

'Group members are intensely concerned about each other's well-being; shared beliefs bind members together. When one joins a group like this they give up the opportunity for independent decision-making. New members are always accompanied by someone. It's their special person, and without even realising it, a close bond forms between them.'

Kim thought of Tiffany and Britney. She was sure Tiff had the sense to see what was going on.

'These groups promote distress and then offer relief. The world is going to end, but not if you join with us. The world is a shit and dangerous place, but we'll take care of you. Most newbies are recruited by invitation to workshops, to creative classes. Many young people are looking for something. Mind control involves little or no overt physical abuse. The individual is deceived and manipulated. There's a circle; behaviour, thoughts and emotion. If you can change one, the others will follow.'

'I don't get it,' Kim said.

'Okay, imagine controlling behaviour through environment: food, sleep, jobs, schedule. Having to ask permission for everything. You're eating and working with the same people. You're given a buddy. There are punishments: cold showers, fasting, being forced to stay up all night.

'Leaders can't command someone's inner thoughts, but they know if they command behaviour, hearts and minds will follow. Same with thoughts. They train members to block out information that is not critical to the group. They practice thought stopping of negative emotions. Chanting and meditating all play their part. When thoughts are controlled, feelings and behaviours are controlled too, but by far the cruellest and the hardest to unlock is emotional control.

'A leader has the ability to manipulate the range of a person's feelings. Members are taught to fear outside enemies: fear punishment. They're kept off balance, praised then punished. Some can be made to have a panic reaction to the thought of leaving. There is an elitist mentality. There is strict obedience and people are manipulated through fear and guilt.'

'What about people who decide to leave?'

Kane shook his head vigorously.

'Actively, and I mean actively, discouraged. Anyone who leaves shows that the system is broken. How can they be unhappy and how was that not fed back to the relevant people so that it could be addressed?'

'Is that why no one will talk about them?' she asked.

'Once a member is gone they are dead to the whole group. No one is allowed to dwell on it or examine their reasons. It may lead to others having doubts about the whole movement. Their rooms will be cleared and any evidence of their time will be removed. No reminders of failure. Never forget that a cult only has two objectives: recruit and make money. That's it.'

'But how do people not see this?' Kim asked, frustrated.

'For a start they don't really want to. You really want me to tell you how unhealthy the pizza is when it tastes so good?' he asked, referring to their earlier conversation. 'Groups engage new members by creating an atmosphere of unconditional acceptance. They then build a wall between them and us. The group's behavioural norms structure all areas of members' lives: work, sexuality, socialisation, et cetera.'

Kim thought about the 'no relationship' rule at the Farm.

'It's all designed to keep control. Outsiders are shunned and all activities are carried out with other members. You see, membership is characterised by levels of sanctity so that a member is continually striving to achieve a higher level of acceptance by conforming all the more with the group's expectations. All information into the group is managed, boundary control is exercised and suspicion towards all non-members is exaggerated.'

'Does all of this come from one man?' Bryant asked.

'The personality of the leader is important as cult structure is authoritarian. Charisma is less important than skills of persuasion and ability to manipulate. Most cult leaders are male and self-appointed. They claim to have a special mission or special knowledge. All cults make the claim their members are chosen, select or special.

'Eventually, the group expects members to devote increasing time, energy and money to the cause. They dictate what members wear and eat, when and where they work, sleep and bathe as well as what they should believe or think. They promote black and white thinking. All or nothing. Isolation and food are the cult's most common mechanisms of control and enforced dependency.'

'Rice and beans?' Kim asked.

'The most basic rations are reserved for underperformers. It's a clear message that hits at our basic need to survive.'

'That's what we found in both Sammy's and Tyler's stomachs.'

He didn't look surprised.

'They were both free of Unity Farm, so were they punishing themselves?' Kim asked as the thought occurred to her. No one had forced that food into their stomachs.

'Very likely. Although Sammy was on the road to recovery she still carried the guilt for not going back.'

'Both Sammy and Tyler were at low points in their lives. Were they actively targeted for that reason?' Kim asked.

'Research indicates that approximately two thirds of joiners come from normal functioning families. Only five to six per cent had major psychological difficulties. Please understand that cults offer instant, simplistic solutions to life's problems. Young adults can feel overwhelmed with too many decisions to make. They're fertile but normally not wealthy. People not in relationships are more susceptible to persuasion. They target foreign students alone with flags on their backpacks; seek out the elderly with pensions and money. Widowed middle-age women have clear titles to houses, cars, et cetera.'

Kim immediately thought of Sheila Thorpe.

'There are thousands of different tactics used to tap into the psychology of the individual but they all fall into one of six categories.'

'Which are?'

'As humans, we like to be consistent. If we've made a commitment then break it, we feel guilty. If someone gives us something we try to repay it in kind, so once you accept food it should be repaid. We try to find out what other people think is correct. We want social proof so we imitate what we see. We have a deep-seated sense of duty to authority figures.'

'Some of us do,' Bryant chirped in.

'So members accept the leader as authority. We obey people we like, so as the object of love bombing, you feel like you should do as you're told. And finally, scarcity. If we come to want something, we can be made to fear that if we wait it'll be gone, so without the group you will lose your stress-free life.'

She thought of Tiff and the fact she'd been with these people for over twenty-four hours.

'But well-balanced, sensible people are immune to all the smoke and mirrors, right?' she asked, feeling a sickness grow in her stomach.

Kane sighed heavily.

'If that's what you think, after all that I've said, you haven't heard a word that came out of my mouth.'

Tiff was guessing that a taxi was not a normal occurrence for Britney, who seemed eager to get back to the Farm. She pushed away the anxiety in her stomach that it was somehow linked to her or the boss's visit and told herself that Britney just felt unwell.

She told the taxi to stop at the external gate like the previous day, but this time there was no excited chatter or pausing at the top of the hill to watch the lights come on. Shame, Tiff thought, she would have liked to see that again, but Britney didn't seem in the right frame of mind for her to ask.

And, a part of her was relieved to see Britney's bad mood. After the consistent smiling and happy chatter, it was good to know she had another emotional level. She just hoped it didn't last for too long. She was hoping to meet more of the family tonight and maybe find Sophie Brown.

Tiff followed Britney into the farmhouse and straight into Jake.

'Evening, ladies, good day?' he asked, with a smile.

'Yeah, great day, Jake,' Britney answered quickly. 'Can I have a quick word before…'

'Maybe later, Brit,' he said, placing a hand on her shoulder. 'I believe that Tiff and I have a pre-arranged meeting to continue our discussion from last night.'

'But…'

'Whatever it is can wait, Britney,' he said, more firmly.

Brit got the message and offered Tiff a half-smile and held out her hand. She nodded towards the backpack.

Tiff removed it and thanked her for taking it to their room. The phone from the boss was still nestled down the front of her trousers.

'Follow me,' Jake said, leading her up the stairs.

After many smiles and waves, they arrived at a door marked 'Private'.

Tiff stepped inside and immediately felt as though the room was welcoming her into a big, warm hug. Dark furniture softened by throws and blankets, walls filled with what looked like first edition books.

'Please, take a seat,' he said, pointing to the plush sofa. She sat facing a roaring fireplace with scented candles flickering on the hearth.

Jake sat in the single chair and rested his forearms on his knees. His shirt sleeves gathered at the elbow, revealing a Rolex watch on his left wrist.

'I hope you don't mind but Brit told me a little about your home situation. She wasn't speaking out of turn but she's grown very fond of you in a short time.'

Tiff shook her head. She didn't mind. She often wondered if she was overreacting to her mother's blatant favouritism, and she'd welcome his view on the subject.

Tiff knew what she was here to do but the reason she'd been upset yesterday was still very real. She hadn't contacted her mother and she hoped Ryan was nice and comfortable in her room.

'You blame them, don't you?' Jake asked, gently. His expression was full of warmth and understanding.

She'd never spoken to anyone about her feelings about her family. There were people with much bigger problems than hers. So what if it made her feel like shit. She'd get over it. She was a grown woman.

'You've always blamed them for your feelings, from that very first injustice that you couldn't justify or explain away to make yourself feel better. Do you remember what it was?'

'Steven's birthday,' she said before she could stop herself. And then realised it was true.

'Tell me about it,' he said, sitting back.

'My birthday was in June. I was nine years old. I had a pair of roller skates. I loved them. A month later it was Steven's birthday and he got a bike, chocolates and we went to McDonald's for tea.'

Something inside her expected him to laugh. The words sounded ridiculous to her own ears.

He didn't laugh.

'Was it the disparity in gift value that stayed with you?' he asked, tipping his head so that the candlelight danced across his face.

She thought about the question. It was what had always stayed in her mind. Her roller skates versus a shiny new bike. And yet it wasn't that that rattled her even now, she realised.

'No, I don't think it was the gift, I think it was the occasion. From the moment he woke up the whole day was about him. Presents, balloons, cards, a rare treat for tea. It was the difference in importance, in priority.'

'So, you began to wonder why you hadn't received the same level of attention. What had you done wrong? Why weren't you good enough?'

She nodded and felt the tears prick at her eyes.

He leaned over and touched her wrist, gently. 'Please don't be upset, Tiff, that's the last thing I want but I do want you to understand. May I continue?'

Tiff swallowed back the emotion and nodded.

'It's hard to look back objectively without the emotion but basically you began to feel inadequate before you were ten years old because of someone else's actions. I bet from that point on you were looking for examples, events that proved your point, things that solidified your view that you were somehow less than your brothers, less important, less worthy?'

She nodded.

'And you found them, didn't you?'

'Yes,' she whispered, trying to stop all the memories from flooding her brain.

'And do you know why you found so much reinforcement of your beliefs?'

She shook her head. Now he was going to tell her what she'd always told herself. He was going to rationalise her childhood by explaining that there was balance, that there were positives too, that there were times she'd received more attention than the boys and that the brain hung on to the negative more than the positive. He was going to tell her that her memories were distorted and that the love had been equal.

'Tiffany, you found so many examples of favouritism because they really were there to find. Your mother obviously treated you differently to your brothers and it has stayed with and affected you your whole life. You were right in your feelings and you were justified.'

'Oh,' she said, surprised.

'But what adds weight to your feelings is your wish to change the facts. You want your mum to wake up and start apportioning her affection equally and that's what holds you back. You're still waiting for a change and it's not going to happen. You can't make it happen.' He paused. 'Because they're your blood family you feel obliged to keep trying, to throw yourself against the wall, but it's not working and every time it doesn't work you suffer the humiliation and hurt all over again. The only one suffering here is you, which makes me incredibly sad, not for you, but for them.'

All kinds of thoughts were going around in her brain.

'I'm sad because I don't think they see just how special and unique you are. We saw it straight away. You're intelligent, energetic, enthusiastic and warm. Any family would be truly blessed to have you in their lives. It's just a pity that your blood family doesn't see what we see.'

He shook his head. 'I hope I haven't upset you but I did want you to understand that there are people here that get it. They also know that the first step to recovery, to discovering the real you, is distance. You have to help yourself to care less about their opinion and, more importantly, their actions. Does that make sense?'

Tiff nodded her understanding.

'It's something we can help you with here but it has to be your choice.'

'I don't… I…'

'Don't think about it now. Give yourself time to think and process what we've discussed. There's no rush,' he said, smiling. 'Now head down to the dining room where you'll find a nice hot meal waiting for you.'

She thanked him and left the room. She was still in a daze when she reached the dining room, trying to examine the feelings that were whizzing around her head like fireworks. She was aware of and returned all the smiles and waves which, while pleasant, felt strange not having Britney beside her. She'd come to think of the two of them as a bit of a team.

For the first time she entered the dining room to the hubbub of the panpipes already playing and people chattering as they ate. The room was already on the second serving.

Oh, well, never mind. She was hungry and would probably eat anything right now. She joined the back of the line.

'Hi, you're Tiffany, aren't you?' asked a voice from behind the tables.

It was the woman who had served her pork chop and mash the night before.

'Yes, yes, that's me.'

The woman reached beneath the table and produced a plate with a cover.

'From the first sitting. Jake asked for a meal to be held aside. Be careful, the plate is hot,' she said, pushing it forward.

'Thank you so much…' Tiff said, as a warm glow spread through her. But she didn't even know the woman's name.

'You're welcome, love,' she said with a smile. 'And just so you know, my name is Sheila.'

CHAPTER 81

'Cults are hard to leave because people feel loyal,' Kane continued, once fresh drinks were before them all. 'There are peer pressures, they believe in the group. They may be exhausted and confused, already separated from their past. They now fear a world without the group. If you put all these things together, it's a powerful force. As exit counsellors we have our own processes but…'

'They don't always work,' Kim finished.

'Of course not. In your own field, Inspector, someone will manufacture a new lock and within hours a savvy criminal will have it open. Same with computer protection. The moment it's written you've got some kid that can hack it. A person resisting exit counselling might say "yes, they told me you'd say that", so you have to remember that the very idea of leaving is terrifying. After leaving people feel guilty, shameful, full of self-blame, fears and paranoia. Many feel depressed, lonely, have low confidence and no longer trust themselves to make good choices.'

'And that's why you thought Sammy Brown wasn't ready?'

Kane nodded. 'She'd been there for two years. In cult years that's half a lifetime. She wasn't ready to address the practical issues related to daily living. They have to face psychological and emotional stirrings that can cause intense agonies, develop a new social network and attempt to repair old relationships. It can take anywhere from six months to two years to get their lives functioning again, and once they do see what went on they suffer a whole new batch of guilt for the people they left behind. They have fear of retribution from the cult and have an inability to trust. They closely watch any family and friends. An ex-cult member can take years to come to terms with the anger and resentment, even if the deprogramming is successful.'

'How does deprogramming work?'

'There's no magic formula or potion. It's about getting a member to question and examine their beliefs. Show them similarities to other groups. Read them books and articles they can identify with. Show them videos on cults. Demonstrate that they're in a trap. Show them they didn't originally choose to enter the trap.

'We focus on the present, not what they've done but what they can do. We have to build rapport and trust. We have to try and access the pre-cult identity. Put them back in touch with the people they were before. We have to get them to visualise a happy future to undo phobia indoctrination. We have to offer concrete definitions of mind control and characteristics of a destructive cult. We have to be patient and persevere. Some ex-cult members describe it as having fallen deeply in love then finding out you were just being used.'

He sat back in his chair. 'You know some people never recover from the experience of being in a cult. They're changed for ever and some would even rather die than try to readjust to normal life.'

'So, suicide is a very real threat?' Kim asked, thinking how Sammy's death had almost been classified as such.

'Very real,' he said, looking at his watch. 'And I'm pretty sure there's nothing more I can tell you.'

'How about your real name?' she asked.

'Not relevant.'

It had been worth a try.

'Well, thanks for your time,' she said, offering her hand.

He shook it in return. 'You know, I really hope you find who is responsible for these murders.'

'Oh, we will,' she assured him.

He nodded and headed for the door. The two females behind the counter watched him go.

Kim waited for five seconds before getting to her feet. 'Be back in a minute,' she said to Bryant over her shoulder.

Did he really think she was as green as she was cabbage-looking?

As she stepped outside the door, she saw him disappear around the hairdressers on the corner. There was a small car park fifty metres down.

She stayed behind him by a good thirty metres, allowing other shoppers to get between them. His height ensured he didn't blend into the crowd. Okay, so he wouldn't give them his name, but his car had to be registered to someone and from that information they could follow a trail. She was surprised he hadn't worked that out.

Suddenly he took a sharp left into a small side street that led back onto the main road.

'What the…' she said, speeding up.

She reached the corner just in time to see the man folding himself into a cab.

Damn it. He had given it thought after all.

Fuck it, she thought, realising she wasn't giving this man enough credit. Everything really was on his terms.

She seethed. She would find him. She was now more determined than ever.

'Well?' Bryant asked, as she got into the car.

'He got a taxi.'

'Clever guy. So, where to now?'

Kim held up her finger as she received a text message from Tiff. She read it and then looked at her colleague.

'Well, I wasn't expecting that.'

CHAPTER 82

Tiff entered the bedroom with Jake's words still swirling around her brain. Could it be as easy as just letting go of her expectation of change? There was something exhilarating in the notion that she had the power to lessen the effect of other people's actions on her by simply caring less.

'Good chat?' Britney asked, with a smile that by now Tiff could tell was forced.

'Yeah, it was actually. Jake gave me a lot to think about.'

'Yes, he can do that. It's why we all listen to him. He knows the workings of the mind so well.'

Tiff smiled as she saw a change of clothes piled neatly on her bed. She'd been wearing the same jeans and sweater since the day before.

'Ooh, lovely. I'll grab a quick shower and get changed.'

'Great, we've got open chat this evening and I'd love for you to come along.'

'What's that?' she asked.

'As many people who want to come along to the great hall and open up about how they're doing and how they're feeling. It's a great opportunity to meet some of the others.'

'Sounds great,' Tiff said, reaching for the clothes which she was not surprised to see were her size.

'You weren't talking to her, were you?' Brit asked quietly.

Tiff stiffened. She could only be talking about one person.

'Who?' she asked, turning to her friend.

'That police officer.'

Tiffany frowned. 'You were there. She barely looked my way; never even spoke to me, bloody rude and…'

'I mean afterwards, in the ladies' toilets.'

Tiff continued to stare at her.

'She was in there too,' Brit continued.

So, Britney had seen them both leave the toilets. Damn it. Her only option was outright lying.

'Brit, I didn't even know she was in there but if I had what exactly would I have said?'

Brit shrugged. 'I dunno. Maybe bad things about Jake and the—'

'Hang on, you think I'd bad-mouth a place and people that have taken me in when I needed it, fed me, clothed me and made me feel good about myself?'

Tiff saw the tension start to drop from her face and tried to drive the point home.

'If she's after negative stuff she's not gonna get it from me,' Tiff said, nudging Brit in the ribs.

Britney laughed as she nudged her back.

'So, you definitely didn't speak to her?'

Tiff rolled her eyes.

'Brit, I swear to you, I didn't speak to anyone.'

Britney smiled widely back at her, and Tiff swallowed the guilt she now felt for lying to her friend.

CHAPTER 83

'Okay, folks, so we now know that Sheila Thorpe is alive and well and cooking up a storm at Unity Farm,' Kim said to two thirds of her team; but by the looks of Stacey's frown she hadn't got the full attention of her reduced audience.

Bryant had dropped her at the door before heading over to Worcester. He had updated her on the developments with Peter Drake and for his own sanity she wanted him to see this thing out.

'Do you mind if I go and tell Sheila's daughter?' Penn asked.

Kim briefly wondered if the woman would be relieved or dismayed to learn about her mother. But she deserved to know the truth.

'Yeah, and if Stacey would like to join us in the conversation…'

'Sorry, boss, but I was just checking a land registry entry, and I can now confirm that Unity Farm is definitely not Jake Black's first cult.'

'What?' Kim asked, surprised. She'd never considered the possibility.

'It was something Penny Hicks said in her message. She said she'd been with Jake for twelve years, and we know that Unity Farm has only been going for ten years. Turns out he started a group when he was twenty-eight years old. It was a religious group with only about twenty members. They clubbed together to buy a small holding in Somerset. Everything was fine until an eighteen-year-old kid named Graham Deavers died under suspicious circumstances when he fell off a roof, while doing repair work. The authorities weren't convinced but could find no proof of murder. An accidental death was recorded by the coroner. Five months later there was a second death. A man in his late twenties named Christopher Brook committed suicide. Twenty people attested to the fact he'd been depressed and had spoken of ending his own life.'

'Which could be true,' Kim said, trying to remain objective.

Stacey nodded but looked dubious. 'This second incident broke the group up and the property was sold. Jake Black then disappeared for just a few months until Unity Farm was born.'

'Bloody hell, Stace. Good work. Pick that up again first thing,' she said.

This new information prompted even more questions about Jake Black. If his previous cult had been religion based why had he changed to wellness for Unity Farm? Did he truly care about anything as much as he cared about being adored?

Kim took a few minutes to update them on her conversation with Kane.

'He seems to know his stuff,' Stacey observed. 'Everything I've learned over the last couple of days confirms what he's saying. Penny Hicks seemed absolutely terrified to talk to me or go into detail about anything to do with the Farm, and when I tried to press her, she just disappeared. And then there's that girl who just threw herself out the window.'

Kim was no longer as shocked by these things after what she'd learned from Kane. It was fair to say that none of them had had any understanding of the lasting effects of places like Unity Farm.

'Permission to speak freely, boss?' Stacey asked.

Kim raised one eyebrow. Stacey knew she had permission to say whatever she liked. This was the constable's way of warning her that she probably wasn't going to like it.

'It's Tiff. I mean, I'm just worried…'

'I saw her today, Stace. She's fine,' Kim reassured. 'I'll text her later, though, just to make sure.'

'Thanks, boss.'

'So, tomorrow we have a concerted effort on identifying our man in the lake, digging on Kane Devlin and delving deeper into the previous cult. Penn, I still want to know where that money went, but for now we call it a night.'

'Cheers, boss,' Penn said, pushing back his chair.

Stacey did the same.

*

Kim waited for Penn to leave the room before she folded her arms.

'So, wedding plans going well, Stace?'

'Yeah, boss,' she said, without enthusiasm as she put her phone into her satchel.

This was not a woman enjoying making preparations for the happiest day of her life.

'So, how much weight you lost in the last month?' she asked.

'Two and a half pounds,' Stacey answered, miserably.

'Why?'

'I dunno. I just can't seem…'

'No. Why are you even trying?'

'I just want everything to be perfect.'

'What was your weight when Devon asked you to marry her?'

'Two and a half pounds heavier,' Stacey said with a wry smile.

'It's not about your weight, Stace. Devon loves you as you are and you know it.'

She glanced at Penn's desk. A space once occupied by DS Kevin Dawson.

'You know, a very good friend of yours once told me that you'd never feel good enough for Devon, and he was right. I think he told you the same thing.'

The whites of Stacey's eyes suddenly reddened.

'Imagine he was here right now. What would he be saying?'

Stacey swallowed. 'He'd be telling me that I was good enough and that Devon was the lucky one.'

Kim pulled her gaze away from the desk and back to her colleague.

'And for once, Stacey, he would have been right.'

CHAPTER 84

Bryant walked into a room full of excited chatter. The desks were littered with small plastic cups, half-filled, and a bottle of cheap wine on the top table. Three pizza boxes lay open, scattered around the work stations.

Travis came forward, holding a mug of coffee, his other hand outstretched.

'Come in, Bryant,' he said, affably. 'Join the celebration.'

Lynne raised her Diet Coke at him in greeting.

'What's going on?'

'He confessed,' Travis said, loosening his tie. 'Peter Drake told us everything.'

'You're kidding?' Bryant said.

Twenty-five years ago the man had hidden behind a lawyer and hadn't spoken a word until he'd stepped into court.

'Nope. A bit of prodding and we got the lot. Lynne and I are going back in there to finish off once he's had a break, but I can tell you that Peter Drake is headed right back where he belongs.'

'Bloody hell,' Bryant said, as the tension he'd been carrying for the last few days released its grip on his body.

'Here, have one of these,' he said, pouring the last of the wine into the cup.

Bryant declined. The bottle and cups were just for show and the people who weren't driving. Bryant knew few police officers who touched a drop if they were getting behind the wheel.

'Do you mind if I watch the tape?' Bryant asked.

Travis's face hardened. 'Jeez, Bryant, you got what you wanted.'

A girl in her twenties had suffered a horrific, brutal murder. He'd hardly call that getting what he wanted.

'Closure, Travis. I'll watch the confession and then I can let it go.'

He saw the man's frustration and didn't care. If he'd learned anything from his boss it was that you saw something through to the bitter end.

'Bob, get the confession up,' he called to a stick-thin officer reaching for a piece of pizza.

Bob looked from one to the other and put the pizza back down before rubbing his hands on his trousers. He sat, loaded the footage, stood and pointed for Bryant to take his seat.

Bryant thanked him and watched as he headed back to the pizza that had his name on it.

Bryant sat and picked up the headphones that were still attached to the machine.

'Hey, Bryant,' Lynne said, leaning against the desk.

'You do the first interview?' he asked.

She nodded. 'I was arresting officer and there are few arrests that have given me more pleasure. I'll sleep better tonight knowing that piece of shit is back behind bars.'

'You and me both,' he said, looking pointedly at the screen.

'Yeah, I'll leave you to it. Just wanted to ask, how's Penn? I hear his mother is quite close to…'

'Penn's Penn,' he said, honestly. He didn't bring his problems to work.

Bryant noted the way she looked down at her feet when she mentioned his name.

'You know, you should probably ask him yourself. I'm sure he'd appreciate—'

'Hey, Lynne, we're up,' Travis called from the other side of the room.

The man's tie was now tightly fixed against his shirt collar and his jacket had been retrieved from the back of the chair.

'Yeah, maybe…' she said, grabbing a folder from her desk, and following her boss from the office.

He pressed play and watched the screen spring into life.

Travis and Lynne entered the room and Travis offered the detail to the camera.

Travis: Mr Drake, at this time you have waived your right to counsel?

Drake: Nodded.

Travis: Please answer.

Drake: Don't want no lawyer. Just a smoke.

Travis: You understand you've been arrested for the rape and murder of Alice Lennox?

Drake: Yep.

Travis: What would you like to say?

Drake: I done it.

Travis: Wh… what?

Drake: I done it. I killed her. You got me.

Ten seconds of silence.

Travis: Mr Drake, are you confessing to the murder of Alice Lennox?

Drake: Sure am. That's what you want to hear, right?

Lynne: Yes if it's the truth.

Drake: Course it's the truth, yer dumb bitch. I killed…

Travis: Mind your mouth, Mr Drake. Now do you want to expand on the admission?

Travis knew his stuff. He wanted the detail that would hold up in court when Peter Drake changed his mind and pled Not Guilty.

Drake: Look, she was a prostitute. She ain't no loss. I approached her when she left the others. She followed me happily to make a few quid.

Travis: She followed you voluntarily?

Drake: Offered her seventy quid for a blow job. Course she followed me. I took her to Spinners Corner and smacked her one to get her down.

Travis: And you raped her?

Drake: Not with my cock. She's a prossie. Could have had anything. Nah, I shoved a beer bottle up—

Travis: And then what?

Drake: I took out my knife and started cutting her. Small ones at first, just enough to see the top layer of skin separate and then harder, deeper. The more she cried out the harder I cut. Slicing and dicing like I was cooking a fucking Sunday dinner. She was a bleeder all right. She started losing consciousness, going in and out so I proper opened her up.

Travis: Can you describe…

Drake: You know. You've seen her. You know what I like to do. I took the blade and sliced her right open from the inside of her thigh right down to her ankle, on both sides.

Travis: And then what?

Drake: I watched her die. My second-favourite part.

Travis: And then?

Drake: I walked away and left her like the piece of shit that she was.

Another ten seconds of silence before Travis turned to the camera and suspended the interview.

Bryant unclenched his fists and removed the headphones, fully aware that the horror of the scene described by Drake would play over in his head for weeks to come.

Travis was right, the sick bastard had confessed and Bryant had what he wanted, but after listening to what he'd done to that girl, the victory didn't feel like a victory at all.

CHAPTER 85

Kim stepped out of the station and headed towards the Ninja parked at the end of the row of squad cars.

Her heart jumped as a figure stepped from the darkness to block her path.

'Bloody hell,' she exclaimed, looking into the red-rimmed eyes of Kate Brown. Tendrils of blonde hair peeked out from beneath the woollen hat she was wearing and curled onto the lapel of her heavy long coat. It was a chilly night but temperatures hadn't plummeted far enough to warrant this mid-winter precaution.

'I'm sorry, Inspector. I j-just needed a word alone. I've been here for a while,' she said, looking towards the station doors.

'Do you want to come inside?' Kim asked, confused.

She shook her head and looked around. 'No, no, it'll just take a minute.'

The woman appeared terrified despite being in the car park of a police station. There were few safer places she could be.

The penny dropped. 'Does Myles know you're here?'

She hesitated. 'No, he's a stubborn man and still feels we should leave Sophie's safety in the hands of Kane.'

'And you don't?' Kim asked, moving her to the side as two constables headed out of the station doors. It appeared that the heavy, long coat and hat were an attempt at some kind of disguise.

She tucked a stray lock of hair behind her ear. 'Every hour that passes makes me more nervous. I can't help feeling that something is going to go wrong.'

'Has Kane confirmed he has her?' Kim asked.

'No, he won't give us a straight answer and it's getting harder to get in touch with him. Every minute without her is driving me insane. I keep getting the feeling that I'm running out of time. That I'm never going to see Sophie again.' Her eyes filled with tears. 'Please help me, Inspector, I cannot lose another child.'

Up until now she had been unable to spend time proactively looking for Sophie Brown. With no missing person's report and no instruction from the parents, she'd had no remit to interfere in the case of a grown adult not wishing to come home.

'Mrs Brown, are you formally asking me to search for your missing daughter?'

Kate didn't hesitate. 'Inspector, please bring my daughter home.'

Those were the words Kim had been waiting to hear.

CHAPTER 86

Tiff followed Britney into the dining room. The long tables and chairs had been rearranged to form a large square like a medieval banquet so that everyone sitting could see everyone else. A selection of soft drinks and snacks were laid out where the hot food normally sat.

'Only women?' Tiff asked, looking around.

'Yes, Thursday is ladies' night.'

'Why the separation?'

Brit guided her to two seats together.

'Because men's problems are different to women's and people need to be able to speak openly.'

Tiff spotted Sheila about to take a seat opposite and smiled. Sheila gave her a little wave.

'Okay, ladies, are we ready?' called out a woman who was closing the dining room door.

'That's Lorna, been here nine years. She's the one who brought me here. She's awesome.'

Tiff took a good look at the woman dressed in pale jeans and a tie-dyed tee shirt. Her long brown hair was pulled back in an untidy ponytail, revealing pearl studs in her ears. Her face was relaxed and pleasant. Tiff took a moment to take a good look around the women. Sophie Brown was not one of them.

Lorna offered a smile that stretched around the room.

'Let me start by welcoming Tiffany to the group. I understand she likes to be called Tiff.'

The smile was turned her way as everyone waved or called out a greeting.

Never had she been in a room full of so many women and felt so welcome and accepted.

'Okay, anybody want to start, or shall I choose? Don't forget. You can say anything you like here and it goes no further. You can be as honest as you want to be. We're all here to offer support and help.'

A hand was tentatively raised from a woman on the table opposite, three seats away from Sheila.

Tiff guessed the girl to be mid-twenties; she had short blonde hair and a fringe that almost covered her eyes.

'Go ahead, Maria,' Lorna said.

'I've struggled this week,' she admitted, looking around the group. 'It's not that I don't want to be here, it's just…'

'Go on, Maria. Anything you say is safe here,' Lorna encouraged.

'It's just that I love my work in the garden and I love being part of the family, but it's my mum's birthday this week and…'

'Maria, don't feel bad for missing your mum. There's no judgement here. Everyone understands and we all miss things from the outside now and again.'

Tiff noticed Sheila glance down at her nails.

'Everyone here sacrificed things on the outside once they decided to focus on themselves. You've been a valued member of this family for seven months now. You know you're where you belong and everyone here loves you.'

Lorna paused to give the room time to murmur whispers of agreement.

'Sometimes, after a while, it's easy to forget the things that brought us here in the first place, the toxic hurtful forces that made us feel helpless and less than the people we are. Even brief contact with those forces can undo all the work we've done to make ourselves whole.'

Maria was listening wholeheartedly to everything that Lorna said.

'I think you're stronger now, Maria, but I don't think you're strong enough to withstand the reminder of what she put you through.'

Tiff could see Maria's indecision.

'Everyone here will support your decision, and if you want to give your mother a call to wish her happy birthday, no one will judge you, but I'll ask you this: did she care about happy birthdays when she was falling over drunk when you were ten years old?'

Tiff realised she was the only person in the room shocked at Lorna's words. It was clear that everyone knew everyone else's story.

'And did she care about your birthday when you were eighteen and visiting her in prison? Did she care about birthdays when she was taking all your wages from the petrol station to buy alcohol?'

The words, although harsh, were wrapped in a gentle layer of empathy and understanding.

Maria had been shaking her head the whole time.

Lorna stood and went to the girl. She placed her hand on her shoulder.

'Sweetie, if you feel you're ready to let that toxic relationship back into your life, we'll support you. We only want you to be happy.'

Tears began to slide down Maria's cheeks. Lorna turned her and hugged her close, stroking her hair.

'It's okay, sweetheart, let it out. You know we all love you.'

Other women began to leave their seats and gather around Maria. A hand here, a touch there.

Lorna extricated herself from what had become a group hug and returned to her seat.

The hugging eventually stopped and Maria raised her head.

Lorna caught her eye. 'Do you want me to arrange the call?'

Maria shook her head decisively and vigorously as nods of agreement travelled around the room.

'Isn't she awesome?' Britney asked beside her.

Tiff nodded, although she would have used the word persuasive.

Tiff continued to listen as women voiced concerns about missing aspects of their former life, and each one was expertly and subtly steered away by using their own histories against them.

After a girl in her late teens had been dissuaded from visiting her pregnant sister, Lorna checked her watch.

'Okay, ladies, let's pause for some drinks and snacks and then I want to tell you about some exciting events we've got planned for next month.'

Everyone stood and headed for the table.

'Be back in a sec,' Britney said, heading towards Lorna, who was still seated.

Tiff found herself next to Sheila in the queue.

'Hey, Tiff,' she said, reaching for a drink.

'Hi,' Tiff replied, doing the same. 'Wow, that was hard to listen to,' she continued, to get the woman's attention.

Sheila moved to the side. 'It can be hard to hear but that's why we have these meetings, so people can be honest and open about the way they feel.'

'Do you miss anyone?' Tiff asked, taking a sip.

A shadow of sadness crossed her face as she shrugged.

'Sometimes I miss people from my old life but right now I know I'm exactly where I was meant to be. Does that make sense?'

Tiff nodded, not sure that was any kind of answer that would satisfy her daughter.

'How about you, family problems bring you here?'

Tiff thought about the boss's earlier text message. It had been brief and immediate.

Find Sophie.

So far, despite searching the faces of everyone who passed her by she had not yet seen Samantha's sister.

Tiff nodded. 'And I thought my friend might be here. You might know her. Her name is Sophie. Sophie Brown.'

Sheila's face hardened as she glanced around the room.

'You must be mistaken. There's no one here named Sophie.'

Tiff felt a tremble in her hand. Total denial of someone's existence.

From what she understood, that only happened if the person was gone or dead.

CHAPTER 87

'Okay, husband, what's wrong?' Jenny asked, peering at him over his glasses.

'Nothing,' Bryant replied. 'I'm fine.'

'No, you're not. You've barely spoken since you came home and the big guys in black just scored a goal and you never even…'

'It's a try,' he responded automatically. As she well knew.

Her mouth twitched. 'Well, you wanna *try* being honest with your wife about why you've been staring at Laura's photo for the last twenty minutes instead of watching the game I recorded…'

'Match,' he corrected.

'Whatever,' she said, putting her craft tray to the side. She'd recently discovered something called diamond painting, which involved a sticky canvas and hundreds of tiny little glittery stones. Some of the buggers managed to escape and constantly winked at him from the carpet.

'Cuppa?' she said.

'Yes, please,' he answered.

'No, I meant do you want to make one?'

'Yeah, I'll go…'

'Oh, jeez, it must be serious,' she said, removing her glasses completely. 'You never make a drink after ten.'

'Jenny, are you trying to…'

'I'm trying to get you to see how distracted you are. Now I know it's not your current case because anything bothering you on that score you would have taken over to chew on with Kim. So, it has to be this Peter Drake business.'

She was right, it was, but what he couldn't fathom was why it was still on his mind.

When he worked a case with the guv there was a nervous tension that burrowed its way into his stomach. It seesawed between trepidation, excitement, anxiety and hope. It was neither pleasant nor unpleasant. It just was. There was little consistency except for one thing. Once they made an arrest the feeling went away. His stomach settled until the next major crime scene. But with Peter Drake it hadn't yet gone away.

'Okay, I have three theories,' Jenny said, tucking her legs beneath her.

'Only three?' he joked.

'My first is that it's all happened so quickly you're waiting for your emotions to catch up with you. Ooh, actually I have four theories.'

Bryant laughed out loud.

'My new second theory is that you're still coming to terms with being right about something.'

'Jen.'

'Okay, scrap that one. My next theory, which you're probably not going to like, is that you're hanging on to this case because you don't know how to let it go.'

It wasn't the first time he'd been told that today.

'And the last theory?'

'Is that you're holding on to it for a legitimate reason. That your gut is trying to communicate something to your brain.'

'And, if you were a betting woman?'

'My money would be on the last. I don't know the case but I do know you. So, take out your laptop, go over everything you know and I'll make the cuppa.'

Bryant watched her go. He really was the luckiest man alive and he always knew when to do what his wife said.

CHAPTER 88

Tiff lay in bed and felt her eyelids drooping to the rhythm of Britney's deep breathing, despite the quiet unease in her stomach.

She couldn't believe that it had only been that morning that she and Britney had visited Hilda in her home. The day had been packed full and it had been one thing after another.

The meeting in the dining hall had resumed and had been a totally different story. The air had been charged with positivity as Lorna had updated them on progress for the building work and the schedule for the new indoor swimming pool, hot tub and steam room. She'd talked of success with booking sessions with a well-known yoga teacher and a reiki master. Also, there were plans to introduce their own selection of livestock. Volunteers had been requested to take responsibility for various tasks and hands had shot into the air.

Last had been the highlight section where everyone was asked to choose their most positive moment of the week. A short clap had followed every one. Tiff had been surprised when they'd asked her to offer one too.

'Meeting Britney,' she had blurted out. She'd been moved to see the colour flood the girl's cheeks as she'd touched her lightly on the arm.

The meeting had broken up amidst excited chatter, laughter and high spirits, the earlier sadness totally forgotten as people's attention was re-focussed on the future. Was it choreographed that way? Were the meetings a monitoring session to see who was at risk of leaving?

It was only now, here in bed, alone with her own thoughts that she had the clarity of mind to ask herself these questions when all she really wanted to do was go to sleep.

When she was amongst the other ladies, taking part in activities, listening to their stories, she kind of understood the attraction of life at the Farm. There was a loyalty amongst these women that she had never witnessed anywhere else.

She could feel herself being drawn in. She felt a part of daily life. Occasionally, it slipped her mind why she was here. At times, she felt as though she was stepping outside herself, shedding something, leaving something behind. It was both exciting and unnerving at the same time.

The thought of Ryan in her room no longer filled her with the same level of rage. The problem now seemed so small and so far away.

And that's the problem, she realised, as her eyes opened wide. This was how it worked. There was no big thing that changed her outlook. It was a gradual wearing away of the person you were. It didn't hurt, it wasn't painful. It was soft, gentle, seductive and above all dangerous.

Tiff turned over, facing away from Britney. She knew she would get no sleep tonight.

She'd done what she'd been asked to do. The boss had texted her earlier to check on her and to ask about Sophie. She'd assured the boss she was fine and reported that Sophie Brown wasn't here.

She was no longer sure she'd answered the first question truthfully.

Tomorrow, once she and Brit reached the college she would make her excuses and leave.

She had to.

CHAPTER 89

'Okay, guys, what have we got?' Kim asked, entering the squad room. Her team had started working while she'd briefed Woody. He'd agreed with her assessment of the case and the direction. With instruction from Kate Brown, and after confirmation from Tiff that Sophie was no longer at Unity Farm, the emphasis was on finding her. Quickly.

'Got him,' Stacey said, reaching for a chocolate chip cookie from Penn's treat box.

'Go on.'

'His full name is Kane Drummond and lives in West Hagley.'

'Stace, how did…'

'Taxi companies. Katrina, at the seventh one I tried, took the booking and they dropped him off at a car park in Stourbridge which doesn't have cameras. No surprise. But the petrol station on the ring road does and I guess he was low on fuel. Got his reg number and full address.'

'Well done, Stace, but keep digging. Now we know his real name we can…'

'And here's his actual phone number,' Stacey added pushing a piece of paper towards her. 'Katrina always logs them, you know.'

'Even better,' Kim said. She was sick and tired of using Myles Brown as the middleman.

'Nothing on the money yet, boss,' Penn said.

'Okay, Stace, priority is identifying our third victim and then getting history on Kane Drummond and Jake Black. I want everything you can find. Penn, stick with the money. We might find something to haul Jake Black in for so we can add a little pressure.'

'Got it, boss.'

'And I'm gonna make a quick call to our superhero. Let him know he's not in hiding any more.'

Kim stepped into the Bowl and dialled the number.

He answered with a single hello.

'Mr Drummond,' she said, using his full name. 'DI Stone.'

'How did you get…'

'We're the police. We're good at this shit. I think we need another conversation. Sophie is no longer at Unity Farm. Now we could come and see you at your home for…'

'No,' he said, quickly. That was the response she'd hoped for. He was silent for a minute. 'Meet me at the usual place. Ten o'clock.'

'I'd rather…'

'Ten o'clock, Inspector, and you'll see why,' he said, as the line went dead.

She looked at her watch. It was almost eight. Which gave her enough time for the other thing she'd been asked to do.

What exactly had he meant about her seeing why? It felt like he was keeping that café in business.

'Penn, change of plan. Get a team over to Kane's address. Wait for him to leave and then break in. You have reason to fear for Sophie Brown's safety.'

'Got it, boss,' he said, thoughtfully. 'That's not too far from Sheila's daughter's house,' he said, glancing at his watch. He looked at her questioningly.

She nodded. The woman deserved to know where her mother was.

He grabbed his coat and left.

Content that everyone knew exactly what they were doing, Kim turned to Bryant.

'You ready?'

He took a deep breath.

'Ready as I'll ever be.'

CHAPTER 90

Tiff fixed a smile to her face and followed Britney into the breakfast hall. She felt groggy from lack of sleep. Once she'd decided it was time to leave, the morning had not come quickly enough. She had even started to wonder if she'd done the right thing agreeing to do this in the first place.

Mixed with her eagerness to leave was the feeling of having let the team down. She'd been trusted to come in and find Sophie. She hadn't found Sophie and neither had she found out anything about the girl. If the Brown family ended up with another dead daughter, it would all be down to her. And she didn't really want to see the boss's face right now, knowing she had failed miserably. She knew she'd never be asked to help this team again.

'You okay?' Brit asked, as they waited in line.

'I'm fine, just missing home a bit.'

'You want to leave?' Britney asked, alarmed.

'God no, I love it here,' Tiff countered quickly. She didn't want to upset her friend before she needed to. She didn't really want to upset Brit at all. Despite her best efforts, she felt closer to the redhead than she had to anyone in quite a while.

'Good, cos I've got a surprise for you after breakfast.'

'Really?' Tiff asked.

'Yeah, but let's eat first. I'm absolutely ravenous.'

'Okay,' Tiff said, following her to the nearest table. Tiff was surprised that Sheila wasn't in the line-up today.

'Where's Sheila?' she asked Brit as they buttered their toast. Tiff hadn't felt hungry until the plate of scrambled eggs and bacon was on her tray, but her mouth now watered at the prospect.

Enjoying breakfast wasn't a sin. It was her last meal here anyway. As soon as they finished breakfast she'd text the boss and let her know she was on her way out. There might be a debrief, which would be very brief indeed seeing as she knew nothing.

'Ah, it's Friday,' Brit explained. 'Sheila and one of the others go and do the weekly food shop every Friday morning. Cream cakes for everyone later on,' Brit said, cutting the fat from her bacon.

Tiff tucked into her own breakfast and the two of them ate in silence.

'Well, that's me set up for the morning,' Brit said, placing down her knife and fork. Tiffany was just one mouthful behind.

'Come on, then, Tiff, we've got a busy day.'

Tiff headed over to the table. She wouldn't need the packed lunch, but it was important to keep up appearances until she was ready to tell Britney she was going home.

'Where you going?' Brit asked.

'To get our lunch.'

Britney smiled widely.

'Ah, that's my surprise. Today we're staying in.'

CHAPTER 91

'You set?' the guv asked him from the passenger seat. 'Do you want…'

'No, stay here. I'll give the nod.'

Bryant got out of the car and headed to the front door.

He turned around and took one look around the street while he waited. This was not going to be an easy conversation. For either of them.

He turned and knocked again. More forcefully this time. The car was parked on the drive.

He tried once more before taking a look through the curtainless window. The lounge appeared tidy and clean.

He looked back to the guv, who pointed to the side of the house.

He stepped away from the front door and tried the gate at the side. It opened.

He knocked the back door after checking. He could see nothing through the drawn-down blind. The back door was locked and a quick glance told him that no windows were open.

He felt his heart start to beat faster. Something here wasn't right.

He headed back around the front. The guv was already out of the car and heading towards him.

'Nothing open?' she asked.

He shook his head as he banged on the door again.

No response.

Bryant leaned down and poked his fingers through the letterbox. There were no brush or flaps to obscure his view.

Just inside the door was a table holding a dead plant, car keys and a couple of unopened letters. On the tiled floor were two pairs of shoes and a pair of trainers. His gaze moved forward to the stairs. His eyes travelled upwards as far as they could go and that's when he saw them.

His stomach lurched into his throat.

'Stand back,' he said, urgently to the guv.

'We going in?' she asked.

'Oh yeah.'

'Okay, you top, me bottom.'

'One, two, three,' he called.

On the count of three the guv threw all her weight against the bottom of the door and he focussed his strength on the top.

The door burst open, slammed against the wall and headed back towards them. Bryant threw his arm in the way and pushed it back open.

'Oh shit,' the guv said, seeing what he'd glimpsed from the letterbox.

The lifeless body of Richard Harrison hung from the upstairs light fitting. A pair of short stepladders had been kicked to the side.

They both stared at the sight before them. There was no doubt that the man had taken his own life.

'Well, Bryant,' the guv said. 'You certainly can't do what you came here to do.'

That was a fact.

He'd been here to arrest the man for murder.

CHAPTER 92

Penn registered the quizzical smile on the face of Josie Finch as she opened the door.

'You again?'

He wasn't offended. It was hardly a surprise. She'd had little to no interest from the police in eighteen months and now two visits in as many days.

'May I come in?' he asked, detecting the faint smell of burned toast in the background.

'Boyfriend changed the setting on the toaster again,' she offered. 'He likes his cremated and I like mine barely touched. Not sure how we've managed… I'm rambling, aren't I?'

He smiled but said nothing as she indicated for him to take a seat.

'I ramble when I'm nervous. You can only be back because you've got something to tell me, and I'm not sure how I'm going to feel about anything you have to say.'

'Mrs…'

'Josie, please,' she insisted.

'You know more about me than most of your work colleagues. See, the problem is, any news you have for me is going to require an emotional response of some kind and I'm not sure what I've got left to give, and if you want the truth in all its brutal glory, I don't know what news I'm hoping for more.'

Penn suspected that was the anger talking; resentment towards her mother for having left in the first place and rage at not being able to let it out. To be able to throw all the hurt at her mother. It was still bubbling away inside her. But she deserved the truth.

'Your mum's alive, Josie.'

She stared at him but he saw her body deflate before him as though she was letting out a breath she'd been holding for a year and a half.

'She's at a place called Unity Farm.'

'Is she okay. I mean, has she?...'

'She's fine, as far as we know, but we also know she's not being held by force.'

Penn watched as her eyes reddened around unshed tears. She deserved the whole truth.

'I understand,' she said, thickly. 'She's alive but she still doesn't want to see me.'

That wasn't a fact he could argue with.

'Josie, if it helps, the more we learn about this place the more we understand how persuasive they are. They don't use threats or violence. They use seduction and promises. They prey on people's weaknesses, their vulnerabilities. They find a small chink and then massage it until it is much more. They preyed on your mum's grief after your father died. They found some vulnerability in her and exploited—'

'She had no one to take care of,' Josie said, suddenly. 'You know I brushed it aside at the time, but every day after Dad died she'd mention that she was lost without him to take care of. She kept offering to come round here to clean and cook and...'

'Cook?' he asked.

Josie nodded. 'My dad never had a takeaway in his life. Mum wouldn't hear of it. She loved cooking from scratch. She was... is a brilliant cook. Her food...'

'It's what she does at the Farm, Josie.'

She smiled sadly. 'I'm not surprised. Mum would always do anything to help other people. She has a very big heart.'

'All is not lost, Josie. Maybe one day…'

'I can't think about that. If I do, I'll start to hope and then it'll just be disappointment all over again. A part of me has to stay angry with her. It's self-preservation.'

He understood. 'I just want you to know that she didn't just up and leave you. She would have been courted, flattered, complimented and manipulated.'

Right then Josie did shed a tear. 'Okay, I'll try and forgive her and then maybe I can forgive myself.'

'For what?' Penn asked.

'I'm afraid I wasn't totally honest with you,' she said, lowering her head. 'It's all my fault, you see. I told you about the last time we spoke, but what I didn't tell you was that we had a huge argument. I was being selfish and was wrapped up in my own grief. I wanted my mum to be as she'd always been – there for me – but my father's death hit her so hard she couldn't offer comfort to me or anyone else. Our grief didn't bring us closer together. I allowed it to tear us apart.'

Penn could hear the shame in her voice. 'That doesn't make you responsible.'

She looked up as tears rolled over her cheeks. 'I told her I never wanted to see her again. I'd just found out I was pregnant and my marriage was in trouble. I wasn't coping and I took it out on her. She tried to ring me the following day and I ignored her calls. I'm still not sure what I was punishing her for; I only know that it was the most painful time in both our lives.'

Penn felt for the torment this woman had put herself through. She wasn't the cause of her mother joining a manipulative cult, but their estrangement had certainly made Unity Farm's job easier. Sheila had been grieving for the love of her life and her only child wanted nothing to do with her.

'By the time the neighbour told me about the man she saw hanging around, my emotions were all over the…'

'Who?' Penn asked, confused. For some reason he'd assumed she'd been recruited by a woman.

'The big man. The man in black. The one with the massive Range Rover.'

CHAPTER 93

Stacey was dividing her time between trying to find out more about Kane Drummond, Jake Black and identifying their third victim.

So far, she'd managed to find out that Kane was a director in three separate companies. All of their details had been sent to the printer while she waded through the next batch of missing persons' reports.

The parameters were the most general she'd ever worked with. Male, five foot four, aged twenty-five to fifty-five, and in the water for between three months and three years. Any physical description further would have been a guess on his part, Keats had said, and so was not prepared to speculate.

A little speculation could be a good thing, Stacey thought, especially if it narrowed down the reports that fit within her criteria.

She sure wished Penn was here, she thought, as the next available record was for a man named Derek Noble, aged thirty-eight when he went missing eleven months ago.

Stacey began to read the detail of his case when her phone rang.

'Hey, you psychic or something?' she asked her colleague.

'I bet I can predict that you'll be having another cookie sometime soon.'

Damn him. She had been thinking about it.

'You on your way back. Please say yes,' she pleaded.

'Will be in a minute. I'm just outside the office of the estate agent who sold Sheila Thorpe's house. Spoke to a lady who wouldn't give me any specifics, but seemed to remember mention of the money being transferred to a company that sounded like something to do with lager. You come across anything even remotely like Stella, Budweiser, Carlsberg or?...'

'Charlsberg,' Stacey said, suddenly, reaching around to the printer behind.

'Stands a good chance, why?' Penn asked, with dread in his voice.

'It's one of Kane Drummond's companies.'

'Damn it,' Penn said. 'That's what I thought you were going to say.'

'So, what did he say?' Kim asked, as they drove towards the café and their third meeting with Kane. Bryant had called Travis as soon as they'd found Richard's body. A team had arrived within ten minutes, and Bryant would need to go into Worcester later to provide a full statement.

'I explained I'd been going there to get him to confess to the murder of Alice Lennox. He didn't sound particularly pleased. I begged him to go over Drake's confession and see for himself that the detail he offered was all in the press reports and that he'd offered nothing that only the murderer would know. I even mentioned the cigarette.'

Bryant had explained the significance of that to her earlier. Nowhere in his account of murdering Alice Lennox had Drake mentioned pausing to smoke a cigarette. He'd detailed everything else but not the one thing that had been withheld from the reports.

'And that's how I know Richard planned it,' Bryant said. 'We both stood and watched him smoke that cigarette outside the prison. I left before Richard so he must have gone and picked it up knowing exactly what he was going to do with it. But there were other things that didn't feel right. Drake never used an object to sexually assault his victims, despite what he said about Alice being a prostitute, and he never admitted so readily to committing the crimes. When questioned about the murder of Wendy and the attempted murder of Tina Crossley he instructed a solicitor and never spoke a word. The only thing that matched were the injuries sustained to Alice, which were identical to Wendy's wounds and which were completely familiar to Richard.'

'But why didn't he just kill Drake?' Kim asked. That was the man he hated.

'He couldn't. He told me outside the prison that he was terrified that Drake would find Wendy in the afterlife and that he wouldn't be there to protect her. Drake couldn't die before he did. He couldn't let her down again.'

Bryant glanced her way as though he expected her to argue or minimise the theory, but she couldn't because she'd had similar thoughts about her mother.

Personally she didn't believe in the afterlife but she lived with the fear that if she was wrong her mother would get the opportunity to torture her brother all over again, that he would be alone and powerless to protect himself.

She shook the thoughts away.

'So, what did Travis say when you told him all this?'

'He thanked me for my theory and said he'd give it some thought.'

'Ooh, brush off,' Kim noted.

'He can't ignore evidence.'

Kim wasn't sure evidence was what Travis had been presented with. She got the feeling it wasn't over for Bryant quite yet.

'He's already there,' Kim said, as Bryant parked in front of the café. Kane had secured a seat by the window. Despite this he sat with his back to the outside view.

Kim couldn't help the half-smile as she noted three cups on the table before him.

'Mr Drummond,' she said, sitting.

'Let's not show off, Inspector. We've already established that you know my real name and I think Kane will do fine.'

'Anything else you'd like to reveal about yourself?'

'No.'

She shrugged. 'It's okay. My DC is very talented. She'll have everything including your shoe size and favourite colour by the end of the day.'

'Eleven and black,' he said, without humour.

'Fabulous. That should save her some time.'

Kim wondered how it was possible that even now, on their third meeting, she detected neither positive nor negative vibes from this man. He was direct, curt and obnoxious but those qualities alone did not make him a murderer. Thankfully for her. But she picked up no empathy either. Everything he said was factual, like a bullet-point list, with no emotion behind it.

'I have a question for you, Kane. Just the one this time.'

'Go ahead,' he said, glancing to his left. Two middle-aged women shared a pot of tea.

'Where is Sophie Brown?'

No reaction. He shrugged. 'Unity Farm, I should think.'

'Apparently not.'

'How would you know? There are over a hundred people in there.'

'And one of them is ours,' Kim said, taking a sip of her drink.

Surprise turned to shock to disbelief to horror, and finally to anger. At last there was proof of emotion.

'You're kidding? Please tell me you're joking,' he said, leaning forward. His gaze was intense as he waited for her answer.

Kim shook her head. 'It was the only way to—'

'Fuck's sake,' he spat. 'At least tell me this person has some experience of cults and their practices; at the very least that they were briefed fully about the dangers of…'

'She's a police officer, of course we briefed her,' Kim snapped, defensively. No emotion for days and then everything at once at the mention of an undercover officer. What was that about? she wondered.

'Except you didn't even know yourself. You didn't even believe it was a cult.'

'We've been in touch. She's fine.'

Kane shook his head. 'Do you have any idea of the level of danger you've put…'

'You wouldn't happen to be trying to deflect attention from the question you were asked here to answer, would you?' she asked, bristling at his tone. 'So, I'll ask it again in case you've forgotten. What have you done with Sophie Brown?'

The shutter had closed once more on his emotions.

'What makes you think I've done anything with her?'

'You said so yourself the other day. Your last words to me hinted that you already had her.'

'And if I recall I also explained that if I did have her, the people paying me would be the first to know.'

'And just how much are they paying you, Kane? Is this one a reduced rate given the fuck-up with—'

'The mistake wasn't mine, Inspector,' he said, as a muscle along his cheekbone did a jig. The man didn't like to be accused of making mistakes.

She was about to goad him further when her phone rang. It was Penn, who knew full well where she was and what she was doing right now.

'Stone,' she answered, knowing he would only disturb her for something she needed to know.

She allowed him to speak without interruption, ensuring no emotion registered on her face.

She thanked him, ended the call and turned to Kane Drummond.

'Well, it appears I do have another question, after all.' She paused and glanced at her colleague before fixing her gaze on Kane.

'Why did Sheila Thorpe give all her money to you?'

CHAPTER 95

Once they'd finished breakfast, Britney had taken her on a tour of the outside space and explained where the pool and livestock were going. Every few minutes Tiff had opened her mouth to say that she was going to leave and each time she saw the raw excitement and animation on her friend's face and the words just wouldn't come.

She cursed herself for her own weakness as Britney guided her into the meditation room in barn 3.

'Ever tried it?'

Tiff shook her head.

'It's beginners' class today. Perfect for you, but I'll do it anyway. I don't need to listen any more and can go quite deep now,' she said, proudly.

After this class she would tell her, Tiff promised herself.

She took a seat on the floor and decided to use the time to get her thoughts straight, make a new plan, an exit strategy that wouldn't hurt her friend's feelings. All she had to do was close her eyes like the others and focus on her own thoughts instead of what was being said.

A woman named Mindy clothed in a maxidress and with a neck full of coloured beads explained they were doing a beginner's class and no one should worry if they didn't go deep first time.

'You learn to meditate by meditating,' she explained. 'You will go deeper over time and the results are better than sex, drugs or even Sheila's rice pudding.'

The seven other women in the room chuckled.

'Choose a mantra,' Mindy said to them all. 'It can be anything you want, a single word, a phrase but something that brings a positive feeling to your consciousness. Got one?'

Tiffany decided on the word 'Evita'. It was her favourite stage show. She'd seen it nine times, and the story of Eva Perón never failed to move her.

'Now, sit comfortably and quietly with your eyes closed. Relax the muscles in your body. Start with your feet, calves and then thighs. Shrug your shoulders and roll your head and neck around. Listen to your own breathing, focus on the breath in and out. Don't try to change it or slow it down, just focus on it. Listen to it. Enjoy the process of the breath entering and leaving your body. Notice that your thoughts will come and go without any effort. Allow them to flow in and out. We'll do that silently for a minute or two.'

Tiffany returned to her own thoughts and wondered what time of day was best to explain to Britney she was leaving. If she was honest the thought had occurred to her to try and persuade Britney to leave with her, but she didn't feel she had enough time to make her understand why. Perhaps in a few days she could meet Britney at the college and try to talk her into…

'Okay, now silently repeat your mantra in the same, simple, effortless way. As you repeat your mantra, thoughts will come and that's okay. Gently return to your mantra and be careful not to try to meditate. Don't force anything. Now let's try that for a few minutes.'

Tiffany allowed the thoughts to come and go. Maybe this was something she could use in her real life to escape the stress of her job and home life.

Evita.

She didn't want Brit to feel as though she was being deserted.

Evita.

But she knew she had to leave this place for her own peace of mind.

Evita.

Maybe Brit would be open to the…

Evita.

If she broached it…

Evita.

Evita.

Evita.

CHAPTER 96

Kane insisted on getting another drink before he'd answer the question.

Both her and Bryant had refused top-ups.

'Okay,' he said, sitting down. 'Sheila Thorpe works for me.'

'What?' Kim and Bryant said together.

'We know how Unity Farm recruits its members, especially the older ones. They read the local obituaries and go for the ones with the least relatives, especially women.'

'Explain,' Kim demanded.

'You've seen them yourself. Arthur Evans will be missed by his daughters, sons, wife, brother, father et cetera. Most relatives are listed. The longer the list, the harder the target because they have more family watching over them. The fewer relatives listed the easier to get to the money. Sheila's husband's obituary mentioned only a daughter and wife. Perfect. Sheila was easy pickings, as she had little family surrounding her.'

'And I suppose her estrangement from her daughter wouldn't have helped?' Kim asked.

'The less people to keep a person connected to their normal life the better,' he answered.

'So, how does it work?' Bryant asked. 'What are the actual mechanics of the manipulation?'

'One of the members will knock the door, offer to do jobs, get their feet inside the door and assess the first weakness to manipulate.'

'So, you got to Sheila first?' Kim asked.

He shook his head. 'Not before she'd already handed over most of her savings. We caught her before she sold the house and contents.'

'So, she sold them and gave the money to you instead?'

He shook his head. 'We have it all, safe and ready for when she leaves. It's all been signed over to her daughter if anything happens to her.'

'I don't get it. How did you turn her away from the cult?'

'Same way we do everyone else. Sheila was still living in her house. She hadn't moved into Unity Farm but was visiting almost daily. We showed her proof of how they work, read her articles about recruitment practices. She felt stupid and guilty and she wanted to help.'

'Did you know she'd had an argument with her daughter?' Kim asked, distaste at his tactics resting on her tongue.

'Yes.'

'Which is what you played on? Her good nature, eagerness to help other people and the fact she felt like she had no one left?'

He nodded without emotion. 'She agreed to carry on with the cult so we'd have someone on the inside. Our organisation is not traceable. We're not listed under Google so parents can't come to us direct, so we armed her, told her everything they'd do to win her over. She was prepared and fully briefed.'

Pieces of the puzzle started falling into place and Kim didn't much like the picture they were forming.

'So, Sheila identifies people inside with wealthy parents who you approach and offer your services for a fee?'

Jesus, manipulation really was the name of the game.

'Almost,' he said. 'Except Sheila's criteria for selection isn't based on wealthy parents, it's about people who may be at risk. It may be someone who is out of favour because they broke the rules. It could be someone being consistently mistreated for whatever reason. It may be someone being pressurised to bring more funds to the farm. There are many reasons.'

'Are you talking physical danger?'

He nodded. 'But, it's not the only kind.'

Kim now understood that he was referring to the long-term effects of joining a cult. 'So, Sheila identifies people she feels are at risk, communicates this to you, you snatch them and bring them back to their senses?'

He nodded.

'But how does she let you know?' Kim asked. Tiffany had already told her that people were not allowed their own mobile phone and Tiff's own phone had been stolen.

'One second and I'll explain,' he said, taking another sip of his drink.

Kim waited patiently as the two women sharing a pot of tea got up and left the café.

Kane walked over and lifted up the tea cup that was nearest to him. She and Bryant looked at each other as he retrieved a small square of folded paper.

Kim's gaze shot to the door.

'That was Sheila Thorpe?' she asked, unable to believe that the woman she'd been searching for in a lake had just been drinking tea behind her.

He nodded. 'She's doing the weekly food shop, but as you can see, she's never alone.'

'So that's a list of people she feels are in danger at the Farm?'

He nodded and opened up the paper.

He frowned.

'What?' Kim asked.

'Three names but very little information on the last one. Apparently she's worried about someone named Tiff.'

CHAPTER 97

Tiff shook the fatigue from her eyes as she headed to the front door of the farmhouse. It was barely one o'clock and she could easily have gone back to the room for a nap. It wasn't because of any kind of strenuous activity, quite the opposite. She had been relaxed to within an inch of her life.

After the meditation session Britney had taken her to barn number 5, to a woman named Violet who was learning Indian head massage and needed to practise. The woman had expertly kneaded sesame oil into her scalp, her strong fingers firmly working the pressure points all around her head. Tiffany had barely been able to form a thought as her mind had followed the rhythmic rubbing loosening tension and pressure. But she had made one decision before she'd given herself up to the experience.

The first chance she got, she was leaving and explaining to Britney would have to wait.

Time to just get on with it, she thought, heading outside. It would be a few minutes yet until Britney realised she hadn't just popped to the toilet.

She had decided to leave the same way they'd come. She guessed it was a longer trek to the road but at least she'd had some sense of direction. As soon as she got to the road she'd call the boss and let her know she was out.

Her stomach plummeted at the thought. Despite everything, she was leaving empty-handed but something inside told her it was more important to just leave.

She headed across the courtyard towards the foot of the hill. There was no one around and she could easily slip away, but a sudden thought occurred to her and she slowed her pace.

As she and Britney had headed in on that first night and stood at the top of the hill, she'd seen something glint in the wooded area. Was there a structure there? A building? Could Sophie Brown be in there?

Her mind wrestled with itself. On one hand was a growing urgency propelling her back towards civilisation and her own life, but the other hand was trying desperately not to leave this place with nothing. She'd been sent in to discover more about the cult and to locate Sophie Brown.

What if Sophie Brown had been here all along?

The anxiety began to grow in her stomach as she realised that she couldn't leave without at least checking it out.

Instead of heading straight for the hill she turned right into the wooded area.

Immediately the daylight receded as the trees entwined and arched above her, blocking out the sun. The shrubbery on either side of the narrow walking path was dense. She moved forward slowly, the whole scene reminding her of some sinister turn in a fairy tale. If she was watching this on the TV screen at home, creepy, ominous music would be growing in volume and warning her to stay out.

She smiled at her own dramatics but the unease didn't ebb away.

She took two more steps forward, heading into the darkness. A stinger caught her bare ankle. She bent down and rubbed it, knowing it was the worst thing she could do.

She straightened and caught a glimpse of some kind of structure up ahead.

She took a few more steps forward. The silence of the woods made way for the heavy beating of her heart, the blood pounding in her ears.

Two more steps forward.

The crack of a twig behind her.

She turned, right into the chest of Jake Black, who was only inches away.

Her heart rose up into her throat.

'Hey Tiff,' he said, peering down at her with a questioning gaze. 'What are you doing alone out here?'

She tried to gather herself quickly and cover up the trembling of her limbs.

Her heart thumped in her chest.

'J-Just getting a little air,' she replied.

He placed a warm, firm hand on her shoulder and turned her around.

'I think it's best if we go back to the house, don't you?'

CHAPTER 98

'Where do you want me?' Penn asked, sliding into his chair.

Stacey breathed a sigh of relief to have her colleague back. She had multiple screens open on her computer and was flitting between them all.

'Can you find out whatever you can about Jake Black, cos I might have a possible contender for our guy in the lake.'

'On it, boss,' he said.

Stacey chuckled. He was higher in rank than her but ranks meant nothing to Penn. He went where the work sent him. Sometimes that was pounding the streets and other times pounding the keys.

She turned her attention back to Derek Noble, the man who had flitted onto her screen right before Penn had called.

Of his thirty-eight years he'd been known to them for fifteen. From the age of seventeen he'd been arrested over twenty times for offences that had escalated over the years. The last seven offences had been drug related, culminating in a violent episode where a man had been blinded. Derek Noble had been put away for his longest stretch of six years in 2012 and had maintained radio silence ever since. The records stated that he'd been released from prison late 2018. Had he been murdered as soon as he walked out of prison? Was it somehow related to his previous crimes; revenge perhaps, and nothing to do with their murders? His life had been anything but normal and he must have made a few enemies along the way.

If this guy wasn't connected to their case, they needed to rule him out straight away. For all she knew, this wasn't even the guy they were searching for. She could be wasting time passing this on to the boss. She made up her mind. She'd pass the information on and keep looking.

CHAPTER 99

'Anything back yet?' Bryant asked as he headed towards Hayes Lane and the address given to them by Stacey. The constable hadn't sounded convinced this was their man and Kim could understand why. There was no indication of him having any link to their other victims or to Unity Farm. But they were close to the trading estate, so it was worth a shot, even if it was to rule him out.

'Nothing since the first message,' she said, glancing down at the phone that hadn't been out of her hand since they'd left Kane sitting in the café.

She had texted Tiff immediately after seeing her name on that piece of paper. Just a short message asking if she was okay. Her heart had been hammering in her chest waiting for a response. It was only minutes until she received a reply saying

Fine, speak soon.

Kim had sent a further message asking where she was but nothing had come back.

'She'll be fine,' Bryant said. 'She knows what she's doing. If she senses any danger, she'll let us know.'

'I hope you're right,' Kim said as Bryant pulled up outside Neeley's Auto Shop on the Forge Trading Estate.

'So, the owner of this place reported our guy missing?' Bryant asked as they got out the car.

'Yep, George Neeley himself,' she said, pushing open a heavy glass door into a small reception area. The space was tidy with two chairs and a self-serve coffee machine. A plug-in air freshener was doing nothing to mask the odour of petrol, grease and diesel fumes, thank goodness. It was a blend of smells that made her feel right at home.

The reception area was unmanned but a bell was attached to the desk. Kim pressed it and heard it sound in the workshop behind.

A man appeared from beneath a ramp and peered at her through the glass window.

He shouted something to a colleague and walked into the reception, wiping his hand on a dirty rag. A blast of lunchtime traffic news filtered through the door behind him from a radio blaring somewhere in the workshop.

'George Neeley?' Kim asked, holding up her ID.

'Depends. If he's in trouble I ay sid 'im for months, if not I'm yer mon.'

Kim worked her way through the thick Black Country accent to understand they were talking to the owner of the business.

'Mr Neeley, we're here to talk about a man named Derek Noble.'

He frowned and glanced up to his left as though that's where he'd find the information.

'You reported him missing.'

'Ah, yow mean Nobbie?'

Okay, Kim thought. Close enough.

'Was he a friend of yours?'

George shook his head. 'Employee. I gid the chap a job when he gor out of prison. Doin me bit for the community and he wore 'alf bad to be fair.'

'Go on,' Kim said.

'Took 'im on to do a bit of sweeping and fetching and carrying, to free up me blokes a bit. Grunt work, really, but for a little 'un he 'ad some stamina and was a bloody hard worker.'

'You knew of his past?' Kim asked, trying to marry the two images of the same man. His life prior to prison read nothing like the picture George was painting in her mind.

'Yeah, yeah but it was a scheme, wore it? It day cost me a penny to employ him for six months. The government paid and I got free labour.'

Kim was beginning to change her opinion on this man's charitable motivations.

'So, you kept him for six months?'

George shook his head 'Nah, by the time the scheme ended Nobbie was wuth his weight in gold. He was driving customers to work, opening up, closing up, keeping the place tidy, the machines clean and valeting the cars before they went back out. We wore never goona let 'im goo.'

Her opinion warmed again.

'Listen, I dow put much faith in our prisons but Nobbie surprised me. He wanted to change. He wore 'alf sorry for all the shit he'd caused and all the folks he'd hurt. He was trying to mek amends.'

Kim just let him talk.

'In fact the last day he was here, he was gooin to see somebody. A wench he'd hurt in his past. He day give me no details but showed me the mek up present he'd bought. Lovely it was. A silver necklace in a red velvet box.'

CHAPTER 100

'Stacey, he's our guy,' Kim said when they were back in the car.

'Find out everything you can about him. We're on our way back in,' she added, before ending the call.

'No obvious link, is there?' Bryant asked, as he headed towards the town centre.

'There's something, Bryant. It's too coincidental that he was found in the same lake as Tyler Short. He must have some kind of link to Unity Farm.'

She turned her attention to the phone still in her hand. Still no further messages from Tiff.

'Stop here,' Kim said, taking off her seatbelt.

She hadn't lied to Stacey. They were on their way back, but she had just one stop to make first.

She strode around the building to the front car park of the college.

Students were streaming out of the entrance, taking an early mark on a Friday afternoon.

Kim stood on the wall, trying to pick out a redhead and a blonde.

She tuned out the excited pre-weekend chatter of the students and looked in every direction.

The crowds began to thin and her suspicions were correct.

Not only was she receiving no contact from the undercover police officer.

She no longer knew for sure where Tiffany was.

CHAPTER 101

Tiff took a deep breath as she sat down on the bed.

As they'd walked back from the edge of the woods, she had talked nonstop about the Farm and all the things she had experienced in her time there. Whether her efforts to distract him from any suspicion of her wanting to leave had worked she had no idea. She wasn't even sure why she was concerned about him knowing that she'd been thinking of leaving but she was.

Jake had told her to go and take a bit of time for herself in her room while he tracked down Britney.

She resigned herself to the fact she was going to have to let the boss know she was coming out. Yes, she'd failed but right now that mattered less to her than getting away from this place and back to some kind of normality.

She'd take the opportunity to text now while she waited for Brit to come back, and later she'd eat her meal, pretend everything was normal and then find a way to slip out and head to the hill. And this time she wouldn't stop.

She reached into her back pocket for the phone. The cardigan she was wearing was longer so she'd been able to move it from the front of her jeans.

It wasn't there.

She checked her back-left pocket but already knew she wouldn't have put it there.

She stood up and looked around the bed. Maybe it had come out as she'd sat down. She moved the quilt around and checked the floor, feeling the heat flood her face.

Damn it. Her one link to the outside world. Gone.

She paced the room as she retraced her steps after sending that short message to the boss.

Just after the Indian head massage, they'd headed to the toilets.

Oh no, she remembered now. She'd taken it from her back pocket and placed it on the sanitary bin so it didn't fall out as she undid her jeans. Damn, if Brit had found it she'd know everything. She'd know that Tiff had been lying to her the whole time. She intended to tell her friend the truth but not until she was safely away from Unity Farm.

Tiff headed out of the room and walked quickly to the toilets, waving and smiling as she went. She had to find the phone. She had no other way to let the boss know she was coming out.

She pushed open the door. Thankfully it was empty as people were making their way to the food hall. She went straight for the middle cubicle. The phone wasn't on the sanitary bin where she'd left it. Maybe it had fallen and been kicked along the floor.

She entered each cubicle, moving the bins and looking around.

By the time she reached the end cubicle, her heart was hammering in her chest and the sweat was forming on her forehead.

The phone was no longer here.

Her one link to the outside world was gone.

CHAPTER 102

Kim glanced at her phone again while she waited for Bryant to re-join them in the squad room. Still no reply from Tiffany, but the tick and the timestamp told her the messages had been read. Why the hell was she not replying?

Kim took a moment to pour coffee while the other two were tapping away furiously at their keyboards.

She glanced outside as the light on the car park began to fade. She peered more closely at the figure pacing and waving his arms around as he spoke on the phone.

Shit, what now? she wondered, although she had a sneaking suspicion she knew, had known what was coming all day.

'Be back in a sec, guys,' she said, leaving the coffee for now.

Kim stepped outside just as Bryant ended the call.

'They've fucking charged him,' he bellowed at her. His eyes were ablaze, his body tense as he continued to pace back and forth.

Yep, that's what she'd thought.

'They know they have the wrong man. He didn't do it, Kim. They're charging the wrong man. We can't let this happen.'

Kim ignored the use of her first name during work hours. It only demonstrated how emotional he was about the Peter Drake situation. She'd given thought to it herself throughout the day.

'Bryant, there's nothing we can do.'

'You're joking?' he asked, incredulously. 'You who believes wholeheartedly in justice?'

She knew this was going to be a difficult sell, especially coming from her. He knew she was a firm believer in the right people being punished for the right crime, but Travis wasn't her and he was never going to entertain anything Bryant had to say.

'Look, you got nothing from Harrison. What do you expect Travis to do? He has a victim and a confession and physical evidence that links the two. How is he not going to put them together when the man you suspect is now dead?'

Every word was leaving a bad taste in her mouth but she had to do what was right for her friend. He had to let it go.

'You don't believe me?' he asked.

Kim didn't hesitate. 'Of course I believe you. You know these people better than I do and I trust your judgement, but you can't try a dead man.' She took a breath. 'Travis has no choice. If he puts blind faith in you, he gets no conviction and he has to let Peter Drake go. A prospect that no one likes very much.'

'But justice isn't always easy, guv,' he said.

'And neither is it always black and white,' she said, sitting on the wall.

Bryant followed suit and sat beside her.

'That man carried out horrific crimes and ruined countless lives. Most people seem to feel he is capable of doing it again. You think he is. Travis thinks he is.'

'But he didn't…'

'Bryant, do you think he got enough time for what he did?'

'Never.'

'You think the public is at risk if he's set free?'

Bryant nodded.

'Then at what price do you get your black and white justice?' she asked. 'It's not ideal but he is going back to prison where he belongs and will never get the chance to hurt anyone again.'

He shook his head. 'It just feels…'

'And you're forgetting one very important factor, Bryant?'

'Go on.'

Thank goodness, he was finally listening.

'He confessed. For whatever reason, Peter Drake has confessed. He either wants to be back in prison or feels he should be. Either way he's going back before he can do any more harm.'

Bryant rubbed at his hair, trying to resolve the demons in his head.

'Okay, guv, just one question, if you don't mind.'

'Go on.'

'Would you have done what Travis has done?'

Kim was saved from answering as her phone rang.

Her first thought was Tiffany.

'Go ahead, Stace,' she said.

'Sorry, boss, but we need you up here, now.'

'On our way,' she said, ending the call.

She and Bryant made the journey back to the squad room in silence. She felt like taking a detour to the bathroom to wash her mouth out with soap.

He didn't push her for an answer to his earlier question.

Because he already knew what it was.

CHAPTER 103

'I think Tiff might be in danger,' Stacey said.

'I might know where Sophie is,' Penn said.

Kim held up her hands as Bryant took a seat. She'd only been gone a few minutes.

'Stacey, go,' Kim said, taking a sip of her cold coffee.

'The second person who died at Jake Black's first cult, Christopher Brook, he was a police officer, undercover.'

Kim froze and a heavy silence settled around them all.

'That fact didn't reach the press until the inquest, which recorded a suicide verdict based on the testimony of people at the cult. The case landed in the news on the same day as the Chancellor's Budget so got no attention. A wrongful death lawsuit was filed by the family against Somerset and Avon Police, which was settled, quietly, out of court.'

'Thanks, Stace,' Kim said, maintaining her composure. One undercover police officer had already lost his life in connection with Jake Black, and she'd sent another one right into the fire.

'Penn?' she said, checking her phone once more.

Nothing. Damn it.

'Charlsberg Holdings, which belongs to Kane Drummond, owns three separate properties. One appears to be Kane's home in West Hagley, the second is a cottage on the outskirts of Pershore and the third is a warehouse in Kidderminster.'

'Does the cottage have outbuildings?' Kim asked, picturing a peaceful, semi-rural location.

Penn nodded and got the property on the screen. 'Just west of the cottage is a small barn and some kind of storage shed.'

Kim stood behind him. The place was perfect for hiding someone until you knew what to do with them. There was no main road for miles and the property was accessed through a couple of miles of single-track lanes.

'Show me the warehouse.'

Penn clicked onto another open tab.

The warehouse was situated on the edge of a disused quarry half a mile out of the town centre. Around it were smaller properties and overspill parking spaces. It was far busier, with more potential to be seen.

'Okay, Penn, Stacey, I need you to go find out if Kane Drummond is holding Sophie Brown.'

'You want us to go to the cottage?' Stacey asked.

She shook her head. 'The warehouse.'

Both officers looked at her doubtfully.

'The cottage is too far. Kane needs faster access. If she's alive she's going to be close.'

She turned to Bryant. 'Grab your coat, Bryant, we're going the other way.'

She'd had enough pissing around. It was time to go get their colleague back.

CHAPTER 104

'You really think she's in danger, guv, given what Stacey said?' Bryant asked, as they headed towards Wolverley.

'I'd feel better if she'd replied to my texts,' Kim answered.

She'd sent another one which had been read immediately, but still no response. How was she able to keep reading them but not send a short one back to confirm all was well?

'What if it isn't Tiff reading them?' Bryant asked, reaching down into her deepest fears. Especially after what Stacey had just told them.

For the hundredth time, she regretted the moment she'd had the idea to send Tiffany in there. Yes, she was a police officer and not a child but she was also up against a force greater than any of them had imagined. After her conversation with Kane she realised she hadn't taken the threat of a cult seriously. And she had sent Tiffany in there alone.

'You know, Bryant, if anything happens to her…'

'I know, guv.'

She turned and stared out the window, allowing Bryant to concentrate on getting to the Farm as quickly as possible. She cursed herself again for sending Tiffany into a situation for which none of them were prepared. Her own refusal to accept the risks of such a group had potentially endangered the life of one of her colleagues.

If anything happened to Tiffany she would never forgive herself.

And the speed of Bryant's driving told her he was just as concerned as she was.

CHAPTER 105

'You know, Stace, I don't like to question the boss but…'

'Yeah, I'm wondering if we're in the right place too,' Stacey replied as they pulled off the main road.

Although it was almost seven there were still people locking up premises and leaving work late on a Friday night right by the warehouse.

Every second gave Stacey more doubts that they were in the right place.

The warehouse looked to be the size of a football pitch and had a large roller shutter door on the front and a single glass entrance door. Any stickers and signs had been peeled off, leaving patches of old glue all around the glass. There was no clue as to what the place had previously been used for, but right now it looked derelict.

'Now what?' Stacey asked.

Penn looked at the lock on the roller shutter door and then hurried around the side.

Stacey moved from one foot to the other.

'I reckon I can get in,' he said, rubbing his hands.

'What, around the side?' she asked.

He shook his head. 'Nah, that one's double locked. I've got a better chance with the roller shutter. Saw a colleague do it once.'

'Penn, that's in full view,' she hissed.

'Stand in front of me and stop looking so guilty.'

'We're breaking in,' she said as he lowered himself to the ground.

'We're the police,' he reminded her.

'Without a bloody warrant,' she snapped back.

'You think any magistrate would issue one given what we have?'

Stacey shook her head. Magistrates issued them providing reasonable grounds had been established to suspect an offence had been committed. They had nothing.

'So, just stand still and keep the blood off your hands.'

Stacey rolled her eyes at the analogy. They might be feet away from another dead body.

She shielded him as best she could while she heard an array of frustrated oofs and aahars coming from his lips.

But the longer she stood there the more she came around to the boss's thinking. They were actively breaking into a building and not one person was taking a bit of notice, so they'd hardly notice the comings and goings of a vehicle.

'Got it,' Penn said, as she heard a metallic snap.

Within seconds the roller shutter was sliding up and still no attention came their way.

When it was about waist high, they both ducked underneath it and pulled it back down, them into total darkness.

'Well, that…' Her words trailed away as a single beam of light shone up, illuminating the immediate area.

'Boy scout,' Penn explained, holding the torch beneath his chin, lighting up his face like a Halloween pumpkin.

'Boo.'

'Stop it, Penn, that's creepy,' she hissed.

'Okay, try and stay close – we don't know what's in here.'

Stacey was about to remind him she wasn't Jasper when she remembered there was only one torch. She took out her phone and aimed the light at his feet and followed.

Penn shone the light around the vast space, which appeared to be empty and hazard free. Breeze-block walls were painted white and there was a vague smell of cleaning detergent. She heard a slow rhythmic dripping sound somewhere in the distance.

Penn waved the torch around until the beam found the very end of the space at the furthest point away.

'What's that over there?' Stacey asked, when the torch rested on something solid in the distance.

Penn shone the torch again while moving slowly deeper into the space.

'Some kind of container,' he said.

'Is that a table next to it?' she asked.

He continued moving slowly towards it. She pointed her phone at his feet and followed the direction of the torch.

The container was made of blue steel. It reminded her of cargo containers but smaller. She'd seen similar ones on building sites.

They reached the table first, which was no more than twenty feet from the container.

Penn stopped walking and shone the light.

'What the hell?' Stacey asked, as the torchlight swept across, illuminating three bottles of water, a bottle of cola, two packs of sandwiches and a few pieces of fruit.

'Shit party,' Penn said.

'Yeah, but for who?' Stacey asked, glancing towards the container door.

Penn shone the torch at the door handle as they stood side by side staring at it.

'Penn, do you think she's in there?' Stacey asked, above the sound of her own beating heart.

'Only one way to find out,' he said, focussing the beam of the torch.

Stacey took a step forward, her hand almost on the cold metal handle.

A low voice sounded behind her.

'What the hell do you think you're doing?'

CHAPTER 106

Britney burst into the room breathless with excitement.

'Ohmygod, Tiff, you're never going to believe what's happened.'

'What?'

'Jake wants us to go meditate with him.'

'Why? I mean…'

'Who cares?' she asked, looking like she'd lost her mind.

Brit bounced down on the bed beside her.

'I know you probably don't get this yet but Jake is on a totally different intellectual and spiritual plane to the rest of us. Jake has a special place on the grounds where he chooses to meditate alone. Occasionally, I mean rarely, he invites a trusted member of the group to share the experience with him. Jeez, Lorna has been here ten years and she's only been invited once. It's an honour and a privilege, Tiff, now come on and get ready. He won't be happy if we keep him waiting.'

Tiffany felt the fear crawl all over her.

The man had caught her trying to snoop earlier and somehow, somewhere, she had lost a phone that gave everything away.

She felt the perspiration begin to prick at her skin.

Lorna had been here for ten years and she'd been here two days. Why was he inviting her now?

She realised her chance to get away was gone, as Britney opened the door to the room.

Tiff had no choice but to follow her friend.

CHAPTER 107

Although she'd never met him, Stacey knew she was looking up into the face of Kane Drummond, who towered above them both. His expression was unreadable but it was on a face that was vaguely familiar to her already. A few things fell into place but now was not the time. They were here for one reason only.

'Sophie's in there, isn't she?' she asked, trying to steady her voice.

Kane said nothing.

'You're holding her against her will?' Penn added.

'It's not what you think.'

Penn glanced around at the desolate warehouse and the locked container door.

'Really? Hardly five star is it?'

Kane regarded them silently for just a few seconds before leaning forward and opening the door to the container. It wasn't locked.

As the door opened a shaft of light reached out to them. Stacey blinked away the brightness that assaulted her eyes. As her sight adjusted, her gaze rested on the unmistakeable form of Sophie Brown sitting upright in a dining chair. The second thing she noticed were the tearstains that travelled down her cheeks.

Stacey took a step forward, noting the similar pretty features and blonde hair of her older sister.

Kane placed a hand on her arm. 'Look and wait.'

Inside the container was another table. On it were more bottles of water and packs of food. Additionally, there were three piles of what looked like freshly laundered and folded clothes. A fan was placed in one corner and a blow heater in the other. Stacey's gaze wandered over to Sophie, her forearms held rigid against the arms of the chair; a cushion had been placed behind her back.

'Wh-who's there?' Sophie asked, moving her head from side to side.

Stacey wanted to go to her, but Kane's hand was still on her arm.

'Pl-Please... who's there? Please take the blindfold off me so I can see you.'

Stacey's mouth fell open.

There was no blindfold.

Sophie's eyes were tightly closed.

'Untie me, you bastard,' she cried.

There were no ties.

Her arms and feet were free to move any time she wanted.

Stacey swallowed hard and looked at Kane.

What the hell was going on here?

CHAPTER 108

The dirt track deposited them at the shed and fenced area as the last rays of sun disappeared behind a hill. Stacey had been unable to locate any other means of entry on Google Earth due to overhanging trees. As Kim had noted the other day, there was no break in the fence line and the fence itself was ten feet high. Even after scaling it they would have a half-mile jog to the farmhouse.

'Bryant…?' she said, looking to him and then the fence.

'Ah, damn it. I need a new car anyway.'

He pulled the gear stick into reverse and backed up about fifty feet.

'Ready?'

Kim nodded as he changed gears and hit the accelerator.

Kim braced herself as the shiny metal fence hurtled towards her. The sickening sound of metal on metal met her ears as sparks flew around them. The car hit resistance for just a second before the metal fencing was ripped from its post and flew across the front of the car.

'Jeez, Bryant. Woody would be so proud of the steadying influence you have on me.'

'More worried about explaining it to the wife to be honest,' he muttered, getting the car onto the line of tarmac that led all the way to the house.

Bryant kept up the speed and pulled up short at the front of the house. A group had gathered having heard the noise of the approaching car.

Kim recognised one woman in particular and headed straight for her. Everyone else moved aside.

'Sheila, where's Tiffany?'

'Who?… I don't…'

'Please don't lie. Kane told us everything. Now, where is she?' Kim didn't have the time to explain.

'Meditating with Jake.'

'Where?'

Sheila nodded towards the wooded area at the foot of the hill.

'A cabin about a quarter-mile in.'

Kim hesitated for just a second.

'For what it's worth, your daughter misses you very much.' She didn't wait for a response but Sheila's words followed her.

'Stick to the path. There are traps…'

Kim threw her hand in the air to signal that she'd heard.

'What exactly are they trying to catch?' Bryant asked, as they hit the trodden-down path, leaving the lights of the Farm behind.

'Ssh…' Kim said, knowing their voices would carry in the silence.

The path into the woods was barely discernible and was only a couple of feet wide. Although it was only dusk, the towering trees blocked out the last of the fading light.

'Stay behind,' she advised her colleague, who was taking the torch from his pocket.

'Too bright,' she said, taking out her mobile phone. One slip and the beam would light up the whole area, alerting Jake to their presence. She wanted the element of surprise on her side.

'Hang on, guv, what's that hanging?…'

'Bryant, don't veer…'

Her warning came too late as she heard the thud of him falling to the ground, dead leaves crunching around him.

'What the hell?'

'Fuck, Bryant, what have you?…'

She stopped speaking as he shone the torch down at his feet. Damn it, he'd trodden on a tripwire leg snare. The cord around his leg stretched up to a thick branch on a tree about twelve feet away.

'Shit,' he said, trying to pull the rope from around his ankles.

The more he pulled, the tighter it got.

'Bryant, stop,' she warned. It was a complex knot and he was going to cut off the circulation if he kept tugging at it. Discomfort was already shaping his face. The only way to free him safely was with a knife.

Indecision tugged at her. One colleague was injured and another…

'Go,' Bryant hissed, in a whisper shout. 'I'll keep still, I swear.'

'You sure?'

He nodded and moved his hand away from the rope.

She shone the phone back down to the ground, locating the exact line of the path.

She would have to face Jake Black alone.

CHAPTER 109

Kane let go of Stacey's arm and moved slowly towards Sophie.

Stacey glanced at Penn, who was as dumbfounded as she was.

She watched as Kane gently touched the skin at the girl's wrist.

'There are no ties, Sophie,' he said, gently. 'You can move your arms and open your eyes whenever you want.'

'Fuck off,' she hissed. 'He told me you'd say that. He told me everything you'd do to try and brainwash me. He told me. He knows all your tricks. He knows everything.'

Kane continued to rub the bare skin on her wrist.

'Is this the same man who told you that your parents didn't really want you, that you were an accident and they'd only ever loved Sammy?' Kane asked, quietly.

A tear forced its way from the corner of her eye.

'Yes, and it was true. I hate them, both of them. They love her more than me and I can prove it. Jake explained it to me.'

A wave of sadness engulfed Stacey as she watched this young girl, lost inside herself.

Stacey met Kane's gaze and he shook his head. She didn't know her sister was dead.

Kane returned to stand beside Stacey. 'Almost five days she's refused to open her eyes. I can't force her. That's the whole point. I have to allow her to understand and realise on her own that I don't have her tied down.'

'How did she get this way?' Stacey whispered.

'My understanding is that Jake played the sisters off against each other. Sophie followed Sammy into the cult because she idolised her, but Jake broke that bond and enforced the separation once Sammy was gone. He's done a real number on her, but forcing her to open her eyes will only reinforce everything she's been told.'

'She doesn't trust you,' Penn said, quietly. 'You're everything Jake warned her against. She's been expecting everything you've said and done. Every time you speak you prove Jake right and strengthen his hold of her mind. You're actually making it worse.'

Kane nodded his agreement. 'With the way she now feels about her parents I'm not sure they'd have any more luck.'

Stacey swallowed back the emotion as she watched the girl fidgeting in the chair but never once moving beyond the invisible ties that bound her.

Of course everything Jake said was true, she thought. If he had convinced her about her parents then she would believe him on everything.

'May I speak to her?' Stacey whispered.

Sophie tipped her head at the unfamiliar sound of a woman's voice. There was something Kane had said that she might be able to work with.

'Don't mention Sammy. She can't take that yet.'

Stacey nodded her understanding and approached cautiously.

'Hey, Sophie, my name's Stacey and I'm a friend of your mum and dad.'

Her face tightened.

'Listen, I don't know Jake but I think he might be wrong about your parents.'

'They proved him right,' she spat.

'By taking Sammy first?' Stacey asked.

She nodded.

Of course the master manipulator had turned that around to poison her mind. Both girls were in the cult and yet they'd chosen to get Sammy out and not her.

'Ah, but I know why they did that. Your mum told me that you were the stronger of the two of you. That's why they took Sammy first.'

Sophie shook her head. 'No that's…'

'Sophie, I have no reason to lie and I'm sure Jake thought he was helping, but even your dad said you'd be stronger and would cope better. They trusted in your strength and asked Kane to get you as soon as he could. They knew Sammy was weaker than you.'

Stacey could see that Kane was uncomfortable with her lying, but the spell that had hung fast for days needed to be broken and the only way to do that was to cast even just a shadow of doubt on Jake's words without calling him a liar. She would not accept that accusation. That could come later but right now all that was needed was an entry point, a way to reach the girl inside.

'Sophie, I'm going to untie your ankles and your wrists, okay?'
Sophie nodded.

Stacey leaned down and fussed around her ankles, making sure she made contact with the skin. She repeated the process around the wrists.

She stood and leaned over the trembling girl, who hadn't moved an inch.

'Now I'm taking off the blindfold.'

Stacey touched the girl's cheeks gently and then fumbled at the back of her head.

'Okay, sweetie, it's all gone. You're totally free now.'

With a hammering heart, Stacey touched the girl's hand.

'Come on, Sophie, please look at me. Trust me that the blindfold is gone.'

Sophie finally opened her eyes.

CHAPTER 110

Kim knew she was just metres away from the cabin. A roaming torchlight and the low hum of voices told her she was getting close.

Being forced to walk slowly and carefully had given her mind a chance to clear. For the life of her she hadn't been able to work out the link to the death of Derek Noble, their third victim. He had no connection to the college or any of the victims. But for his body to be found in the same place as Tyler had to mean something. And now she knew what it was.

She stood perfectly still as she reached the trees that circled the cabin. Two Victorian street lamps either side of the wooden structure lit up the small clearing and the leaves already being shed from the overhanging branches. Two figures sat on a fallen log. The glint of something in the lamp light confirmed her suspicions.

She was close enough to hear every word.

'I'm sure he'll be here in a minute,' the redheaded girl said.

'That's not true at all, is it, Britney?' Kim asked, stepping out of the shadows.

Both Tiff and Britney turned to stare at her, one expression bathed in relief and the other rage.

In a split second Britney whirled around, grabbing Tiff's hair and forcing her to the ground.

'Get away from us,' Britney cried out. 'You're just trying to take her away from me.'

Tiff cried out in pain as Britney wound her hand further and further into her hair. Britney reached behind her and took a knife from her back pocket.

'Take one step and I'll slice her throat.'

'Like you did with Sammy?' Kim asked, not moving an inch. 'Was she your best friend too?'

The fog had cleared in her mind as she'd left Bryant behind. She remembered Kane's words about newbies being flattered and showered with love. How potent that was and the power it had on the individual receiving the attention; but how powerful for the person showering the love, especially if they themselves were vulnerable too.

'You recruited Sammy, didn't you, from the college?'

Britney said nothing.

'There was no way she wouldn't allow you into her flat. She trusted you and you killed her.'

'She left me,' Brit said, as though that explained everything.

'And what about Tyler? You liked him, didn't you? Even though you weren't supposed to find love at the farm, you fell in love with Tyler?'

'He loved me too,' she growled, pulling tighter on Tiffany's hair.

'But he left after Sammy went, didn't he? He followed her into the cult and he followed her back out again. He may have loved you but he was obsessed with her, had been for years.'

Britney began pulling back and forth on Tiff's hair. The hand holding the knife was flailing around all over the place.

'He shouldn't have left me,' she said, her face creasing into an ugly sneer.

'Like your father did?' Kim asked, glancing at the butterfly hanging around her neck.

'Everyone leaves me,' she said. 'And Tiff was going to leave me too. I saw the messages between the two of you. She never liked me from the first—'

'Is that what you think?' Kim asked, trying to divert Britney's hatred away from Tiffany. She tried to think quickly and prayed Tiff had said nothing.

'You read the messages and so you know why Tiff was here, but did you look at the call register?'

Brit's face creased in confusion.

Thank God.

'She called me earlier,' Kim said, being as vague about the time as she could. She didn't know when Britney had gotten hold of the phone.

'Yeah, she called. She told me she didn't want to leave. She said she'd met a new friend and she wanted to stay here for a while. She said she wanted to be with you.'

'No, no, she hates me, just like…'

'Britney, no one hated you,' Kim said, realising that she had to keep talking. She had to throw as much doubt and uncertainty at her to douse her rage at Tiffany before she did something stupid.

'Even your father didn't hate you. Yes, he left when you were young. He was in a bad state but he came looking for you, didn't he? Bought you that necklace. He told all his colleagues about you, about how…'

'I don't believe you,' Brit said, as the strength returned to her voice.

Too abstract, Kim realised. It was a man she had never really known. She'd veered too far off track but she had one last ace to play.

'Brit, Sammy didn't leave you either.'

'Of course, she did. She hated…'

Why the hell was the girl convinced that all the people who had left hated her?

'She was snatched,' Kim explained. 'She didn't run away. It was all arranged by her parents. Sammy didn't have any choice. She didn't even know it was going to happen.' Kim paused. 'She didn't hate you and she didn't leave.'

'No… no… no,' she cried, shaking her head. 'It's not true. She left me. They all left me. Tiff was going…'

'I wasn't Brit, I swear,' Tiff said, trying to move her head with Britney's erratic actions.

'She's right, I called and told her I wanted to stay. I wanted to learn more from you. We've had such a laugh and I love being with you.'

'You do?' Brit asked, in a voice that held hope that it had all been a misunderstanding and everything could go back to the way it had been earlier.

Britney's hesitation was all Tiffany needed to turn herself one hundred and eighty degrees and head-butt Britney in the stomach.

Britney's hand unwound from Tiff's hair as she fell backwards.

Kim took the opportunity to lurch forward and wrestle the knife from Britney's hand by applying pressure to the wrist.

Britney bucked and flipped, but Tiffany was already straddled across her, in a move that Kim had used herself once or twice.

Kim felt the knife drop from her hand as a force from behind knocked her to the ground.

CHAPTER 111

Kim turned to see Jake Black standing over Tiffany and Britney with the knife in his hand.

'Get off her,' Jake said, touching Tiff between the shoulders with the blade. His expression was unreadable.

'Do it,' Kim said, turning herself to a sitting position. The person who held the knife held the power.

Tiff moved aside and Britney sat upright.

'Oh, Britney, what have you done?' Jake asked, gently.

'She was going to leave me, Jake. Just like the rest of them. I had to stop her,' Britney said, staring up at him. Both she and Tiff were forgotten, and the girl only had eyes for the man towering over her.

'We don't hurt people, Brit,' he said, softly.

Kim studied his face. The words were gentle but the expression in his eyes was hard. His right hand gripped the knife tightly.

A shiver ran down her body. Jake Black was not here to help.

She had no idea what he planned to do with the knife in his hand and until she did, she couldn't move. He was too close to Britney and in striking distance of Tiff.

'But you said they all hated me, you told me where Sammy lived and…'

'I told you so that you'd know she was safe. I knew how close you two were. I wanted you to know she was okay.'

'B-But… you said they needed to be punished… that they had let us down. That they were ungrateful and that they were going to say bad things about the farm… about the family.'

'I didn't mean that *we* had to punish them, Britney,' he said, smoothly.

'You told me they hated me, that they'd never liked me.'

Kim's heart broke for the child in Britney that was speaking as the depth of Jake's manipulation became clear.

He shrugged. 'They didn't stay for you, did they? No one stayed for you.'

The tears were now running fast over Britney's cheeks. Tiffany gazed at her with concern and then turned her head to Kim.

Kim shook her head. Jake was still holding the knife and neither of them was close enough to get up and wrestle it from him before he could do any damage.

'I told you everything, about my father and...'

'Yes, you told me how you arranged to meet him at the lake and that you killed him. We talked about that. You were sorry for what you'd done. How could I know that you had it in you to do it again?'

He'd known exactly which buttons to press to get this girl to do his bidding, Kim realised. All she wanted, had ever wanted, was a family and he had given her that, in return for hurting the people he felt had betrayed him. Everything came at a price.

He knew full well that Sammy had been snatched. His problem had been that she hadn't returned; however slowly and steadily, Sammy had been trying to make normal life work. Something either Kane or her parents had said had registered in her brain.

This man had destroyed countless lives through manipulation and coercion. He had destroyed this girl and was continuing to do it now.

'What about your last Farm, Jake?' Kim asked, to get his attention away from Britney. 'People died there too, didn't they?'

He turned towards her, as though surprised that she was still there.

'Accidents happen,' he said, without emotion.

'Graham Deavers falling from the roof was an accident, and Christopher Brook really did kill himself?' she pushed.

'So the inquests said,' he offered with a smugness that crept into his eyes. It was the expression of a man who knew he had got away with murder. He would never admit to what he'd done.

'Did you know Christopher was a police officer?'

He shrugged, leaving her in no doubt. 'No good ever comes to snoops.'

'Did Graham want to leave you?' she asked. 'Did he hurt your pride and your ego?'

His expression darkened.

'You're no different to Britney. You build a family and people leave. That hurts Britney because of her past, but it only hurts your ego not your feelings; it's proof that you failed. How could anyone want to leave you and what you've created?'

She saw a muscle jump in his cheek as he turned towards her.

'You use vulnerable people to get revenge,' she spat, knowing that Britney was going to have to pay a high price for the things she'd done, for him.

If she could just get him to move a couple of steps away from Britney, she could take her chances and rush him for the knife.

'You use people to build your empire. You seek out vulnerable people and take everything you can: their money, their families, their free will and you call that a family. It's not a family,' she taunted. 'It's a dictatorship and you're going to lose everything you've built.'

He laughed out loud and took a step towards her. 'You think anyone is going to believe a word she says?' he asked, waving the knife towards Britney. 'I have a hundred people back there who will…'

'Yes, a hundred people who also knew Sammy, who also knew Tyler and have known Britney. You really think you can convince them all that you had no part in this? Do you really think your intelligence is superior to everyone back there, that not even one of them will doubt you? All it takes is one person, Jake, and your house of cards…'

He took another step towards her.

Britney sprang from her seated position and grabbed the knife from Jake's hand. She turned it and thrust it into his stomach.

'Noooo…' both she and Tiff screamed running towards her.

In her frenzied state the girl landed another two wounds. Blood stained his white shirt immediately as he stared at Britney in shock.

'He has to die,' Britney screamed, as Jake fell to the ground.

Kim grabbed the knife and threw it as Tiff pulled Britney away.

'He used me. He had to die,' Britney cried as she tried to wriggle out of Tiff's grip.

'Jesus,' Kim said, assessing the mess before her. The blood was pooling either side of Jake's torso and his colour was fading fast.

Kim ripped open his shirt as his eyes rolled back in his head. Of the three wounds, the first and last seemed to be spewing the most blood.

She placed both hands over the wounds and tried to apply pressure. The blood seeped over her hands as the wounds tried to suck her fingers down.

'Damn it,' she said, trying to move her hands around to keep the blood from leaving his body. All the while she could see the pools of blood growing deeper and wider around him.

'No,' she cried out as she felt the life ebbing away from him. 'Don't you dare,' she growled, moving her hands again. She knew a person could die from loss of blood in as little as five minutes, less if the wounds were serious, and right now she had two serious wounds from which she couldn't stem the blood.

She knew he had lost consciousness.

She moved her hands again, the warm stickiness leaving hand prints everywhere she touched.

'Stay with me, Jake,' she breathed, as his torso gave a sigh before stilling completely.

'Fuck it,' she called out, tipping his head back.

'Boss, can I?...'

'Stay where you are, Tiff,' Kim instructed. They couldn't risk Britney getting away.

'Keep still, Brit,' Tiffany shouted, and Kim could hear the emotion in her voice.

Tiffany had gotten closer to this girl than Kim had imagined but she couldn't think about that now.

She linked her fingers and placed the heel of her hand in the middle of Jake's chest. She pressed down thirty times and then gave two breaths directly into his mouth.

She checked his chest. Nothing.

She repeated the process and checked again.

Nothing.

Part of her knew he'd gone, but she had to keep trying.

Sheila and three other women appeared at the edge of the trees followed by her limping colleague.

The women looked on in horror as Bryant approached her. Two beads of sweat dropped onto the unmoving chest of Jake Black.

'He's gone, guv,' Bryant said, touching her shoulder.

Kim sat back and took a proper look, seeing what Bryant had seen straight away. His complexion was a deathly white and the circles of blood around him were like storm puddles. No one could survive that level of blood loss.

She wiped her hand across her forehead and felt the stickiness of his blood on her skin.

'What the hell happened here?' Bryant asked, looking around.

'I'll explain later,' she said, getting to her feet. 'Nothing to see here, folks,' Kim said, stepping in front of Britney and Tiff.

Bryant took over and began shepherding them away.

Britney had stopped struggling once Kim had stopped working on Jake, as though she now knew for certain that it was all over.

The girl looked up at the woman she thought had been her friend. Hurt shone from her eyes.

Kim stepped to one side.

'Britney, I don't hate you,' Tiff said. 'In spite of what you've done, I still don't hate you. You welcomed me and took care of me and made me feel as though I'd met someone I could totally trust. I was going to leave, but I was leaving this place. I wasn't leaving you.'

Kim heard the sob that came from the girl on the ground.

Kim was satisfied they had their killer but there would be no celebration in the squad room tonight.

Britney was not a mindless, ruthless, brutal murderer but a kid damaged by being abandoned. She had found some measure of security at the Farm, where her weaknesses and vulnerabilities had been manipulated and used to satisfy the feeling of betrayal of someone else.

Kim tapped Tiffany on the shoulder.

The officer looked back up at her with reddened eyes.

'Okay, Tink, time to step aside. I think it's best if I take it from here.'

CHAPTER 112

It was almost eleven when Bryant stepped out of the taxi.

The boss had insisted he get himself to hospital for a check-up, but he'd diverted the taxi she'd ordered. His ankle was a bit stiff from the initial jolt of the rope but his years on the rugby pitch told him that nothing was broken, and there was something he needed to do before he could put Peter Drake and the week from hell behind him.

Damon Crossley answered the door on the second knock.

'What the fuck?...'

'Oh, Damon, shut up and let me past,' Bryant said, in no mood for his hard man act. He was hungry and tired and he still hadn't told Jenny about the car.

Bryant had thought long and hard about what he was going to do, especially when he'd been sitting alone in the woods with a trap around his ankle.

Bryant knew that Richard Harrison had killed Alice Lennox and that Peter Drake was innocent of the crime, despite his confession. In his own twisted mind, Richard had not understood that in taking the life of an innocent girl, he had been doing exactly what he'd feared Peter Drake would do himself. He had only seen that the man needed to be punished further for the horrific murder of Wendy. Whether his suicide was from the guilt of what he'd done or to reach the afterlife to protect his daughter, Bryant couldn't say for sure but he suspected it was a mixture of the two.

Richard had never been able to free himself of the horror, terror and pain his daughter had suffered. He had relived it every day, allowing the guilt to eat away at the decent person he had once been, although that knowledge did nothing, in Bryant's mind, to absolve him of the brutal murder of Alice Lennox.

He had no proof except for the feeling in his gut that would not go away. If he pursued his suspicions, there was a chance someone might listen if he shouted loud enough. There was no person to charge with the crime because the man was dead. Alice Lennox's family would never have closure.

Peter Drake would be allowed to walk the streets again and the Crossleys would never again know a minute of peace. A lot of lives ruined in his quest for black and white justice.

The other way only he carried the burden of knowing the truth.

Bryant looked at the empty space where Tina had sat before attempting to kill her husband; the man who acted hard as nails to protect the woman he loved.

'So, the bastard struck again, did he?' Crossley asked, dropping one layer of hostility.

And this was where he made the final decision.

'Yes, Damon, Peter Drake struck again. He confessed to the whole thing.'

Bryant prepared himself for the onslaught about shit police and crap parole board before being ordered out of the house.

Damon remained uncharacteristically quiet and stared sadly at Tina's empty space by the window.

'Time to drop the charges and bring her home, Damon,' Bryant said, wearily.

Damon said nothing.

'Nice wound you gave yourself, mate. Took some guts but you didn't much care about yourself when you were trying to get her put back in the only place she's felt safe in decades. You knew just the thought of him being free was putting the fear of God into her and it was the only thing you could do to make her feel safe.'

Damon let out a long breath before dropping down onto the sofa.

'She's always been waiting, you see,' he explained. 'Every day she's known he'd be free someday. It's shaped her life, the fear.'

'Well, she doesn't need to be scared any more. He'll never see the light of day again.'

'Thank God,' Damon breathed into the hands that covered his face.

'Be prepared for a serious bollocking at the station but just tell them the truth. They're expecting it.'

Bryant looked at the empty space.

'And then it's time to go and fetch Tina home.'

Damon Crossley stood and offered his hand.

'You're all right you,' he said. 'Not like the other bastards.'

That was high praise indeed.

The decision he'd made would always stick in his craw. He'd stepped into the grey area of justice and he consoled himself that for everyone around him, he'd done the right thing.

And for him that would have to do.

CHAPTER 113

Kim had found herself thinking about Britney long after she'd charged her with the murder of her father, Tyler Short, Samantha Brown and Jake Black.

Britney had waived the right to legal counsel during questioning, and Kim had felt like insisting, but that wasn't her place. She surmised that the girl wouldn't trust anyone who was appointed to represent her. Everyone was a stranger, a zombie, and zombies weren't to be trusted. Britney had looked so much younger, sitting across from her in the interview room as she had freely added detail to her crimes.

She explained how her father had reached out to her and it was only once she met him at Himley Park that the rage overtook her and she pushed him into the water and held him down. Seeing him again had brought back the abandonment of both her mother and her father, the loneliness, the despair she had felt as a child. Feelings she'd buried for years while she simply survived. Kim had compared Britney's rage to the man's slight build and understood how she had physically outmatched him.

She had recited how easy it had been to get to Samantha with a housewarming gift. Her old friend had pretended to be pleased to see her. But she'd known it was just an act. Jake had explained that Sammy was just another person who had used her and then left her. They had talked and laughed and caught up, and Britney had persuaded Sammy to lie on the bed for a foot massage, something they'd done for each other after a long day standing on the college car park. Once Sammy's eyes had closed she had taken the knife and slit her throat.

Tyler had been easy enough to find. Britney knew from their time together that before he'd followed Sammy to Unity Farm he'd cadged the occasional free meal from the Subway in Dudley. He'd left the Farm with no money and no place to live. She'd only had to wait a couple of days before he showed up. She'd persuaded him to meet her at the lake to talk. At first she'd tried to coax him to return, but he'd refused and in doing so had sealed his own fate. She'd admitted to borrowing Sheila's shoes that day, as was the culture at Unity Farm, after her own had become sodden in a thunderstorm the day before.

Britney would now be living in a prison cell, though Kim couldn't help feeling that she really needed to spend some time with Kane. How the hell could she unravel all this on her own? Had she really seen Jake for what he was before she'd killed him? If so, how would she come to terms with that? Had it been a momentary lapse of anger that she would later regret when he returned to the godlike status in her mind? Same question. How would she come to terms with the fact she was responsible for the death of her idol?

There had been no joy in the process of charging her. Kim had even lacked the sense of achievement she normally felt. She only knew that she had done her job. In an ideal world, she would hate every person she put away; she would despise them and never think of them again.

But that wasn't the case with Britney Murray. The girl had been damaged at an early age, which had prompted her to look for a place to belong, a group of people that would not let her down. But they had let her down. Jake Black had used her to punish people he felt had wronged him. He had massaged her insecurities and her weaknesses until she was powerless to resist his subtle guidance. She had believed him when he said he'd never instructed her to kill anyone. He hadn't needed to but she had no doubt that the man himself was just as much to blame as Britney. He was dead and they would never prove it. Her case would be for the prosecution, but she hoped her defence lawyer called someone like Kane Drummond to testify.

Kim looked down at her hands. Three showers later she could still feel the warm stickiness of Jake Black's blood on her hands. Although she had tried her hardest to save him, there was not one bone in her body that was sorry he was dead. She knew they would have struggled to link him directly to the crimes, and he would have remained free to continue the shaping and warping of young minds.

There would be further questioning at Unity Farm but as Kim saw it no serious offences had been committed by anyone else there. She knew of no accomplices, there were no accessories and it appeared that no one was being held there by force. Hilda would be informed about Britney's true motivations and efforts would be made to uncover any other elderly, vulnerable targets of the Farm. Recent events had catapulted Unity Farm from obscurity and into her cross hairs. From this point on, they would be watched closely. She understood that Lorna had taken over the day-to-day running of the Farm while they all came to terms with Britney's crimes and Jake's death.

Penn had received a call from Josie to say that her mother had returned safe and well and after emotional apologies on both sides they had simply fallen into each other's arms and cried. Maybe that's all some of the folks at Unity Farm needed: a reminder of the people who loved them. If Kane intended to continue his current business, he would need to recruit someone else for the informant role.

She had called him late the previous evening, once Britney was in custody, to update him. Although he'd said little, she could sense the sadness for the girl stretching along the line between them. He had shown no such sadness for the demise of Jake Black and she had understood why.

'Graham Deavers was your brother, wasn't he?' she'd asked, gently.

Stacey had made the connection when she'd come face to face with Kane for the first time in the warehouse.

'Half,' Kane answered.

'That's why you know so much about cults. Did Graham want to leave?'

Kim knew the silence was filled with his indecision in opening up to her.

'Graham was one of the group's beggars,' Kane said, surprising her. 'He'd dropped out of school and was unskilled but still useful. He was an inexpensive body that survived on rice and beans and was sent out every day to beg as much money as he could. The only advantage was that it meant I could get to him. I could see him. While I was learning about how cults work, I was talking to him, almost daily. He was starting to believe me.'

'Until?' Kim asked, feeling her breath gather in her chest even though she knew the outcome to this story.

'Until he told Jake that he was thinking of leaving. Later that day he was asked to fix a section of guttering on the roof.'

'Kane, I'm…'

'And Christopher Brook was sent in because of me. I was insistent that there was something going on there. I was the one who made a nuisance of myself until someone would listen. I was the one…'

'That's why you work alone, why you won't involve the police?' she asked, finally understanding it all, including his aggressive reaction to them having sent in an officer undercover.

'No one else will get hurt because of me.'

Kim closed her eyes and thanked God that she'd got to Tiffany in time.

She could feel his pain, but that wouldn't stop her asking the question that was in her mind and was the real reason for the phone call.

'You know what, Kane, you can't bring that police officer back but you can do a favour for one right now.'

Silence. 'I'm listening.'

Kim had told him what she wanted and ended the call.

During the investigation they had uncovered many more victims than the ones who had lost their lives. She thought of Eric Leland and his mother. Would his hatred for the woman ever dissipate? Would his connection to the Farm and his loyalty to a dead man ever ebb enough for him to lead some semblance of a normal life?

She thought of Sammy Brown and Tyler Short; one with a loving family and the other with nothing. Their backgrounds hadn't mattered. They had both been vulnerable and had sought to belong. Funerals for both were due to be held in the coming week. She would attend both and so would Myles and Kate Brown, who had asked if they could attend the burial of Tyler Short. She had been touched at their wish to pay their respects to a lonely young man whose only crime had been to fall in love with their eldest daughter.

She thought about Sophie Brown. She recalled the shock she'd felt at what Stacey and Penn had explained they'd seen in the warehouse. That Jake had maintained such complete control over Sophie from a distance was both disturbing and terrifying. Sophie was now back at home and Kane had recommended a female colleague to help the family. He accepted that Sophie would not trust anything he had to say. The poor girl had been informed of her sister's murder and was having to try and navigate her way through a whole new world. Kim was sure the Browns knew that it wasn't going to be a short process. It could be years until they got the old Sophie back, if ever. The whole family may have to contemplate that a totally different Sophie might emerge from the fog, while also adjusting to a life without Samantha. She doubted that the family would ever recover from their involvement with Unity Farm.

If there was one thing Kim now understood, it was that involvement with a cult always left its mark. Sophie had a long road to recovery. Over time she would have to learn to deal with her own thoughts, her own ideas. She would have to face the pressure of making her own decisions, living amongst strangers and dealing with everyday stress.

Those thoughts led her to Peter Drake and, although she hadn't voiced her opinion to Bryant, she felt that was the real reason he'd admitted to the murder of Alice Lennox.

After nearly twenty-six years in prison, Peter Drake was now institutionalised. He had lost his freedom but he had been part of a world he understood. He knew the routine, he knew the inmates, he knew the guards. He probably knew what he was going to have for his evening meal on the second Thursday of every month. His cell was his prison but it was also his safety. There were elements that transferred across both cases.

She knew that Bryant would struggle with the decision he'd made, but she'd have supported him whichever route he'd chosen. Because she now knew that's what friends did.

*

So, the statements had been written, her team had been sent home to enjoy what was left of the weekend and in Bryant's case go and look for a new car.

The boards in the office had been wiped clean and there was only one thing left to do, she thought, as a figure appeared in the doorway.

'Come in, Tink, and take a seat.'

Tiffany did as she was asked with a tremulous smile.

Kim had read her statement a few times. It was accurate, factual and bore no hint of the emotion behind it. Tiffany was a professional and Kim respected that.

'So, how are you doing?'

'I'm fine, boss. Eager to get back to work.'

A little too bright and a little too quick.

'Yeah, Tink, thanks for the answer you think I want, but now I'd like the truth.'

'I feel like I let you down,' she blurted out and then looked away. That wasn't what Kim had been expecting.

'You know what, Tink, I feel the same way.'

Tiffany's eyes opened wide. 'But I didn't get anything on the cult. I didn't uncover anything that…'

'Tink, you were with the murderer the whole time and I put you there,' Kim said.

Tiff opened her mouth, but Kim held up her hand.

'No, listen. I allowed, no persuaded, you to enter into a situation that I didn't know enough about. I threw you into the face of danger because I was uninformed and ignorant to the kind of damage these places can do. I sent you in there and for that I'm sorry.'

'But I wanted to help. I was flattered that you asked me, and I'm fine, I didn't get hurt and now life can go back to normal.'

Not quite, Kim thought, folding her arms.

'So, what kind of stuff did Jake say to you?' she asked.

'Aah, it was all just bullshit,' she said, looking away.

'All of it?' Kim probed.

'Yeah, yeah, I didn't listen…'

'Tink, I've been honest with you and I'd appreciate the same courtesy in return.'

Tiffany took a deep breath.

'He told me that it wasn't my fault that my mother favours my brothers over me. It wasn't my fault that she loves them more.'

'And does she?'

'Well, Ryan's in the box room instead of me,' she said, with a half-smile.

Kim frowned, having no idea what that meant. 'Is that important?'

'Yes, it kind of is.'

'So, you listened to him? Jake got you to take notice of everything he said?' Kim asked.

'I suppose so. He did seem to know…'

'He seems to know that targeting family relationships is the quickest way to emotional vulnerability. It's his favourite party trick.'

Tiff looked surprised.

'But how did he reel you in, Tink?'

'I think from the second you're involved you feel important. They make you feel loved, wanted. They make you feel that everything you say is valued, that they want you. They make you feel like you matter.'

'You always mattered to us, you know,' Kim said, gently.

Tiffany swallowed, hard. 'I know and I think I felt that. It kept me grounded. I knew why I was there and I think that stopped me falling over the edge. It would have been so easy.'

Kim tried to push down the guilt that rose in her stomach.

Unwittingly she had put this girl in danger both physically and psychologically. Tiffany's eagerness to help had blinded her to the dangers to herself.

Tiffany may only have been at Unity Farm for a couple of days but the impact was something that even the girl herself wouldn't understand.

And Kim wasn't going to let her down twice.

The shadow of Kane Drummond loomed in the doorway.

'Tink, there's someone I'd like you to meet.'

A LETTER FROM ANGELA

First of all, I want to say a huge thank you for choosing to read *Killing Mind,* the twelfth instalment of the Kim Stone series and to many of you for sticking with Kim Stone and her team since the very beginning. And if you'd like to keep up to date with all my latest releases, just sign up at the website link below.

www.bookouture.com/angela-marsons

I've been interested in cult psychology for many years and have read many books and personal accounts. Like most people, I always felt there was some kind of aggressive, physical method of brain-washing innocent, naïve individuals into a totally different way of thinking. The more I read, the more I learned and understood that the expertise lies in persuasion and manipulation and that we are all subject to subtle forms in our everyday life.

In *Killing Mind* I wanted to explore the tools used by cults to remove people from their everyday lives, friends and family and also to look at the challenges in trying to bring those people back to what they were before.

My research covered many of the well-known cults and sects both in the past and in operation today, but it became increasingly clear that these groups always dress up as something else to lure unsuspecting victims into their ideology. They are more commonplace than we imagine.

As ever the normal team were present, as well as a character that seems to have won over both the team and readers (and me too). I hope you enjoyed reading it as much as I enjoyed writing it.

If you did enjoy it, I would be forever grateful if you'd write a review. I'd love to hear what you think, and it can also help other readers discover one of my books for the first time. Or maybe you can recommend it to your friends and family…

I'd love to hear from you – so please get in touch on my Facebook or Goodreads page, Twitter or through my website.

Thank you so much for your support, it is hugely appreciated.

Angela Marsons

angelamarsonsauthor

@WriteAngie

www.angelamarsons-books.com

ACKNOWLEDGEMENTS

I can not begin to thank people before I acknowledge my partner, Julie, by my side every step of the way, not only now but for the last thirty years. She treats every book as a new adventure and shares my enthusiasm from the excitement of the first seedling of the idea. Unlike me, she maintains that enthusiasm even when I am questioning everything about the story and my ability to tell it. Somehow, she always makes sure we come out at the other end. Truly my partner in crime.

Thank you to my mum and dad, who continue to spread the word proudly to anyone who will listen. And to my sister Lyn, her husband Clive and my nephews Matthew and Christopher for their support too.

Thank you to Amanda and Steve Nicol, who support us in so many ways, and to Kyle Nicol for book-spotting my books everywhere he goes.

I would like to thank the team at Bookouture for their continued enthusiasm for Kim Stone and her stories and especially to Oliver Rhodes, who gave Kim Stone an opportunity to exist.

Special thanks to my editor, Claire Bord, whose patience and understanding is truly appreciated and always available. We have now ascertained that Claire can no longer peruse the Amazon charts at key times for fear she may endanger herself. Her continued excitement and passion inspires me every day to write the very best books that I can.

To Kim Nash (Mama Bear), who works tirelessly to promote our books and protect us from the world. To Noelle Holten, who has limitless enthusiasm and passion for our work.

Many thanks to Alex Crow and Jules Macadam for their genius in marketing the books. Also to Natalie Butlin and Caolinn Douglas for working hard to secure promotions for the books. To Leodora Darlington, who works hard on the books behind the scenes, and to Alexandra Holmes, who looks after the audio production of the stories. Huge thanks also to Peta Nightingale who sends me the most fantastic emails.

A special thanks must go to Janette Currie, who has copy-edited the Kim Stone books from the very beginning. Her knowledge of the stories has ensured a continuity for which I'm extremely grateful. I am equally grateful to Loma Halden, who proofreads the books wonderfully. Also need a special mention for Henry Steadman, who is responsible for the fabulous book covers which I absolutely love.

Thank you to the fantastic Kim Slater, who has been an incredible support and friend to me for many years now, and who, despite writing outstanding novels herself, always finds time for a chat. Massive thanks to Emma Tallon, who has no idea just how much I value her friendship and support. Also to the fabulous Renita D'Silva and Caroline Mitchell, without whom this journey would be impossible. Huge thanks to the growing family of Bookouture authors who continue to amuse, encourage and inspire me on a daily basis.

My eternal gratitude goes to all the wonderful bloggers and reviewers who have taken the time to get to know Kim Stone and follow her story. These wonderful people shout loudly and share generously not because it is their job but because it is their passion. I will never tire of thanking this community for their support of both myself and my books. Thank you all so much.

Massive thanks to all my fabulous readers, especially the ones that have taken time out of their busy day to visit me on my website, Facebook page, Goodreads or Twitter.

Printed in Great Britain
by Amazon

82814645R00214